Secrets of C...

Three siblings, three ...

Royce leads Clan Cameron with honor, respect and integrity. But he's never wanted to burden anyone else with the responsibility, so the guarded laird often goes it alone.

Susanna Cameron has no trouble speaking her mind. And when she sets her sights on something, there's nothing that will stop her.

Rolf Cameron is a warrior. He fights for what's right. But fighting for what he wants could be a different matter...

The siblings are all about to uncover secrets that have been hidden, not just from them but from their entire clan... Will their determination to discover the truth lead them to change their philosophies on life, leadership...and love?

Read Royce and Iona's story in
A Laird without a Past

Discover Susanna and Rowan's story in
The Lady's Proposal for the Laird

Both available now!

And look out for Rolf's story
Coming soon!

Author Note

Some books write themselves and this book was one of those. Ironically, Rowan was a hero I have had in my heart for over ten years, and I think his book was never published before because I had him paired with the wrong heroine.

Perhaps he knew this well before I did.

It wasn't until Susanna appeared in *The Highlander's Secret Son* that I had even an inkling of a new love match for him. Then, once I wrote Iona and Royce's story, *A Laird without a Past*, I realized Rowan and Susanna were the perfect pair. Each of them was fierce, relentless, and full of emotion and passion that teetered on the edge of chaos. All in all, they needed a partner with equal fire, not complementary parts.

It is like that in life sometimes as well. You wait and wait, rather certain you are on the right path, and then suddenly you blink and a different route appears. It is only then you realize it was the one you should have been on all along.

Wishing you the right path at just the right time, my dear readers.

The Lady's Proposal
for the Laird

———

JEANINE ENGLERT

ISBN-13: 978-1-335-59610-9

The Lady's Proposal for the Laird

Copyright © 2024 by Jeanine Englert

Harlequin Enterprises ULC
22 Adelaide St. West, 41st Floor
Toronto, Ontario M5H 4E3, Canada
www.Harlequin.com

Printed in U.S.A.

Jeanine Englert's love affair with mysteries and romance began with Nancy Drew and her grandmother's bookshelves of romance novels. When she isn't wrangling with her characters, she can be found trying to convince her husband to watch her latest Masterpiece/BBC show obsession. She loves to talk about writing, her beloved rescue pups, and mysteries and romance with readers. Visit her website at jeaninewrites.com.

Books by Jeanine Englert

Harlequin Historical

The Highlander's Secret Son

Secrets of Clan Cameron

A Laird without a Past

Falling for a Stewart

Eloping with the Laird
The Lost Laird from Her Past
Conveniently Wed to the Laird

Visit the Author Profile page
at Harlequin.com.

Prologue

October 1745.
Loch's End, Glencoe, Scotland

'She must marry, brother. It is the best way to protect her. In truth, it may be the *only* way to protect her.'

Susanna Cameron scoffed and halted her descent on the stairs at the sound of her eldest brother's voice from the cracked door of the study below. Her blood cooled as her hand clutched the wooden finial of the railing, her slippered foot hanging in mid-air, frozen by his words. Moonlight streamed in through the stained-glass windows, casting blotches of colour on the stone and on her dark gown, as she stood on the landing and listened. Surely her brothers were not discussing *her*. She needed no husband, nor any man's protection. She was a Cameron after all. She frowned. But who else would they be desperate to marry off for protection? Her youngest sister was already married with her first bairn due next year.

'She will not have it, as you well know. *Especially* if you attempt to force it upon her.' Rolf answered with a chuckle rounding out the end of his words.

Susanna smiled as her younger brother Rolf came to her defence, and then frowned with the realisation and confirmation that it *was* she who was being discussed. She squared her shoulders, turned on her heel, and took a step onto the bottom set of stairs prepared to tell them exactly what she thought about their scheme to marry her off. In simplest terms, she wouldn't agree to it.

Ever.

'I do not want to force it upon her, you know that, especially after Jeremiah,' Royce added in low tones. 'But surely her safety trumps all. She must have another family to back her in case the worst happens—and we are no longer here to protect her.'

Susanna stilled. Her throat dried and her stomach dropped. She blanched. *No longer here to protect her?* She had never heard her brothers talk in such a way. The politics and unrest in the Highlands were precarious now to be sure, but Royce, her eldest brother and laird of the clan, feared nothing and no one. The Camerons were one of the most powerful clans in the Highlands, if not *the* most powerful. Who would dare attack or threaten them, especially now? And what reason could they possibly have to do so? They had alliances with almost every surrounding clan.

'You cannot even entertain such thoughts. You have a bairn on the way.'

'That is exactly *why* I must think such,' Royce countered. His boots echoed along the stone floor. 'And you must prepare yourself. Our sisters may become targets once all is revealed. So might Iona and our babe. If something happens to me, you must be ready to carry on. No matter what.'

'You know I will protect all of them with my life, but such talk is extreme. It may never come out, brother. All this worry and planning may be for naught.'

'While I hope you are right, Rolf, my gut tells me otherwise,' Royce replied. 'And once all is revealed, the Highlands may become the battleground we feared, and instead of the British being at odds with us, we will all be fighting one another.'

Chapter One

Two weeks later.
Argyll Castle, Glencoe, Scotland

Laird Rowan Campbell slammed the forging hammer down with force, the clash of metal against iron reverberated through his body. He relished the ache the repeated pounding created in his forearm. His nightly visits to the forge had become his place of peace, not unlike a religious man's house of worship. He set aside his hammer and turned the rough metal blade that would become a sword in his grip and frowned. The piece was becoming too cool to shape and would fracture if he wasn't careful. Setting it aside, he grabbed the shovel, scooped up a heaping pile of hot bright orange coals, and then added them to the forge before sliding the metal blade beneath them.

'This is the last place I thought to search for you, yet here you are.'

Rowan stilled at the sound of the familiar female voice behind him. It was a voice he had not heard for over two years. One he had not ever wished to hear again but wishes were fickle things prone to shatter much like hot metal when it cools too quickly and isn't properly tempered. And that was Susanna Cameron: fire and ice within the same breath and a woman quite prone to breaking things and relishing in her destruction.

'Susanna,' he replied, shifting the coals evenly over the flame in the forge, not eager to face her. He needed a moment to gain his bearings and counted to five as he ran his soiled hands down the leather apron protecting him as he worked. Then, he turned, and his body thrummed and heated at the sight of her like the first time he'd set eyes on her when he was fifteen years old with the beginnings of scruff on his cheeks. She stood framed by the doorway of the forge, covered in her signature dark hooded cloak, her glistening ice blue eyes gathering all the light in the room while her pearly skin and lush pink lips reflected the firelight and sent a surge of need straight through him.

Deuces.

His body didn't remember what his mind always did: her cruelty. He fisted his hands by his sides.

'You look far better than the last time I saw you,' she said, her gaze slowly assessed him head to toe as she pulled at the tips of her gloves one at a time to remove them from her hands.

She'd skilfully landed her first blow. He knew more was to come.

'What do you want, my lady? And how did you manage to get past my guards? And where are yours?' He wiped his forearm across his brow to keep the sweat from stinging his eyes as they swept the room. She was alone.

'Always to the point,' she replied, smiling at him as if she were about to steal from his pocket. Knowing Susanna Cameron, she already had, and he just didn't know it yet.

'Merely eager to get back to my work.' It had been over two years since his last bout with insanity, and he planned to keep it that way, despite her prodding. The forge brought him calm, salvation, and sanity, and his nightly visits were a necessary part of his recovery. Her presence was interrupting all of that.

She scoffed, her gaze flicking about the forge as if it were a dirty, forlorn place. 'You are laird. You have men to tend to these needs.'

'Perhaps it is *I* who need *it*.'

Her brow lifted for a moment, her interest evident, before she cast it aside. 'I need your assistance.'

'I doubt that. You have men to tend to your every need, and you have a way of bending them *to* your needs. Otherwise, you would not have been able to enter this forge.' He would deal with his men that allowed her entry later. Much later, after his temper had cooled.

She frowned. 'Perhaps, but not for this task. It requires discretion.'

'Then why come to me, a man who would relish in the idea of exploiting your clan's secrets for my own benefit.'

'Because I have no other options.'

She looked away and fidgeted with her hands, an odd display of weakness from a woman never prone to it. Her cool, calm, and icy demeanour slipped away to reveal a brief momentary glimmer of the young vulnerable lass he had known and thought he once loved many years ago before her mask fell back into place.

Curious. Now he *was* interested.

'A Cameron without options is an odd situation indeed,' he replied. 'Why would I be willing to help you? Perhaps you have forgotten our last exchange?'

Susanna's gaze met his, but she didn't answer. They both

knew well what that last exchange was, but she was loath to speak of it. So was he.

He set aside his tools and turned away to shovel a new scoop of coal into the forge and the blast of heat sent goose-flesh running along his wet skin. His tunic stuck to his flesh, soaked in sweat from his hour of labour. The sun had long gone down, and the nearby families in the village were tucked in preparing for bed, but not him. He had another hour in the forge, perhaps two, before his body and mind would be exhausted enough for sleep. This unexpected visit might well set him back another hour.

The barn door slid closed, and he lifted his brow in surprise as he stoked the coals and used the tongs to hoist a new strip of metal he needed to shape into the bright orange heap. There was a slight sizzle as sweat from his forehead dripped onto the hot embers.

'Do you not worry about your reputation? Being an unmarried woman alone with a laird in a forge, especially a man like me.' He faced her and was stilled by the desperation and agony in her gaze. He had only seen that expression once before.

'Instead of plaguing me with your barbs, I need you to listen,' she replied, her tone softening.

She had his attention now. He came closer, so close he could see the dark circles under her eyes and the tight agitated hold of her hands in front of her waist. She hadn't been sleeping and probably not eating either. He knew well the signs of prolonged desperation and worry.

'I am listening,' he said, crossing his arms against his chest.

'My brothers are keeping something important from me and my sister, and I need you to unearth what it is.'

He chuckled. 'You came all this way in the dead of night because you need me to find out a secret for you?'

Surely there was more to it. Susanna Cameron was not prone to care about such trivial matters, and nothing was ever as it seemed at first glance with a Cameron. Ever.

'Aye. It is undermining our family, and I don't know why. It consumes my brothers, especially Royce. I fear it will shatter us if I do not figure out what it is that plagues them so.'

'They are probably scheming as you lot are prone to do,' Rowan added.

'Nay. It is far more than that. I know it. They are even conspiring to marry me off to ensure I have the proper protection, whatever that may entail. Imagine me, a Cameron, in need of protection.' She shifted on her feet, another symptom of her growing agitation. He set aside his annoyance.

'And when did this change in their behaviour begin?' he asked.

'After they returned from Lismore a month ago, but it has grown worse in the last two weeks. They have been secretive and meet for hours at a time locked in Father's old study. They will not utter a word about it to me, and with Catriona no longer at Loch's End, I find I am shut out of my own family. I want to know why.'

'That merely sounds like Royce to me,' he replied with a frown.

Susanna's eldest brother was serious and rather unyielding like Rowan was. He had heard the rumours about Laird Cameron's disappearance over the summer. It was an odd recounting of Royce having suffered a head wound and memory loss before returning to his home at Loch's End with his brother Rolf after being missing on the mysterious isle of Lismore for over a month. No one knew why he'd travelled there in the first place.

'The old Royce perhaps, but when he returned from Lismore he was a changed man, and he still is. He is kinder, happy even except for this. He is married now with a bairn on the way. It is this one secret that I do not trust. I still do not even know why he was there. He will speak of it to only Rolf.'

'Why are you asking me to help you? Why not enlist a trusted warrior or guard within your ranks to assist you in this intrigue? Surely, they are better equipped to gain access to and information from your brothers.'

'Nay,' she shook her head. 'It is too great a risk. My gut tells me it is of a far more serious matter than what can be trusted to a soldier, even one within our clan.'

'And to ask my question again: why me, and why on earth would I help you?'

She lifted her chin and pulled back her shoulders like a bird splaying its feathers to make itself appear larger. It didn't really work for Susanna as she was far too petite, but her intention was clear: she would not be refused. 'Because I was promised a favour by your brother when he was laird years ago, any favour of my choosing when I need it, and I plan to collect on it. Tonight.'

'As you well know, my brother Brandon is not laird any more. I am.'

'But as *you* well know you are beholden to fulfil the promise he made to me two years ago as the new laird of Clan Campbell.'

He clenched his jaw. *Devil's blood.* He knew exactly what promise she was referring to. She had offered up her men to help rescue Brandon's son and the babe's mother

Fiona in exchange for an open favour that could be claimed for whatever purpose Susanna needed later. Without her men, Brandon's now wife and son would have been killed. Her assistance had saved their lives.

But that didn't mean it had not been a foolish and risky promise to make as a laird. The Camerons could not be trusted. Rowan had found that out when he had begun courting Susanna when they were teens. His opinion upon them had not wavered. If anything, it had grown more resolute.

He sighed, fisting his hand by his side. Brandon would want and expect Rowan to uphold their end of the agreement with her, no matter how much he wanted to deny Susanna. Honour was not something to be trifled with. She knew he could not balk at fulfilling such a request as it would put his lairdship and clan at risk.

One's word was almost all that mattered in the Highlands, especially now. And he still had much to prove as the reinstalled laird. Even though two years had passed since he had regained his title, the clan elders and villagers still scrutinised him and his decisions.

The woman had him finely wedged between duty and honour and she knew it. Exasperation didn't begin to describe his feelings. He felt trapped and his skin began to itch. He had to find some means of escaping her demands.

'And if I were to fulfil this promise, how do you plan for me to get your brothers, who generally despise me on a good day, to share their most pressing secret with me? I feel you have not thought all of this through, Susanna. Your brothers will see me upon their doorstep and slam the door in my face before I dare utter a syllable. I should know. I would do the same.'

Her gaze lifted to him, and her slow, seductive smile warned him of the danger that would fall next from her lips, but nothing could have prepared him for her words.

'You will offer for my hand, and we will be betrothed until I discover the truth.'

Chapter Two

Rowan's laughter surprised Susanna most. It was a deep, heavenly sound, and it echoed through the large, heated barn that served as the clan's main forge. Despite the ugliness that had passed between them before, her attraction to him had never waned, ever since the first time she'd seen him when she was a young lass on the cusp of womanhood. He was a large, powerful, handsome man used to getting his own desires met, and that ferocity had always made her pulse quicken and throat dry. She was glad to see him back to his old self. Remembering him as the fragile broken man of two years ago in Argyll Castle made her shiver. Rowan was never meant to be anything other than the substantial, formidable wolf amongst men that he was now.

While she knew he would balk at her request, she hadn't expected this odd response. He had always been overly serious and prone to brooding just like her eldest brother. She wasn't quite sure how to manoeuvre. Ranting, refusal, and dismissal she could counter, but laughter?

Curses.

Finally, his laughter subsided, and he wiped the wetness from his eyes. 'I must thank you. I have not laughed aloud like that in years. Now, please tell me your *real* plan.'

'That *is* my real plan.'

He scrubbed a hand through his dark, damp, wavy hair that had grown a bit past his shoulders, far longer than she could ever remember. His muscles rippled along his torso and forearms exposed by the rolled sleeves of his shirt; her gaze unable to resist following the movement. His body strained against the transparent material of his tunic that was soaked through by his labours. It had been far too long since she had been comforted by a man's touch, and sadly her body had always had an overly strong reaction to him. She pressed her thumbnail into the flesh of her index finger so she could focus on the pain of it rather than her emotion. A trick she had learned and mastered over the years. It quelled the flush of heat rushing through her skin and helped her focus on the task at hand: gaining his agreement.

'Susanna, there is no way this will work. Surely, you realised that before travelling all this way to me.'

'Nay, it will work, but it will require your commitment to the role. They are eager to find me a husband, and your clan is powerful enough to fulfil that need.'

'I am no performer. You have the wrong laird for such a part.'

'Nay. You are the perfect candidate for the role. People fear you and wouldn't dare question you. And because of your recent past, people will not doubt your—changefulness towards me.' She bit her lip on her word choice. It could have been better. Perhaps he would not pick up on her allusion.

He looked down at his hands and shook his head before finally lifting his bright blue gaze to glare at her. 'Ah. You believe this will work because of my previous bout with insanity. No man will question the irrational acts of a man who has struggled with his faculties once before.'

He winced. 'Quite the cut, even from you.' He rubbed the back of his neck.

Her skin heated. Aye, it was a cruelty to use his weakness against him in such a way, but she was desperate. Far more desperate than she wanted him to know.

The future of her clan might rest in his hands. The thought of it turned her stomach.

'And what shall you tell your family?' he asked. 'How will they believe you have fallen for a laird whose reason and sanity are questionable at best, especially after our fractious history together. You rejected my proposal to marry you more than ten years ago. We ended on horrid terms. We are not even friends. How and why would they believe *you* have changed *your* mind and chosen to attach yourself to *me*?' He pointed a finger to his chest.

She had practiced this part, knowing full well he would challenge her scheme and attempt to poke holes in her plan. 'For power. I will tell them you are weak and that I can control you once we are married and use it to further our claim in the Highlands.'

He cursed and walked away from her. He stoked the coals and turned the metal he was heating with the tongs. She knew this would be the most perilous part of their conversation. No man and no laird would want to be perceived as so weak and without control, especially a man like Rowan. But she had no choice. 'You cannot expect me to agree to this, promise or not.'

'Aye. I do. Your brother and I had an agreement, and I will hold you to it.' She lifted her chin.

He glared back at her.

'If I had other options, I would seize upon them,' she offered, her confidence gaining even as his agreement waned.

'But I have thought through them all. It is either you or my family, and as you well know, I will always choose them.'

He turned and his steely gaze seared through her. 'Aye. You made that clear to me when we were teens and you rejected me. I have not forgotten. But this—this is low even for your standards.' He threw down the tongs and stalked towards her. He stood so close she feared, and half hoped he might touch her or kiss her, but he did neither.

'If you *knew*…if you truly understood what I have been through to crawl back from the pit of grief I was in after losing Anna and our son four years ago. If you understood what I have been through to get to where I am now as laird after all I lost, you would not ask this of me. You would not ask me to put myself in such a position of weakness amongst my clan.' He swallowed hard. 'Not even you would be so cruel.'

'As I said,' she whispered, commanding herself to stand her ground under the swell of heat and emotion in his eyes. She could not acknowledge his past grief for fear of being dissuaded by her mission. 'You are my only option, and your brother promised me I could call in the favour I am due at any time for any reason. And this is how I wish to do it. You do not have to like it, but you must uphold your end of his agreement to me as the Laird of the clan.'

'And you are as cold of a wench as they come, Susanna Cameron.' His eyes glistened in the light, the hatred for her burning brightly in his gaze.

She held fast, gripped her cloak, and absorbed his words. Too much had passed between them to be unwound now and she dared not try. She almost had his agreement despite how repulsed he was by her tactic of calling in her brother's favour. It was time to lay her final card out on the table to seize his agreement. She stepped closer.

'What if I said in return for your agreement in this and as a gesture of good faith, I would aid you in your revenge upon Laird Audric MacDonald? He does not venture out of his lands much these days, as you well know, but he will be meeting with my brothers in the coming weeks and months to recommit to our alliance and to set a firm boundary to a disputed portion of our shared border wall. If we are betrothed, your access and presence at Loch's End will not be of consequence, and he will be within your grasp finally. I am sure you could concoct a plan for his demise that would not be suspected, especially at his advanced age. You could finally avenge the death of your wife and son and so many others from that horrid day.'

Rowan stilled and an eerie unnatural quiet fell throughout the forge. His gaze met hers, his cobalt blue eyes brilliant and fierce in the light, as he spoke to her. 'Then, I would say, you have your betrothed. When do we begin?'

Now that she had his agreement, Susanna scarcely remembered what to say and do next. She blinked back at him mesmerised by the rhythmic rise and fall of his chest, the heat emanating from him, and the ferocity in his gaze. Those eyes of his had always had a way of seeing through her and she had to fight against the unnatural pull she always felt in his presence and resort to what had always helped her gain her objectivity: cold and brutal detachment. She took a step back and turned away from him as she nestled further into her cloak. The distance helped, and soon she felt her blood cool and pulse settle.

'When can you come to Loch's End?' she asked. 'How soon would a visit be possible?'

'You think me simply arriving at your doorstep and asking for your hand will make this believable?' he scoffed.

She turned to him. 'Aye. Why would it not?'

'I have not been an unattached man for some time, but even *I* remember a man must court a woman properly to be taken seriously before one offers for her hand. Especially, if that hand is to be yours. Your family never approved of me or our previous relationship, and you have refused a proposal from me already. They will suspect this sudden change of heart and reject it if it is forced upon them too soon without merit. They are not fools.' He untied his leather apron and sat on a nearby bench. He leaned forward and pulled his soaked tunic away from his chest, revealing a glimpse of the hardened muscles that hid beneath.

Susanna averted her eyes, unwilling to address her past treatment of him. She also didn't wish to tell him the truth about it. Not yet. 'What would you suggest then?'

'When is the next sizeable Highland clan gathering?' he asked, staring down at his hands before wiping them with an old rag. 'One where it might seem that we could run into one another naturally?'

She frowned. 'I do not keep up with social events.' Such manoeuvrings were quite taxing and boring to her.

'Perhaps now is a fine time to start. For both of our sakes. Look at your recent invitations and I will as well. Then, we can craft when we will encounter one another at one such gathering. Choreograph a scene, if you will, of where and when we meet again for all to see.'

She shook her head and lifted her brow in surprise. She had not expected such forethought from him, but perhaps she should have. He was smart and a soldier. Strategy came naturally for him. Perhaps too easily. She would need to be careful. 'And here you said you could not play such a part?'

He lifted his head and met her gaze. 'To finally have revenge against Audric after four long years—' he paused '—and to have the opportunity to punish him for killing my wife and son during his attack on Argyll Castle and our clan, I can and will do anything. I will hold you to your promise, Susanna. Nothing will stand in my way of finally ending him. Not even you. Do you understand me?'

The hatred in his stare cooled the room, and she froze before she nodded in agreement. She would not begrudge him his revenge. Not after what he had lost that day. Even she was not so heartless, even if the rage emanating from him frightened a small part of her. She had to use it as the weapon it was to gain what she needed: information from her brothers about what secret they held from her and her sister before it fractured them entirely.

'Say it,' he ordered, rising to his feet, and walking towards her.

She held her ground as he approached, her pulse beginning its uneven cadence once more. Lifting her chin, she did not yield to him. Not yet. She needed to maintain the power she had over him as long as she could. Otherwise, he would overwhelm her with his sheer will, and she would not allow anything other than an equal share of power in their pact.

'Say it,' he ordered again, a pitch lower this time as he stood before her. Desperation and rage duelled in his eyes, and his lips parted. His fingertips skimmed the back of her hand, and her pulse picked up speed. He gripped her wrist, the pressure firm but not hard, eliciting a slow pooling heat to travel through her. He leaned in close to her ear. 'Say it,' he whispered.

Her eyes closed and she savoured his touch, the feel of his warm, strong fingers along her skin, the calluses from his labours in the forge gliding along her smooth unblemished flesh. It had been far too long since any man had touched her and somehow even after all these years her body remembered him and longed for his touch as much as she was loath to admit it.

As much as she hated to acknowledge the power he held over her.

'Aye,' she whispered, leaning even closer before she could halt the reaction, the heat from his body warming her own. Her lips almost touched the skin along his collarbone. 'I understand,' she answered. 'Nothing will stand in your way.' Her breath hitched. 'Not even me.'

Rowan closed his eyes at the feel of her warm breath along his shoulder. He dropped her wrist, commanding himself to withdraw from his proximity to her. Susanna always did this to him, and he didn't know if he hated himself or her more for it. Perhaps he hated the heavens that had made her the most. She was a force that could pull him in and drive him to say and do things he didn't like: such as commanding her to say she understood, as if he had any right to touch her or demand for her to say anything at all.

Devil's blood.

He held his breath and stepped back. Scrubbing a hand through his hair, he turned away from her and faced the forge, resting his hands along his waist. The heat and flickering flames beckoned him, and he needed to hammer out his budding desire and rage before he would be able to sleep at all this eve.

'I'll be in touch,' she said before leaving. 'Do not tarry

in your reply to my letter. You know I do not like to be kept waiting…for anything.'

The barn door slid closed behind her, and Rowan exhaled in relief. He leaned against the work table, clutching at the solid, steady presence it provided him with, and counted to ten.

Focus on the present. Focus on the present. Focus on the present.

He chanted the phrase in his mind over and over until his pulse slowed and he felt calm again. Then, he donned his leather apron and set about the task of finishing the blade he had hoped to complete this eve. He would craft strategy as he worked.

If he was to survive this plan with Susanna to be her betrothed *and* exact his revenge on Audric, Rowan would need to utilise his mind and body and focus them both on strategy *while* maintaining his sanity. He had come too far to lose the foothold he had regained in his life. And he sure as hell would not relinquish it now. Not even for the likes of Susanna Cameron.

His mind spooled back to the memory of her as a bonnie lass when they'd met. The first time he'd seen her, all of him had stilled. His body, his heart, and his gaze had been absolutely transfixed and arrested by her beauty and the power that had emanated off her as if she were fire itself. It had been a cold, autumn day, the trees burnished gold, and mist had swallowed up the rolling green hills of the meadow coloured with the last lingering purple hues of heather. He had stormed out of the castle, angered by his father's demands of him, and walked down to the meadow to explore the grove of rowan trees that had been planted when he was born, a tribute to his future but also a noose of expectation of what he was expected to achieve for the clan. Such expectation hung tightly around his neck, despite the beauty and peace the sight of the grove always brought him.

Susanna had been a dark ethereal cloaked creature amongst the black, silvery tree trunks and their reaching limbs, and the setting sun had glowed out of her as she had turned and faced him. Her blue eyes, pale skin, dark hair, and full rosy lips made her the most beautiful and enchanting woman he had ever seen. When he discovered she too had fled the castle walls of Loch's End due to a dispute with her controlling father, Rowan had thought they were kindred spirits. He had seen himself in her and recognised her struggle and she had seen his own. He had kissed her that day, his first kiss as well as her own. The feel of her warm lips on his and the slight pressure of her hand against his chest had made his body feel weightless as if they had transformed—into the mist themselves. He released a breath at the memory. Even now, he didn't know if it had been a trick of the light or her sheer power and beauty that had reflected just so in that moment.

Did it even matter?

He blinked back to the present. Despite that heady kiss and the many that followed after that, she had refused him when he had asked for her hand in marriage. Soon after, she had fallen in love with a Cameron soldier named Jeremiah and made her affection for him well known. Unfortunately, their affair had a brutal end as he had died in battle.

After Susanna's rejection, Rowan's heart had healed— ever so slowly. A year later, he had met Anna, and married her soon after. *Anna.* A woman he had loved more deeply than he ever thought possible. They had shared a life and built a life together with their two children. Her brutal death and the death of their son had brought Rowan to his knees and thrown him into the depths of grief and madness.

Aye, Susanna had been his first kiss and first love, but she had made her decision to be without him long ago. So had he. Much time and heartache rested between them now, and none of it could be undone.

Fool.

He slammed the hammer along the metal blade and smothered the memory of the moment of their first meeting, knowing full well it was the romanticised version of his youth, not reality. The real Susanna Cameron was the one he saw today. Cold. Heartless. Selfish.

She was the woman who had rebuked him when he was at one of his lowest points of grief and loss two years ago. The memory of their brief encounter at her and his brother's sham of an engagement celebration still stung. Not only had the engagement been orchestrated by Susanna's father to punish her for not marrying the man of his choosing, but it had also been a reminder to Rowan of how low and useless he had become after losing his title as laird. The only blessing of the eve was that his brother Brandon had come to his senses and such a marriage to Susanna had never happened—and that her harsh words that eve had set Rowan about a different course. One that may have saved his life.

'You do not deserve to be a laird or a father,' Susanna had seethed, her ice blue gaze taking in the sight of him, roving from the tips of his boots to his face with disapproval. *'Despite your fine clothes this eve, I know what you have become, Rowan. Perhaps no one else dares to tell you such truths, but I will, despite how estranged we*

have become. You are weak and selfish and no father for that wee girl. It is as if the lass has lost both of her parents, but do you even care or notice? What Anna would think of you now,' she'd said bitterly. *'I for one am glad she is dead, so she doesn't have to look upon you like this. You are not the man you used to be.'*

She'd held his gaze for one more beat of time before turning away from him, the tail of her long dark cloak whipping around and making her look like the serpent she was.

In that moment, her words had cut through him and set him alight with anger. Who was she to challenge him, especially after not seeing one another for so many years? But, as he watched her go, her cloak gliding along the stone castle floor, her words had echoed in his mind and shaken him to his core—for deep down he knew they were true. He was no longer the man Anna had married and was no father to his daughter Rosa. He'd been stripped of his title as laird due to his own ineptitude. Consumed by anger and self-pity after his wife and son's deaths, he had cast all responsibilities aside, even that of being a father. All he had thought of was his need for revenge against Laird Audric MacDonald, the man responsible for killing them. No other life or purpose had mattered to him at the time: not even the love of his daughter.

The realisation had stopped him cold.

Later that eve when he'd had the choice to rescue his nephew or chase after Audric for revenge, he had chosen to save his nephew, wee William. It was a decision he had never regretted. It had led him back to the journey of remembering his duty as a father and laird. Soon after, Brandon had stepped down as laird and convinced the elders that Rowan was a changed and capable leader once more.

All because he had been able to set aside his grief and rage for the purpose of saving William.

Something he should have instinctively wanted to do.

But if Susanna hadn't spoken to him that eve, would he have made a different choice? Would he have cast aside his nephew's welfare and sacrificed him to kill Audric and have his revenge?

Rowan shuddered to think upon it. He wanted to believe he would have done so without her words, but in truth, he would never know.

The irony of Susanna lobbing the option for him to now fulfil that quest for revenge against Audric was not lost on him. Perhaps that cruel moment years before had been her putting him and what was best for him and his daughter first for once although it hadn't felt that way then. Could she have said it to help him?

Was she capable of such a kindness? Of such friendship even after how their relationship had ended over a decade ago?

It was hard to imagine, but perhaps she was. Perhaps some small part of her had still wanted him to be happy and cared for him and his daughter Rosa despite all the unsettled and rocky past between them. He scoffed and shook his head. Now *that* was a fool's musing. One he should keep at arm's length. Just like he should keep *her* at arm's length.

Susanna was the same cold, calculating woman she had always been. And he would do well to remember that, lest he get his heart ripped to shreds.

Chapter Three

Midnight kicked up dirt and mud as Susanna rode her filly hard across the valley, cresting one hill and then the next in a flurry of speed. The wind whipped along her cheeks and tugged strands loose from her dark plait, the hood of her cloak having fallen back to rest on her neck miles ago. Her two most trusted soldiers, Lunn and Cynric, rode ahead of her as the pastel streaks of dawn threatened. She slapped the reins to close the gap between her and them. She had to be back inside Loch's End before her brothers rose. No one could know of her adventure, except her two guides, and they had even been sworn to secrecy. She only hoped they would mind their word to her out of duty to Jeremiah, the man she had loved more than any other. A man they had been loyal to until his untimely end in battle almost five years ago. Their mutual affection and loss had bound them to each other in an odd way, but she never took their loyalty and care for granted. They knew how much she had loved Jeremiah and how deep her grief had been when her father had stood between her marriage to him and sent him away to fight to punish him for daring to offer above his rank for her hand. Her chest tightened. And such actions had ultimately led to his death.

Even when her father lay dying a few months after her

botched engagement to Rowan's brother Brandon and asked for her forgiveness for keeping her from the man she loved, she had not granted it. Now, she would have released him from such guilt and grief as her heart had finally loosened its fierce and angry grip on the past. She understood regrets and had her own about Jeremiah's loss. But she could not undo such regrets. No one could.

Not even God.

The glorious looming profile of Loch's End came in view, and she breathed a sigh of relief. She would make it. As she crested one rolling meadow and then the next, she slowed, clucking her tongue at Midnight as they approached the large new barn erected in honour of another fine fallen soldier: Athol. The man had given his life to protect her older brother and laird, Royce, just as she would risk all to keep her siblings and clan safe. The reminder of Athol's sacrifice only steeled her resolve and affirmed that she was doing the right thing for them all.

She stared upon the smooth silver crest with its crossed dirks above the door honouring him. She could not help but think he was now alongside Jeremiah still watching over her, her brothers, and dear sister. That they were warriors even in spirit guiding them alongside their journeys. She didn't wish to imagine them as buried in the earth in foreign lands. A shiver lit up her spine and she shook off the unease such a flicker of thought gave her and followed Lunn and Cynric towards the barn. Lunn dismounted and approached her, reaching up to assist her in descending from Midnight. His gaze reflected the resolve and strength it always had. 'Was your journey a successful one, my lady?' he asked.

'Aye. I achieved all I hoped for. Now, I must be patient and let things play out.'

As her boots rested on the ground, he released her hand and chuckled.

'I know. Patience is not my strong suit, but I shall try.' She pulled off her gloves and breathed in. The cool air invigorated her as it always did. So did the possibility that she might be one step closer to figuring out what her brothers were up to.

'That will be a sight to behold,' Cynric added with a smirk as he approached them.

Such informalities between them were common although they reverted to utter formality whenever anyone else was near. She smiled. 'Aye. It will.' She stepped closer. 'Thank you both for daring to accompany me this eve. As always, I owe you far more than I can ever repay.'

'And you know we would do anything for you, my lady. 'tis what Jeremiah would want.' Lunn glanced down and shifted on his feet.

'I am grateful for such loyalty,' she answered quietly.

'You shall always have it,' Cynric replied with a nod.

Emotion tightened her chest, and she pressed her lips together. She did not know if they would despise her once they realised what she had done. Even they didn't know all her plan. Only Rowan did. It was risky to not include them, but she didn't want to lose their friendship. They were a tether to her past with Jeremiah, and she wasn't ready to let go of it or her memory of him.

She doubted she ever would be.

For it was one thing to feel attraction and desire for a man like she had this eve with Rowan, but it was quite another to give a man her heart. And the one time she had done that with her beloved Jeremiah and lost him, it had broken her. It was best to never take such a risk again.

Ever.

'I will take care of the horses if you'll escort her in,' Lunn said, taking the reins of Midnight from Cynric.

'Aye,' he answered. His other hand rested atop the hilt of his blade in his waist belt. Even now, he was on his guard scanning their surroundings for any possible threats. Times were perilous in the Highlands. Even such a short distance to the castle was one Susanna no longer took alone at night. Desperation and unrest had made once good men into thieves, and the grief caused by the British pressing in ever closer to them all made it even worse. Even her sister-in-law Iona had ceased her daily swims in the loch, no longer willing to risk such with her bairn on the way.

Susanna's hand slid to her stomach. She wondered what such a blessing would feel like. To have a wee bairn growing within her belly. She had had so many dreams with Jeremiah. One of them was being a young mother and carrying a babe with the best of them both. Perhaps a wee son with his crooked smile or a daughter with his solitary dimple. Her eyes filled at the reminder of what she had lost. Her hand dropped away, and she pressed her thumbnail into the fleshy pad of her index finger once more until she collected herself and blinked away any possible tears.

As she reached the back entrance to the castle, she pulled up her cloak to help her hide within the shadows of the many corridors. No doubt some of the servants would see her, but they would never tell Royce. Over the years, she had either earned their devotion or their fear. Both suited her purpose: their silence. Cynric opened the door for her, allowed her to pass through, and sealed the door tightly behind her. Knowing Cynric, he would stand watch for ten more minutes just to ensure her safety. She smiled at the thought of it. Jeremiah's friends were the best of men, just like he had been.

She rounded the corner, removed her cloak, and added it to the many hooks near the door. She travelled silently through the main foyer, her gaze casting left and right, but she saw no one. As she approached the hallway to Royce's study, light emanated from the room. His lanterns were already lit.

Curses.

She stopped, lifted her skirts, and turned back to take another stairwell to her room.

'Up so early, sister?' Royce called. The mild censure in his voice was mixed with amusement.

She stiffened. While subduing the desire to curse aloud, she let go of her skirts and turned to face him. Her brother sat in shadow behind her in a large, oversized chair before the hearth, which had yet to be lit. She shivered and alarm set her on edge. Would her ruse with Rowan end even before it began? Was her brother here to tell her the name of her future husband? Had he attempted to tell her last night and noted her absence even then?

She swallowed hard. She needed to choose her words carefully. Royce was no fool.

'Aye. Just taking Midnight out for an early ride,' she offered. It was *almost* the truth.

'All night long?' he asked and rose from his seat. He was impeccably dressed as if he had just awoken, but his eyes held a fatigue that warned otherwise.

She said nothing, but clasped her hands in front of her

and waited for whatever further questioning was to come. Or whatever news of her future remained.

'No answer?'

She pressed her lips together.

He lifted his brow and sighed. 'And here I thought we were building bridges back to one another and not keeping secrets.' He rested his hand on the back of the chair.

She scoffed. 'Says the man who hides with Rolf for hours in your blasted study and will tell me none of your clan dealings.'

'That is not the same.' His voice hardened.

'Oh, no? It seems such to me.' She crossed her arms against her chest. 'If you and Rolf have secrets, then so shall I.'

''Tis your choice, sister,' he replied, a weary edge to his tone. 'I have far more pressing issues to tend to this day.' He let the matter drop, which concerned her. It was very unlike Royce to drop anything. Her pulse picked up speed.

'Has something happened?' she asked.

He nodded. 'Iona cannot keep down her meals as of late.'

She approached him and sat across from him on the edge of an identical chair, her heart fluttering with unease. Iona's carrying had been more difficult than expected. Her sickness in the morning these early months of her pregnancy had been as difficult as what Susanna remembered for her mother, who had lost not one, but two babes before they were due. It struck urgency in Susanna, but she tried to suppress it for Royce's sake. He would no doubt remember what the outcome had been for their mother as well.

'The doctor only left an hour ago,' he added. 'I had gone to your chambers to fetch you for help. You have a way of comforting Iona that she prefers.' He chuckled and scrubbed a hand through his hair, sending strands in all directions. 'She says I fuss over her too much and make her worry more. When you were not there, it only compounded my worry.'

She squeezed his hand. 'I am sorry, brother. What did the doctor say? What can I do now?'

She would not explain herself, but she would help. She cared deeply for her sister-in-law and her eldest brother. She also could not wait to have a sweet niece or nephew. She secretly hoped for one of each.

'She needs rest. He also left some tonics to set her stomach at ease. She had one and now sleeps. We will try to get her to eat again later when she wakes. I am utterly helpless to her, and I hate it.'

'Aye. You are, but just be there for her. She and the babe will be fine. I know it.' She met his gaze and smiled. While she did not know anything for certain, she would do her best to will a happy outcome. The two of them deserved nothing less than a beautiful, healthy baby.

'So, you will not tell me what you were about this eve?' he asked.

'Nay. But you do not have to worry about me, brother. I can take care of myself.'

'That is something else I wished to speak to you about. Perhaps it is not the perfect time, but there will not be one, as I know you do not wish to discuss it.' He rubbed the back of his neck as he was prone to do when worried. She braced herself for the words she feared.

'You must take a husband. It is time, Susanna. Past time if I am to be honest. Long enough has passed since Jeremiah. You must marry and be settled—and protected,' he added.

'Why now?' she scoffed.

'Why not now?' he countered.

'You know I do not wish to marry,' she pushed her nail into the pad of her thumb, trying to quell the emotion bubbling within her.

'Aye,' he sighed and met her gaze. 'But you must. I have begun enquiries as to possible matches. Ones that may benefit you and the clan since I know you will not marry for love.'

'And why might that be, brother?' she countered, her anger getting the better of her.

'Susanna,' he replied, his voice softening.

'Why did you not just allow me to marry Jeremiah? Why did you have to side with Father? You could have stood up to him.' Her words were sharp prickly arrows she hurtled at him.

'I was not strong enough then, Susanna. I did not understand,' he replied simply. 'I am sorry. I know you loved him. And when I think of how I would have felt if Iona had been taken from me in such a way…' he could not finish but looked upon her with sympathy.

To his credit, he absorbed her censure without rebuke. He was indeed changed. It made her eyes well and she bit her lip, trying to keep the emotion at bay. She was moved by his kindness but embraced her anger instead. 'Then, you shall marry me off to a stranger to make it up to me?' she rose from the chair and paced the room, her energy vibrating through her.

'Nay,' he replied. 'I will give you some time to offer up some additional candidates for us to consider for you. It is the best I can do right now. Times are perilous for us.

You must trust me.' Royce's tone held a pleading note that softened her. The rebuttal she had planned faded away.

When she did not answer, he rose from his chair and approached her.

He pulled her into a side hug and kissed the side of her head before releasing her. 'I know you do not understand, and I know I cannot bring Jeremiah back. Just take this opportunity to choose and try to open your heart to the possibility of it.'

She cherished this new Royce and his kindness, but the idea of a husband was unfathomable.

'I must get some sleep before Iona awakes. I will expect your list in a week or so. Promise me?' he asked her before pulling away.

'I promise,' she replied crossing her fingers behind her back. She watched him turn the corner, and then hustled up the opposite staircase to her own chambers, lifting her skirts so she could climb the stairs two at a time. She had much to attend to. Sleep could wait.

So could that blasted list of his with the names of future husbands.

Susanna opened the door to her chamber and her lady's maid, Tilly, cast her a curious glare. One she was quite familiar with. Susanna looked away and pressed her lips together. The woman had been more of a mother to her than her own, and she knew all facets of Susanna, even the ones she wished she could have kept hidden. To her credit, Tilly completed folding the extra bedding before lobbing her first question.

'And just where have ye been, lassie?' That single solitary eyebrow that Susanna had grown to fear as a girl raised its ugly head at her. The censure and judgement obvious. 'Ye are not a young woman any more. What ye do at night outside of this castle could cause ye ruin, but ye know that already, don't ye?' Tilly gave the folded sheets one final blow to pat them into submission, a bit harder than necessary, before she tucked them into a drawer.

How many times had they had a similar conversation? Enough that if these words were coin, she would be swimming in money.

Susanna rolled her eyes and flopped dramatically on the bed. Nothing could send her back to her teenage self faster than a rebuke from Tilly. Suddenly, she was thirteen all over again having sneaked out for the first time and been caught upon her return. She refused to answer Tilly's questions for she knew it would aggravate her maid further.

Old habits were hard to break.

'Nothing to say for yerself?' she walked over to Susanna and popped her hands to her plump hips, a few wisps of grey hair escaping her cap.

Susanna blinked up at Tilly's looming figure and shrugged.

'Exasperating as always,' Tilly muttered and shook her head before turning to open the large heavy blue curtains that framed the double windows that looked out at the loch far off in the distance. 'Suit yerself. Ye know where to find me if ye have need of me.'

'Thank you, Tilly,' Susanna called as the woman left the room.

Sun swathed the room. Susanna stretched and stared at the ceiling, the large wooden beams solid and sound like every inch of Loch's End. The castle was an impenetrable fortress in the Highlands just like her clan itself. Or at least she had always thought it was. But the way her brothers had spoken that night she'd overheard them in the study unnerved her. What if they were not as strong and protected as she always believed? What would she do then?

She sat up.

She would refuse to concede to such a thought. Period.

Facing the loch with its rising sun, she squinted. It would be a very long day, but she could not begrudge its beauty or what she had accomplished with her evening meeting with Rowan. Soon, she would know what secrets lurked in this castle and her family would be safe.

And that was all that mattered.

She settled into her writing desk, delighting in the cool smooth wood of her favourite chair and the orderly arrangement of parchment, ink pot, and quill. Sleep would have to wait its turn for she had far more important matters to attend to, namely crafting her betrothal plan. If she was to create a believable match, she would have to be careful and thoughtful in her approach and tread carefully with Rowan. A fragility still rested in his eyes. One akin to weakness. And weakness might lead them both to ruin.

And she would not allow it.

She scratched out her list:

Phase One: The Accidental Encounter
Where?
When?
How accidental should it be?
How many observers should be there to make the encounter worth the effort?

She frowned. She hadn't thought much past getting him to agree to the ruse. Now that she had his agreement, it did sound a bit complicated. But it was necessary. She had to know what her brothers were hiding from her, and she had to prevent some unseemly marriage arrangement by implementing their fake betrothal sooner rather than later despite how abhorrent the idea of being anyone's betrothed was. She shivered.

In the last week, correspondence had been heavy, with a larger than normal volume of letters coming in and going out from the castle. And a bit of investigating had led her to note a trend in the enquiries: eligible lairds and second sons. There was also only one reason a sea of enquiries were sent out to so many lairds and second sons at once: to see who dared take her as a bride. Royce had confirmed her suspicions this very morn.

She hoped the list would be small. Very small.

And most likely it would be. She smiled. She'd done her part in distributing her share of rejections and refusals when she had tried desperately to marry Jeremiah, much to her father's displeasure years ago, and no one would mistake her for a soft, compliant bride.

Bride.

The thought of it made her throat dry.

She gripped the quill, sat forward, and straightened her back, newly inspired to work on her plan. While she was fine with being someone's fake betrothed for a while, the idea of being a real bride turned her stomach. Even though motherhood appealed to her, she had no one in mind that could fill the role of husband. And one seemed to preclude the other, did it not?

She sighed, staring down at the dark blot of ink on the parchment from where she'd stilled the quill. The ink bled out much as her grief had years ago.

Jeremiah.

He had been the one to win her heart, and when she lost him, her heart had been buried with him. And she planned for it to stay that way.

Chapter Four

'Papa?' Rosa called from outside the study door.

'Aye, love,' Rowan answered without looking up from his work. Soon, he heard the worn study door creak open, the familiar pitter-patter of small bare feet on stone, and giggles bubbling in the air as his eight-year-old daughter climbed up his legs and crawled onto his lap.

He set aside his work and smiled.

This was his favourite part of the day: these first moments when his daughter was awake and she looked upon him like he was a good man, hell a great man, and he could set the course of his day by trying to prove her right, trying to be the father she deserved. The one she believed he was.

Nothing else mattered.

She wrapped her soft warm arms about his neck and pressed a sweet wet kiss to his cheek. Her small hand scrubbed along his scruffy face, and she giggled again. 'It tickles,' she said.

'Aye. Your papa needs a shave,' he answered, wrapping his arms around her as she settled into his lap and stared up at him.

'Did you sleep well, my little pitcher?' he asked, running a hand over her long chestnut hair, the curls lopsided and still rumpled from sleep.

She shifted on his lap and nodded. 'I dreamt of Mama,' she said and rubbed her eyes. 'She looked just like the painting,' she said turning around to point to the portrait of Anna that hung in his study on the opposite wall, where he could stare upon her whenever he wished. 'It was lovely,' she continued. 'We played along the meadow and made daisy chains. I could feel the warm sun on my cheeks.'

Rowan's heart lurched in his chest, and he caught his breath, steeling himself for the emotion that always swelled within him at the mention of his late wife. He counted to five and answered. He knew talking of Anna was important to Rosa, and he wanted dearly to keep the memories of her mother alive and well within her no matter the cost to him.

'Do you remember such a day?' he asked gently as she snuggled her back against him, so they could both look upon Anna's portrait.

'Aye,' she answered. 'She made me a beautiful crown and I made her a necklace.'

He chuckled. 'Aye. I remember now. You made one for me as well as Mr. Hugh.'

She cackled. 'And Mr. Hugh broke his. Flowers went everywhere.'

'Aye. They did.'

She leaned back against Rowan's chest and sighed. 'I miss her, Papa.'

His throat clogged with emotion, but he swallowed it down. 'I do too.'

She turned and smiled at him. 'I love you, Papa.'

'And I you, my Rosa,' he murmured, pulling her into a tight hug.

She returned his embrace, and he smiled. 'What do you plan to do today?' he asked.

She pulled back. 'Cook said she would teach me how to make pies.'

'Pies?'

'Aye.' She leaned close and whispered in his ear. 'Auntie Trice's birthday is in two weeks, and I want to learn how to make her a pie. Don't tell her,' she added. 'It will be a surprise.'

'Your secret is safe with me. Off with you to Cook then. And if it helps, apple pie is her favourite.' He winked at her, and his daughter scurried out.

'But put on some shoes first,' he called after her, but she was already gone. He chuckled and shook his head. His daughter hated shoes just as he had when he was a boy. In truth, he couldn't blame her. He was tempted to pull off his own and savour the feel of the cool stone beneath the soles of his feet right this minute. Something about it always made him feel anchored to the world.

'Good morn, Mr. Hugh,' Rosa called down the hallway.

'Good morn to you, my lady,' Hugh replied. The sound of his heavy booted footfalls growing louder as he approached.

Evidently, Rowan's fancy of having bare feet this morn would have to wait.

With his brother away on clan business with his family in the northern Highlands, Rowan had much to discuss with Hugh Loudoun, the clan's second in command. Namely this farce of a plan with Susanna that he'd agreed to last night. *Deuces*. How exactly would he begin to explain? He scrubbed a hand through his hair. He wasn't altogether sure, but he would have to. Hugh was no fool, and if Rowan didn't enlist his help with crafting such a charade, it would fail before it even began. Rowan couldn't do it alone. It would require far too much coordination.

And subterfuge.

He set aside the maps that cluttered his desk, glanced at Anna's portrait, and stilled. What had he been thinking? He hadn't been. The thought of exacting revenge on the man that had stolen Anna's life and the life of their son had consumed all reason and he'd agreed in an instant. That was what the thought of Audric did to him. In a moment, he'd been set back years in his recovery of grief. The flash of hate and vengeance had lanced through him like a thunderbolt in the sky, hungry to hit its mark and singe whatever was in its path. Even now the thought of it made his pulse increase in anticipation. He rolled his shoulders. He was well enough that he could do this. He just didn't dare do it alone. Hugh would keep him in check and ensure he wasn't drifting too far afield from sanity. That he was staying focused on his health, his daughter, and the well-being of the clan. It was a daunting task, but if there was a man who could muster it, it was Hugh.

The man might also try to change Rowan's mind and convince him to fulfil Susanna's favour without exacting his revenge on Laird Audric MacDonald. Rowan shifted in his chair. Even in the wee hours of the morn after a night's sleep, his desire to follow through with Susanna's plan to exact his revenge on Audric had not wavered. The peace and healing it would give him would allow him the sleep of a lifetime. As ridiculous as it was, he still wanted and needed justice despite how hard it would be for him to maintain his well-being.

Managing extended periods of time with Susanna Cameron would break any man.

He almost chuckled aloud at his own joke.

'What has you smiling this morn?' Hugh asked as he crossed the threshold to the study.

'Ah, a new plan. Close the door,' Rowan commanded without making eye contact with Hugh. His friend would be none too pleased when he heard of his arrangement.

'I had to speak to the men on duty at the forge last night,' Rowan began.

'Oh?' Hugh asked, crossing his arms against his chest, his stance prepared for the unexpected.

'I had a surprising visitor.'

Hugh furrowed his brow and his jaw tightened. He said nothing but waited for Rowan to continue. As expected, Hugh would wait until all was revealed before commenting on anything. It was what made him such a great leader and strategist. He listened while others talked, and he had no compelling desire for power.

Unlike most soldiers he knew, Hugh desired peace above all else.

A solely unexpected and unusual trait for any soldier in the Highlands. And one Rowan never took for granted.

'Susanna Cameron.'

He shook his head and craned his neck towards Rowan. 'Sorry, did you say, Susanna Cameron?'

'Aye. She appeared in the forge close to midnight as I was working. Sneaked past our soldiers and entered unbidden. Seems her soldiers created a compelling distraction that allowed her to sneak in. Our men still don't even know she was here. Only you and I do.'

Hugh sat in the chair opposite Rowan with a thud. 'Why?' He shifted in the chair. 'She has not set foot on these lands since her sham of an engagement to your brother two years ago.'

'I remember. I was just as surprised to see her.'

Hugh studied Rowan's face for a few moments and frowned. 'I'm not going to like her reason for being here, am I?'

'Most likely not. She asked me to marry her.'

His friend's eyes widened, and then he laughed.

Rowan smiled and waited for the laughter to dissipate before he continued. 'I had the same reaction, but it is no jest. Even called in her favour from Brandon to compel me to follow through with it. *This* is what she wants in return for helping us to rescue Fiona and William the night of that sham of an engagement.'

Hugh leaned forward in his chair and narrowed his gaze at Rowan. 'But she hates you. Why would she *compel* you to marry her? Does she truly wish for you to be unhappy that much? Seems extreme even for a woman such as her.'

'Although I am not entirely clear as to what has made her so worried, she says it is so I can help her extract information from her brothers. There is a secret troubling her.'

'All of this to unearth a secret?' Hugh scoffed. 'Are you sure there is not a different motive at play here? It seems too far-fetched to be believed, and she is a Cameron after all.'

'I thought the same. The added threat to her is that Royce is threatening to marry her off to keep her safe from whatever this secret danger may be. By pretending to be engaged to me she can keep that from happening as well.'

'A pretend engagement? Now you've lost me.'

'Aye. I am to *pretend* to be engaged to her until we discover this secret of her brothers. Then, our affair can run itself into the ground and be over. She has no real desire to *actually* marry me, which is quite a relief, truth to be told.'

'To me and you both.' He ruffled his hair and sighed. 'Night and day with her might put us both into an early grave.'

Rowan laughed.

'But this still seems an odd plan. No one will believe you are serious about one another, especially after your last encounter here.'

'I said the same to her, but she is quite determined, and she made an additional offer I could not refuse.'

'Oh?' He leaned backwards in his chair. 'Now I am intrigued. I could not imagine there would be anything that could make you agree to such a farce, especially with her.'

'She can give me access to Audric. I can finally have my revenge.'

Hugh stilled and studied him before shaking his head. 'Rowan, you cannot entertain such an idea. Killing him would incite a war we would never recover from. It would turn the Highlands into a battleground, and not with the British, but with ourselves. You cannot be responsible for such despite how much he deserves such a fate. You know this.'

Rowan dug in. He knew Hugh wouldn't like this part. Perhaps he shouldn't have told him, but the man was no fool. He would have deduced it soon. 'This is the chance I have been waiting for. Surely you can see that?'

'I can see your pride talking. *That* is what I see.'

Hugh's words hit their mark.

'Aye,' he answered. 'I would be lying to pretend otherwise. But it is also what Anna and my son deserve.'

Hugh's gaze softened. 'But is that what they would want for you and Rosa? For the clan?'

Rowan stared upon Anna's portrait. He knew the answer. She wouldn't have. But she wasn't here living with the brutal agony he carried each day. Knowing he hadn't been enough. That he had failed at his most important duty: protecting his family.

But he couldn't say that aloud. Not to Hugh. Or anyone. It cut too deep and wide, and even now he could hardly breathe at the mere thought of it. He steeled himself and clenched his jaw.

'Then it is a good thing you don't have to make such a decision,' Rowan replied, his tone hard and unyielding. While there was much he could be persuaded to do, letting this go was not one of them.

Ending Laird Audric MacDonald was a mission as necessary as his love for his daughter, and he'd not let it go. Not while he drew breath.

Hugh nodded and let the matter drop, as Rowan expected he would. There was providing counsel to the Laird and then there was contradicting him, and Hugh knew his place as second in command. He'd not challenge Rowan on it further.

'But as to the matter of Susanna,' Rowan continued. 'I will need your help in devising a strategy to make our farce believable. That is why I have enlisted your help. As you know, I am far removed from the expectations of courting.'

Hugh chuckled. 'And you think I know better?'

'You know something of it, which is more than I can say. You also have a bevy of men you could ask such advice from and not be questioned, whereas such enquiries from me would create quite a stir, especially from Trice.'

Hugh laughed at that, the good humour and rapport between them easily restored. 'Aye. Your sister would love it, and you would never hear the end of it. I will see what I can find out. What thoughts do you have so far?'

Rowan turned the parchment he had been writing and sketching ideas on for hours around so Hugh could see it. He smirked and squinted at it before glancing back up to Rowan.

'This looks like a battle plan.'

Rowan smiled. 'It is.'

Chapter Five

'Yer correspondence, my lady.' Lunn murmured close to Susanna's ear, pressing a small letter into her palm as he helped her down from Midnight after their morning ride. A glimpse of the maroon wax seal stamped with what looked to be the Campbell crest sent her heart fluttering, the response surprising her.

It was about time. A week had already passed.

'Aye. Thank you for asking. I had a lovely ride this morn,' Susanna replied, loud enough for any stable boys to hear as she alighted to the ground and handed off Midnight's reins to Lunn. She slipped the note into her gown pocket quickly before removing her gloves in case other gazes were upon them. While she wished to rip into the note unbidden, she dared not risk being seen. Without secrecy, her plan would fail before it even began.

Her heart skittered with a mix of relief and irritation. While she was thrilled to finally receive some correspondence from Rowan, his lack of urgency had tested the limits of her withering patience. Her brothers continued their daily talks without her, despite her protests, and the uncertainty fed her doubt much like air to a starved fire.

She ran her fingers over the edge of the letter in her pocket. She would have to break her fast and wait before reading the letter in private. Too many eyes and tongues were about Loch's End.

Climbing the hillside, she took in the glorious, lush green grass and soft turning of the leaves on the trees. Soon, the valley would be awash with autumnal shades of reds, golds, and browns. And not long after the once violet fields of heather would be dark green hillsides carrying the winds of winter along with their subtle whispers and howls along the loch. Her favourite time of year was almost here. She sighed and her heart slowed. This was the quiet peace she sought.

If only she had the man she had loved at her side to share it with.

Even now she could feel his touch heating her bare skin and the feathery trace of the back of his hand along the nape of her neck. She shivered as a breeze kissed along her cheek.

Jeremiah.

She smiled.

'When the wind whispers softly along your cheek, it is me, love, sending my kisses until I return.'

Her chest tightened and she blinked back the tears burning the back of her eyes. Those were the last words he'd spoken to her before he'd left for battle. His gaze revealing he had little hope of returning to her. If she were honest with herself, she had known it too. Her father had been angry, and he was a brutal man. Jeremiah had dared love her, the daughter of the Laird, a woman well above his station, and Father would not suffer such insolence.

He had sent Jeremiah to a battle along the Borderlands as punishment, but they had both suffered and lost. Lost one another. For ever. She clenched her fists at her side. While she'd always been prone to hardness and suppressing her feelings, a consequence of her father's own coldness and cruelty, Jeremiah's death made Susanna's edges rougher and her anger sharper. She'd turned into a woman who preferred to use her sharpness and edges to keep all other suitors at a distance, for there was no replacing Jeremiah and no one who would ever be worthy of giving her heart to again.

She frowned. The joyous mood from her ride and the walk through the beautiful early morn of the day was evaporating away like the morning dew the closer she came to the castle. Rolling her shoulders, she set her mask of indifference in place and entered, nodding to those servants she passed, as she headed to the dining room. If she were lucky, her brothers would have already broken their fast and she could eat alone.

Entering the room, she frowned. She was not to be so lucky this morn.

'Sister,' Rolf said, nodding to her in greeting before popping what remained of a piece of bread into his mouth.

'Good morn,' she replied, her gaze flitting briefly to meet his. When his eyes cut to their brother Royce and then back to her without a word, her heart skipped a beat and then sped up. It was her younger brother's way of warning her that Royce was not to be trifled with this morn. They had used such code since they were children. She walked quietly to the buffet to see the spread set out for them. The usual meats, cheeses, breads, and jams greeted her. She picked up a plate and set a slice of bread upon it before Royce launched into his speech.

'It has been a week since we spoke, sister. I have granted you time. Have you prepared a list of suitable candidates for marriage as we agreed?'

She clutched the plate, hoping her fierce hold would not shatter the fine porcelain into bits. Rather than fear, anger filled her gut. She counted to ten and then answered. 'Aye. I have a list.' After plunking a sausage, cheese, and a slathering of marmalade to her plate, she dropped her plate loudly on the table, sat down with a rather unlady-like plop, and set what she hoped was her best withering gaze upon him.

'And?' Royce asked, matching her ire.

She glanced to Rolf who shook his head slowly at her as if in warning to swallow the angry words brewing from her lips, but she lifted a single brow at him instead and he sighed, knowing what was coming for they had spoken about such a list just the evening before.

She removed the small, folded paper from her pocket, careful to leave the correspondence she'd received tucked safely within. After setting the note on the table, the maid poured her some tea, and Susanna thanked her.

Royce opened the note and sighed.

Susanna stifled the smirk on her lips and took a sip, the liquid scalding the tip of her tongue. Perhaps it served her right.

'Close the door upon your leave,' he ordered. The maid nodded and sealed them within the room.

'It is blank,' Royce stated coolly.

Rolf met her gaze, also suppressing a chuckle.

'You knew as well?' Royce set his glare upon her younger brother.

'Did you expect anything else? I didn't.' Rolf toyed with the rumpled linen napkin beside his empty plate.

'Aye. I did,' Royce answered, his tone dark and deep. 'I provide you the option to pick your husband and you lob the offer back in my face in reproach with a blank piece of paper. Perhaps I shall marry you off to Dallan MacGregor. I hear he has not secured a match.'

Rolf intervened, a growl entering his voice. 'That is too far, brother, and not a joke to be made.'

Royce shook his head. 'Apologies. You are right. I never should have said such. Not even in jest. Not after what happened.'

Or *almost* happened to their younger sister, Catriona. Thank God Ewan Stewart had saved her that day at the Grassmarket in Edinburgh. Otherwise... Susanna's skin crawled at the thought of such a horrid man like Dallan MacGregor being anyone's husband.

Royce scrubbed a hand through his hair, and the room stilled.

'Despite the crassness of what I just said,' Royce began, 'and how lack of sleep is impacting my judgement, the re-sult is still the same. You *must* pick someone, sister. While Rolf and I cannot divulge the entirety of why, you must marry within the year, for your own safety. The High-lands is an uncertain place now. We need to know you are protected.' His gaze was soft, his voice pleading, and the alarm that was slowly bubbling within her started a slow boil. Angry, roaring Royce she knew and understood, but this—this she did not, and it terrified her.

Rolf reached over and squeezed her hand. 'We know you do not wish to marry after losing Jeremiah, but it is important, sister. Please choose someone and soon. Please.'

The second please and desperation in their gazes cut her to the quick. Before she knew it, she was nodding. 'Aye. I will. And soon.'

Her hunger was squashed by their conversation; she rose from the table.

'You did not eat,' Rolf said and gestured to the spread of food.

'I find I am no longer hungry,' she answered. 'And there are other matters I must attend to.' She left before they launched into any enquiry. The last thing she needed was more poking and prodding or encouragement to choose a spouse. Her stomach soured, and she climbed the stairs, reaching her chambers in record time. Tilly assisted her with changing into a more proper day gown and out of her riding clothes, the hems now soiled and splattered with the mud and dirt from her extended ride.

After Tilly left, Susanna walked to the window and opened her palm. She had hidden the letter there while she'd changed, and the parchment had warmed and softened, moulding to the curving shape of her hold.

She pressed her lips together before breaking the wax seal on it, a feather of worry clouding her. It had been a week since her visit to his forge. Had Rowan changed his mind already? Or perhaps he had a plan in play? With Rowan, her chances of success equalled her probability of failure. Despite his agreement at their initial meeting, uncertainty had consumed her. It was a large request, and he was a man known for his moods well before losing Anna. Her loss had only exacerbated his changefulness. He was unpredictable, which made him a dangerous choice for such a secretive plan, but he had been her only option for this ruse for three reasons. First, he was the only man who would never really marry her because he despised her because she had refused him before. Second, he was so honest that he was incapable of going back on his word.

Lastly and to Susanna's chagrin, despite all that had happened between them, he was the one man she dared trust outside of her family, Lunn, and Cynric, and she could not involve Jeremiah's friends in such a scheme.

Unfortunately, that had not changed. Over the last week, she had thought upon her options for a real husband, and they were—less than appealing. She said a quick prayer and opened the letter.

> *Suze,*
> *I have thought further upon your request and made some plans which may interest you. I dare not risk including them here. Meet me at the old grove two nights from now at midnight.*
>   *If I do not see you, I will assume you have had a change of heart and abandon any further plans.*
> *Ro*

Susanna's heart skipped at the sight of his use of their nicknames for one another when they were young. No one had called her that in over a decade. Some small part of her flickered to life at the memory of his voice calling her that all those years ago, as if her young self was reawakened and yawning to life.

She bit her lip and swallowed before reading it once more and closing it. Who knew what sort of plan he had concocted by now. Rowan was a creative strategist and strong warrior. Or at least he used to be. Grief had dulled his sharpness. She had seen that even at their initial meeting. The Rowan of old would not have been startled by her arrival at the forge. He would have heard the first squeak of the barn door sliding open and drawn his blade. But the

Rowan of old also would have dragged her out of the forge and not heard her out at all.

She'd have to take both sides of his newness as they came and hope the damage from grief years ago had weakened him just enough to be malleable but not so much that he could not lead her in such an endeavour when required. Only time would tell.

She sat at her writing desk and began a sketch of her own plans, so she'd have a clear idea of her own thoughts before she heard out his own two nights from now.

Ugh.

Her shoulders slumped.

She'd also need to do the unthinkable: ask for any social correspondence. Perusing the latest invitations was essential, despite how much she loathed the idea of being a part of societal manoeuvrings. Although, such a display and effort would set her brothers more at ease as she would seem to be complying with their latest request: to attempt to find a husband. She tugged on the rope near her writing table to summon one of the servants.

While she was quite capable of going down a flight of stairs and sorting through the correspondence herself, making a show of the request would work in her favour. Word would spread through the servants at Loch's End and filter on to her brothers about her renewed and unexpected interest in the upcoming social events of the season. If she were lucky, it might even spread well beyond and out into the Highlands. She smiled widely and wriggled her toes in her shoes.

This would look exactly as she wanted it to.

She would appear to be soft and compliant, while scheming and setting her own plan in motion.

It would be perfect.

A knock sounded at the door.

'Come in,' Susanna answered.

One of the maids entered and stopped before her. 'Aye, my lady?'

'Can you bring me all the recent social correspondence from the last week or so? I'd like to peruse it.' Susanna smiled and attempted to look as innocent as possible, which felt far more forced than she expected.

The young lass's eyes widened briefly before relaxing again. She paused and then replied. 'Aye, my lady.'

'Thank you. That will be all.'

The young woman took a moment to move, but soon she regained her faculties and left.

Based on the wide-eyed disbelief in the young woman's gaze, the first move in Susanna's plan was now well in motion. She could sit back for a minute and watch it unfold.

She had scarcely begun to sketch out a list of ideas for her plan when a knock sounded at the door again.

'Come in,' she replied, shoving the used parchment into the drawer of her writing desk before closing it softly.

She stood and stilled at the sight of her sister-in-law Iona at the threshold. She smiled deeply and hurried to her.

'You shouldn't be up,' Susanna fussed.

Iona flashed her a wicked smile and glanced behind her before quietly closing the door. 'I have made an escape from my room while Royce was downstairs,' she whispered as she stepped further into the room. 'I cannot spend one more hour in that chamber. I fear I am watching the dust settle with boredom,' she continued in her normal voice. A few rogue waves escaped her long dark plait of hair, and her eyes gleamed with mischief despite the hollow pallor of her skin.

Susanna grasped Iona's hand and pulled her into a gentle side hug. 'But you must rest, sister.'

'I know, but I do not have to wither away. I am restless and my limbs ache to move about. I dream about swimming in the loch once more, but I know Royce will have none of it. Nor would the doctor. Perhaps you could walk with me outside? Take in some fresh air?'

'Aye,' she replied. 'Although we will take one of my men along with us, so Royce does not fret.'

Iona met her gaze, her brow furrowed.

'So he will fret *less*,' Susanna corrected and chuckled.

Iona glanced over Susanna's shoulder at the open writing desk and the materials upon it. 'But I have interrupted you. I can come back later.'

'Nay. You will do no such thing. Your arrival will aid me in postponing the inevitable.'

Iona smiled. 'And what is that?'

Susanna sighed. 'Reading through correspondence once it arrives and deciding which social endeavours I shall attend.'

Iona's mouth gaped open, and she stepped back. 'Why?' she asked, a note of suspicion in her voice.

Despite not knowing Iona long, she evidently knew Susanna well enough to know her disdain for such a task. 'To find a husband,' she replied, her voice dropping so low and in such an indiscernible murmur that it was indecipherable.

Iona cocked her head. 'To find a what?'

She felt like stamping her foot like a three-year-old demanding more sweets, but she didn't. She squared her shoulders and said clearly, 'To find a husband.'

Iona crossed her arms against her chest and frowned. 'Why?'

When Susanna failed to answer, Iona surmised the truth. 'Because of Royce,' she muttered, settling on the settee near the writing desk. It was more of a statement than a question.

Susanna nodded and sat next to her, settling back into the soft cushions.

Iona rolled her eyes. 'You would think he would have learned after Catriona. He pushes and shoves his notions into decisions without thinking sometimes. I will speak with him.'

Susanna smirked at Iona's certainty in being able to sway her husband. Before her, Royce could not be swayed into much of anything. The petite healer was strong, intelligent, and formidable, and Susanna was often in awe of how easily she had slipped into their family after bringing Royce back from certain death after being ambushed on her tiny isle of Lismore.

Despite being far too rational now to have such romantic notions, Susanna couldn't help but wonder at how fate had brought the two of them crashing together, much like the waves upon the shore of where Iona found Royce that night. If she hadn't rescued him and nursed him back to health, her eldest brother and laird of the clan would be dead. The thought of such a loss made Susanna shiver. She had come to love this new and improved brother of hers. Iona had softened his hardened edges, well some of them, which was far more than she could ever ask for.

'I appreciate your willingness, but I do not believe Royce movable on this issue. He claims it is for my own safety and well-being.'

'A man would say such,' she said with a chuckle of her own. 'But I believe we both know not every man can provide such comforts, but the right man can. I do wish that for you.'

'I do not hold out such hope for myself,' Susanna replied.

'I had not either but look at me now. Seems I just had to get out of my own way. My doubt almost cost me everything.'

'Meaning?'

Iona met her gaze and gifted her a soft smile. 'I did not believe I deserved his love or your family's love for that matter. That is why I did not come when he first invited me here to be his wife.'

The confession stilled Susanna.

That wasn't her, was it?

She didn't have a husband because there was no replacing Jeremiah. The two things were not the same.

Were they?

She looked down at her hands and picked at her nail.

'Sometimes I wonder if you have denied yourself for the same reason.' Iona's words were soft. 'But it is not for me to say. Just know that I will support you in whatever you do. You are my sister.'

Tears heated the back of Susanna's eyes. Why did she feel like crying? She never cried.

Perhaps she did need some fresh air, despite returning from a ride only a few hours ago.

'Still longing for a walk?' she offered, avoiding the implication of Iona's statement.

'Aye,' she replied, gripping Susanna's hand. 'Although I cannot promise I will not be sick in the bushes at some point.'

Susanna laughed aloud, the feeling of it a joyful re-lease of emotion in the moment. 'And I promise not to tell Royce if you do.'

'Deal. Let us go before anyone can stop us.'

Correspondence could wait.

Chapter Six

Crunch. Crunch. Crunch.

Rowan frowned at the sound of leaves being crushed beneath boots. Despite her usual stealth, Susanna and her guards were as loud as Rosa trying to catch him in a game of 'Where am I?' where he hid, and she tried to find him. Rowan clenched his jaw and stared at the bright moon above him and the intermittent clouds that eased effortlessly across the navy sky. Tiny stars dotted the darkness, like an array of breadcrumbs leading to the heavens. He smiled. Or at least that was what Anna always used to say.

He blinked back the emotion that accompanied the memory and remained hidden behind one of the many large rowan trees spaced along the hearty grove and watched Susanna advance. He wished to observe *her* this time before they spoke as opposed to what happened during her visit to the forge at Argyll Castle. He needed to see if she could be trusted before he ventured further into their plan together.

A Cameron was a Cameron after all.

Perched high in the opposite direction from the hillside, Rowan spied Hugh scanning the surroundings to ensure Rowan's safety and determine who else accompanied Susanna. As a skilled soldier and bowman like himself, Hugh could fell a man from a great distance with impressive accuracy. And despite his reluctance to take part in this scheme with Susanna, Hugh was loyal and willing to protect Rowan and the clan at all costs, even in this ridiculous ruse.

The crunching grew louder and the upper leaves on a tree quivered to his left as a bird took flight, spooked by her approach. Rowan held his breath as Susanna slowly emerged into his sights. Cloaked in all black, her steps were careful, methodical even, and she scanned the area before her as she advanced. A glimmer of metal flashed from a drawn blade, and Rowan caught sight of one and then the other Cameron soldier accompanying her this eve. They had fanned out behind her in a 'V' formation to ensure privacy but were also close enough to strike quickly in her defence if needed. While the men's facial features were too far in shadow for him to discern their identity, perhaps Hugh would have better luck at distinguishing who they were. He wanted to know who the woman trusted enough to accompany her. It would help him with his backup plan, if indeed he needed to use it.

Susanna stopped and stilled like a doe in the wood as it listens for a predator. Rowan watched, unable to look away at her exquisite yet fragile profile set in the darkness. A small curling of chilled breath escaped her lips, otherwise she might have blended into the surroundings of the wood and disappeared entirely. This duality of her strength and softness had been a fascination for him since their first meeting all those years ago when they were young, and even now he held his breath.

A slow smile formed on her lips. 'I know you are there,' she said just above a whisper. 'I can feel you watching me.' She turned in his direction a quarter step and pushed back her cloak hood to reveal her face and the loose dark locks framing her features.

Gooseflesh rose along his forearms as her gaze met his own.

He stepped from behind the tree and set a glare upon her, frustrated at being discovered before he wished to reveal himself and by the thrumming attraction his body had to her presence.

'You may need to work on your stealth, my laird,' she murmured as he approached.

'As you may wish to work on your couth, my lady,' he countered, glowering at her.

She shrugged. 'I have never claimed to be kind. Why would you expect such now?'

'Because we are to pretend to be betrothed,' he said as loudly as he dared, so as not to be overheard. 'No man would allow themselves to be cut and cuckolded by the woman he plans to wed. Surely even *you* know such.' He lifted his brow at her and settled his hands along his waist belt. 'Otherwise, this ruse of yours shall be over before it begins.'

She said nothing and pressed her lips into a thin line, a tell that his words had hit their mark and served their purpose.

'Your plan?' she finally asked. Her light blue eyes set upon him as cool and piercing as a pike thrust into frozen ice.

He looked away and pulled the rolled parchment from his waist belt and gestured for her to follow him up to a small spot in the grove where they could be partially hidden by the canopy of two trees yet still sit on the large boulder there and read by the full light of the moon. This was not his first midnight rendezvous, and he knew the grove as he knew the battle scars along his body. Every tree within the neatly arranged orchard had grown in unparalleled precision just as he had and this place had become a haven and part of who he was, as if it were a fixture of his identity.

For all intents and purposes, it was, for it was planted on the day of his birth. A tribute to him from his father and a beacon of hope and luck for a clan attempting to recover from its troubled past. Just as he was now.

He gestured for her to take a seat on the large boulder, weathered smooth by wind and rain. Her cloak flared out before she sat, reminding him of a peacock showing its feathers to assert itself. He smothered the beginnings of a smile. While they had both changed, in some ways they were each profoundly the same. When he joined her on the boulder, there was little room between them. He frowned. He didn't remember this boulder being so small and…intimate. Shifting away from her a bit, he unrolled the parchment. She leaned closer to him, and he stilled before turning to glare at her.

She matched his glare and lifted an eyebrow. 'I cannot see it clearly with you so far away. Either I move closer, or you do.'

'We both will,' he conceded, and they both slid in until they were seated hip to hip. Her warmth was an unwelcome distraction. After a few moments, he commanded himself to focus on the plan at hand: settle upon terms for their arrangement, agree to the first step in said arrangement so it can be set in motion, and leave. His gut told him to skip the first two steps and leave, but he could not sacrifice the idea of exacting revenge upon Audric and giving Anna and his son the justice they deserved. He ran an open palm down his trews to centre himself and began.

'This is the plan I wished to share with you,' he whispered. 'Once we agree upon it, we can set the first step in motion.'

Susanna scanned the document and then frowned. Shifting closer to him, she rummaged in her right gown pocket, teetering into his side. He clutched her shoulder to keep her from rocking back and toppling off the boulder before righting herself. 'And here is *my* plan,' she countered. She unfolded her document slowly and then held it out to him. 'I will analyse yours and you mine, and then we shall come to some sort of an agreement.'

He sighed, making no effort to accept the parchment she held out to him. 'I am a laird. Making battle plans is what *I* do. We need not look upon yours. I have a well thought out plan that can be easily executed.'

'And may *I* remind *you* this is *not* a battle plan, but a betrothal,' she replied, letting her parchment drop to her lap. 'It requires more…delicacy.'

'Are you sure?' he asked. 'Neither of us excels with delicacy.'

'While you are not altogether wrong, we must try. Just read it.' She extended her plan to him again. 'Please. The outcome of this is important. It must be successful.' The desperation he saw at their first meeting came into her gaze again, and he shifted, uncomfortable with and unused to her pleading. He preferred her demanding and irrational.

He took the document from her. 'Under the condition that you will agree to the best plan, not your own.'

'As long as you agree to the same.'

'Aye. I will.'

They settled into silence as they read. While her plan was sound, Rowan preferred his own much as he expected he would.

'Meow?' Susanna said murmuring under her breath and chuckled.

Rowan paused his reading and turned to her. 'What?'

She laughed. 'Your plan is M. E. O. W. As in 'meow' like from a cat.' Her laughter intensified until she had an unladylike snort. Then, she met his gaze, her eyes as bright blue as a clear summer sky, and his breathing faltered at the simple joy in her features. Had he ever heard her laugh so? Perhaps when they were young, but since then? Never. He stared at her transfixed and bewildered all at once. What had her in such a state?

'I don't quite…' he began, but she interrupted.

'My apologies. I am reading. Do not mind me.' She breathed out and collected herself, smoothing back her hair from where it had fallen about her face.

He shook his head. He had no idea what she was on about, but it had given her some joy. Perhaps that was something. He twisted his lips. But he couldn't remember crafting anything that was even remotely entertaining or humorous.

'Are you laughing at me or my plan? Or both?' he asked, his words tainted with a bit of anger, in case she was mocking him.

'Neither' she replied, setting the plan aside. 'It is a solid plan. I just happened to have made a word from the first letter of each of your steps, a memory tool that has served me well over my years, and it happened to reduce to 'meow'. And knowing you, since you are nothing close to a cat at all, well, it made me laugh.'

'Meow?'

'Aye. Your steps break down as Meet by chance, Engage with the enemy, Openly woo, and Win her, meaning my, hand publicly. If you take the first letter of each, it creates the new word meow.' She awaited his response as if what she had said made all the sense in the world, which of course it didn't. Not even close. In truth, she sounded like a woman too deep in her cups or addled, but he knew she was neither.

Or was she?

He sniffed her breath. 'Have you been drinking? I know you enjoy—' He coughed as she elbowed him in the side.

'I've not been drinking you fool. Let us get on with our discussion otherwise we might be here until dawn.' Her eyes darkened. Her mood soured as quickly as it had previously sweetened.

He cleared his throat and straightened back up. 'Your thoughts on my plan other than meow?' he asked.

'Reasonable. Although I do think you have left out many details such as *when* we will meet by chance, *when* you will engage with the enemy, *how* you will openly woo me, and *how* you will win my hand. Care to share those finer details with me?'

'I left the details of what we needed to work out and agree on together for our meeting now. How would I know what events might be suitable for a woman such as yourself to go to for our first 'meet' or how you would like me to engage with Audric and your brothers, as enemies to our future relationship?'

'Simple. First, I will go to whatever social event is the soonest, so we can begin this ruse as quickly as possible. It has no bearing to me as to which one it is. I loathe them all equally. Second, you must remain an enemy to them all, at least at first. Audric and my brothers will instantly distrust any kindness you relay to them too soon. But your meanness and arrogance?' she chuckled. 'Such behaviours will put them at ease, and they will not expect the web we are beginning to spin around them.'

'You speak as though we are a spider and they insects caught in our netting.'

She pondered the suggestion and then nodded. 'They are. And my well-being and the clan's well-being depends upon how well we thread and weave our deceit.'

His stomach soured. The more she spoke of their 'deceit,' the more ill he felt. He was a man of honour, not deception. To win at battle through skill and strategy was one thing, but to win through deceit was quite another. 'Are you not at all worried about what will happen when our deceit is uncovered? Are you sure you wish and need to proceed in such a manner? Perhaps there is another more direct and ethical solution.'

'I have thought upon it over and over into the wee hours of the morn. This is my only option.' Her tone was level and serious with an edge of certainty that surprised him.

'You do not fear your brothers' anger after such deception?' Curiosity was getting the best of him. His gut still told him there was more to her story than what she had shared.

'Aye. They will be livid,' she corrected. 'But I would rather deal with their anger than for them to be dead.'

'Dead?' He faced her. She glanced away from him, worrying her hands in her lap. He clutched her forearm gently. 'Look at me.'

She didn't at first, but when he gently squeezed her forearm, she turned back to him, her eyes bright and wild.

'What are you talking about?' he asked. 'You said you feared for *your* well-being, not theirs? You said you did not wish to marry. That you wished to uncover a secret. Why are you now talking as if the lives of your brothers rest in our hands and the success of this plan?'

She held his gaze before answering. 'Because they do.'

'Explain.'

'I have told you all I can for it is all I know. My brothers will not reveal to me all that threatens them and us, but merely their urgency for my union.'

She still held back from him. He could sense it. But why?

'Then, I will be myself and allow them to see the arrogance and anger that hounds me each day. Shall that work?' he asked, anger roiling in his gut. This meeting with Susanna was becoming even more vexing than expected. He needed to know everything if their plan was to be successful.

'Then, plan on bringing your anger and self-righteousness to the Tournament of Champions at Glenhaven at week's end.'

His head fell back in exasperation briefly before casting her a glare. 'Why must *that* be our "meet by chance" moment? I am no young buck in search of haughty praise by lasses as I throw a hammer. And you are no young prize to be won. Surely there is a better event than that.'

Her back stiffened. 'While you might be no prize, my laird, I am the unmarried daughter of the previous laird of Cameron and sister to the current one. I *am* a prize. And if my brothers are to believe I am serious about finding a husband and you serious about claiming a new bride, we must go to an event that has been flaunted as such a meeting place for decades.' She levelled her gaze at him, and he shifted on the rock.

She was right and he hated it. He held his tongue.

'And besides, gossip has it this may be the last year they host the event. Why not enjoy the last endeavour of it?'

He frowned. 'Perhaps because I never enjoyed the previous *endeavours* of it.'

She scrunched her brow and bit her lip. 'But you met Anna there.'

His chest tightened. 'I know, Susanna. And that is exactly why I do not wish to attend again.'

'I well understand your hesitation. I am not insensitive to it. But think of how much romance and believability it would provide our scheme weeks from now. Us meeting there after a decade when you met your first wife there. Me suddenly opening my heart to you after not doing so with anyone else for years after losing Jeremiah.'

He hated her for asking so much of him.

But he couldn't begrudge the logic of her plan. It *was* a fine strategy from a battle standpoint. He scratched his head. But it would wreak havoc on him. 'On one condition.'

She waited for him to continue.

'My sister Beatrice, Hugh, and my daughter will accompany me. Hugh to maintain my sanity and Trice to help care for Rosa. This could be an opportunity for Rosa to see a part of the Highlands tradition she has not yet experienced before it is gone.'

He could also share with her some of his past with her mother. They could experience and remember Anna together. He swallowed hard. If he could bear it.

'As long as you do not become too sentimental or act too much a grieving widower,' she countered. 'Our awareness of each other must be noticed.'

'Susanna…' he warned.

'You are doing this for Anna are you not?' she asked leaning towards him.

'Aye. But I will not dishonour her memory in the process,' he replied, his tone harsh and low, his face a whisper from her own. His pulse increased as he continued. 'I cannot pretend she was not my wife, that I did not love her, that I am not a widower.'

Susanna touched his face, a gentle wisp of fingers along his cheek as one might do to calm a child. 'And I would not ask you to,' she said softly. 'This is a deception, nothing more. All we must do is make people believe in it. So, a small part of us must believe in it too. That is my point. You must act as I must for this plan of ours to work. For me to discover what secrets plague and threaten my family and for you to finally excise the devil that has wreaked havoc upon yours.'

Her touch ignited longing in him, and he fought the urge to cover her hand with his own and hold it to his face. Despite how much he still missed Anna, there was no denying his loneliness and how much he missed the consoling soft caress of a woman. He leaned forward yearning for the touch to continue, but her hand was gone before he blinked again. His cheek was cool, vacant. When she stared back at him quizzically, he started and pulled away abruptly.

'Seems we have a plan, my lady,' he said coolly. 'I will arrive at Glenhaven on Friday in time for the evening meal. If our chance meeting doesn't happen then, find me on the fields for the games on Saturday.'

'Shall I pretend to swoon at your hammer throws?' she replied with a playful eye roll.

'Nay,' he replied. 'You shall not need to pretend.' He turned away and caught himself smiling as he went to find Hugh.

Then, he cursed himself for being such a fool and his smile fell flat.

They *were* only pretending, and he'd be wise to remember it was a small part of him fulfilling his clan's promise for a favour as well as his larger plan for revenge for Anna and their son.

Nothing more.

He had to stay focused on his purpose.

Chapter Seven

'I still cannot fathom that you are here in Argyll with us, sister,' said Catriona Stewart as she enveloped Susanna in a fierce tight hug. Susanna returned her sister's warm embrace on the landing of Glenhaven, the site of the Tournament of Champions to be held this weekend. Despite it being only a year since Catriona's marriage to Laird Ewan Stewart, Susanna still felt that she was making up for all the lost time between them. Catriona had been lost to their family for well over a decade due to the cruel fates of the sea. Having her back in her life had renewed some of Susanna's belief in goodness and hope. Susanna looked up to Catriona's resilience, kindness, and strength.

Susanna pulled back to look upon her sister's face, the glow of expectant motherhood reflected in her fuller physical features just as happiness reflected in her eyes. Contentment flooded Susanna's heart, and there was nowhere else she wished to be in this moment. She swallowed back her reservations about lying, and then answered, 'I felt it was high time to find a husband, and this seemed the best place to begin my search. I also thought it was a fabulous reason and excuse to come see you. I hope you do not mind the last-minute request to come stay with you and Ewan.'

'I could not have been happier to receive your letter and

to see you here now.' She clutched Susanna's hands in her own and squeezed them. 'The bairn continues to grow and the doctor says we should expect a February arrival.' She winked at her and tucked her elbow within her own as they walked further into the castle. 'So why are you really here? I do not believe for a moment it is to find a husband.' She narrowed her amber eyes at Susanna, and her lips quirked into his smile.

Susanna stiffened momentarily and then released a nervous chuckle. While fooling her brothers might not be so challenging, convincing Catriona of her plan might be near impossible. The woman was gifted in reading people and discerning the truth, a skill that had kept her alive in a string of difficult circumstances prior to Ewan finding her a year ago at the Grassmarket in Edinburgh.

'I will explain everything, sister, but first I would love to get settled, change into more appropriate clothes, and refresh myself before we dine. I want to take advantage of what time I have with you and Ewan this evening before everyone else descends upon Glenhaven tomorrow for the Tournament.'

'Aye. I will take you to your chambers. But I will still wriggle the truth out of you,' she replied.

'Alas, I know you will.'

Which was exactly what Susanna feared.

Susanna did her best to hide her displeasure at Rowan not being in attendance for the evening meal the previous night or this morn as she broke her fast before the games began. How had the man not been here in time for two such optimal moments for them to formally meet again in front of her family? Time was slipping away, and they needed to take advantage of every moment of this weekend to make their plan a success. She lifted her skirts and strode down the familiar hillside to the events, assisting Catriona as they went. With every heavy footfall, she reminded herself that she could throttle the man later—after he arrived.

'Thank you for helping me,' Catriona offered. 'I find myself a bit more unsteady now that I struggle to properly see my feet.'

'I wonder how you will be able to walk upright once Hogmanay comes,' Susanna replied with a chuckle. Leave it to her sister to distract her from her worries.

'We've had quite the turnout this year,' Catriona added, gesturing to the fields full of young lairds and their men preparing for events, unattached ladies watching from afar and whispering to one another, and a scampering of children all hustling about as the events were being set up for the day.

'It does look rather crowded. Is this the norm or because rumour has it that Ewan is set to give them up next year?' Susanna added.

Catriona laughed. 'I knew such a rumour would catch fire if he let it.' She shook her head. 'He has no such plans.' She leaned closer to Susanna and whispered into her ear. 'But he also took no pains in dispelling the rumour when he heard it. He was hoping it would attract more people to help bring us together this season with all the strife and unrest throughout the Highlands. It seems to have worked.'

'I would say so by the looks of it.'

'Just this morn, Laird Campbell even arrived with his daughter in tow. Who would have thought that possible? Ewan has told me many a story of the man's past. I was pleased to see him here and looking so well.'

Susanna's hold on Catriona's arm tightened and then relaxed in relief. *He was here*. All was not lost. She released a long breath as they reached the bottom of the hill. 'That is a surprise. He is not a very social man. Why is he here do you think?'

'I have some theories, but I will keep them to myself. I have gossiped far more than I should have already. Ah, Ewan is waving me over. I will catch up with you in a few minutes. I am overjoyed you are here.' She released Susanna's arm and pressed a kiss to her cheek.

'Aye. As I am pleased to see you.' Susanna replied and watched her sister and Ewan heading towards one another. Seeing them so happy was such a blessing. One she never took for granted. He was a good man, and she would always be grateful for what he did to save Catriona and return her to her family and the Cameron clan. But she also knew Catriona was a Stewart now. She was on the cusp of beginning a family of her own, and soon her attentions would be upon that. Being a Cameron would become second.

Susanna bit her lip, watching the couple walk hand in hand down to the playing field. Could she have that? Did she even want it? Her heart ached with an answer she didn't wish to acknowledge.

Aye. She did.

But creating a family of her own would be risky. Susanna sighed. She'd need to find a man she could trust, dare to rely on him, and wade into the murky waters of marriage and hope she could even carry a bairn. Her mother had had her own difficulties with such matters, having lost two babes to miscarriages in the first months of pregnancy after having Susanna and before having her younger sister Catriona. Would Susanna face the same challenges? And would she be able to handle them? Her mother had struggled greatly after the back-to-back losses of her bairns.

'Beautiful day, is it not?'

The familiar husky, deep voice from behind stilled her, shattering her thoughts and musings over a future she dared not long for. She wasn't up to such disappointment, not right now, anyway.

She closed her eyes and set her veil of indifference in place, despite the relief coursing through her. Now that he had finally arrived, their charade could begin.

'About time, I might add,' she replied and turned to him, crossing her arms against her chest.

He narrowed his gaze at her but flattened the irritation she spied through his flared nostrils. 'If we are to appear to be enjoying our little meet here, then you will need to set aside that glare you have upon me now. No one will believe we are anything like a couple, if you only send me daggers, my lady.' He nodded and gave what may have been his version of a smile, as lopsided and awkward as it was.

She fidgeted and let her hands fall to her sides. *Drat*. He was right. She squared her shoulders and lifted her chin to him, pushing back the hood of her cloak. 'Good morn, my laird,' she said, sending him what she hoped was her most dazzling and affecting smile, before offering her hand to him.

His gaze heated and he smiled as he lifted her hand into his own and kissed it, a soft but ardent pressure of his warm lips against her flesh. A tingle of awareness travelled along her fingers and arm. She fought a shiver. As he let her hand go, he lowered his voice. 'That is the bewitching minx I know. Just do be careful not to flash your intentions too brightly. It must be believable after all. We have not been in each other's lives in a long time. Or at least that is what everyone else will believe. Our attraction and intent cannot be too sudden, despite how attracted you may be to me.'

She wanted to stomp her feet and shout in frustration. 'Are you trying to bait me?' she replied in a low voice matching his own, her teeth almost clenched. 'You just asked me to soften to you, and so I did.'

'This is a wooing, Susanna,' he said, taking a step forward. 'It will take time to make it believable, especially *you* softening to the likes of *me* with our history—and if I remember correctly, you are not a patient woman on any count. This shall be great practice for you in building that skill.'

Now she wanted to throttle him. She resisted the urge to grab him by the tunic or pound a fist against his chest. The man was infuriating. 'Aye. It shall take some effort on my part.' She smiled, turned on her heel, and took one step to advance down the rest of the hillside.

'Do you not wish to send me some good luck?' he called. 'Or perhaps provide me a ribbon of your favour before I set upon my first event, the stone put?'

'I do not wish to appear too eager, my laird, do I?' She continued, smirking before she could stop herself.

He was an arse. Plain and simple. There was no manoeuvring around such, but perhaps this ruse of theirs could be a distraction against her real worries about her brothers, an arranged marriage, and the clan's welfare. She paused. She might even have fun. She shook her head and continued. That was yet another ridiculous notion. This was Rowan Campbell she was talking about. He didn't know how to enjoy himself—neither did she.

Together they would be lucky if they could create anything close to the believable farce of being a couple. The man was impossible.

Chapter Eight

The woman was impossible. Rowan stalked down to the field and joined the other competitors, most of whom were almost a decade younger and scarcely had scruff that would make the likeness of a beard. He grumbled, attempted to stretch before the first event, and was grateful to spy Hugh chatting with Garrick MacLean, a man well respected in the Highlands. One of the few lairds Rowan liked. He was honourable and had brought his clan back from the dead after losing everything years ago while he was a soldier away in the Borderlands. While he'd been a second son and never destined to be laird, he had taken on the mantle of duty without complaint or issue when his father and elder brother had died.

Rowan walked over to the pair of men, so similar standing side by side with their sandy brown hair and large build that they could be mistaken for brothers. 'Morn, you two. Good to see you, MacLean. It has been a few years.'

Garrick MacLean gifted an easy smile and shook Rowan's extended hand. 'Far too long. I am pleased to see you here.'

Rowan replied to his unspoken question. 'As am I, but I felt it was time to get out and enjoy this last Tournament of Champions before it ends.'

Garrick chuckled and stepped closer. 'Brenna tells me

it is only a rumour and not truth, but it has brought us all together has it not? Ewan's plan has worked.'

'Oh? What plan is that?' He furrowed his brow.

'It was in an effort to have us all united in the Highlands. There are murmurings that a battle against the British is imminent. Based on the last few years, I am not surprised to hear such. Neither are you, it seems, by your lack of reaction.' Garrick sighed.

'Nay. Not surprised.' Although it was the last thing Rowan wanted. Years of strife within his own personal life had taken their toll on him along with the Campbells' historic feud with the MacDonalds. He was eager for peace, despite how unpopular the idea would be. The Highland lairds were hungry to end the British hold over them, and war seemed the only way it might be obtained, but that didn't mean he wanted it. Great men would be lost, and he'd had his fill of loss.

'Where is your wife, MacLean?' Hugh asked, scanning the area.

Garrick smiled. 'She is ill.'

Hugh balked. 'Is that something to smile about?' he enquired, his confusion evident.

Rowan was equally baffled by the man's jovial statement of his wife's sickness.

Garrick shook his head. 'Aye, but nay,' he sputtered. 'She is carrying another bairn and has the sickness before she breaks her fast, like she did the last time. I am pleased to have another babe on the way, not that she is ill.' He ran a hand through his hair and a slight colour rose in his cheeks.

Hugh clapped him on the shoulder and smiled. 'Congratulations. That is fine news.'

'Aye,' Rowan echoed, also pleased for his friend's good

fortune. While he had never known his wife well, he assumed her to be a good woman to have caught the eye of MacLean.

'Thank you. We are expecting the bairn next summer. June perhaps.'

Rowan's chest tightened. Would he ever have another bairn? Most likely not. Loving a woman and risking the birth of another child along with the thought of possibly losing either again immobilised him with fear. Rosa was enough, he knew that. But it did not take the sting of the loss of his wife and son away. Nothing ever would.

'Rowan?' Hugh asked.

'Aye?' Rowan replied as his friend's voice pulled him back from his memories.

'They are lining up. Do you still plan to throw?'

'Aye,' he replied begrudgingly. He had no desire to be shown up by young bucks, but he had also promised Susanna he would make his presence known and participate in some of the events. The stone put seemed harmless enough.

'Papa!' Rosa called cheerfully.

Rowan turned to the growing crowd a distance from the throwing field. When he spied his daughter waving at him with Trice by her side, he couldn't help but wave back, his heart filling with pride at having her here. He pulled back his shoulders and walked to the line. He would throw well for Rosa's sake.

Catching Susanna's gaze as he walked to the line, the heat from her stare sent a thrill of awareness through him all the way through his core and down to his fingertips. He opened and closed his fist. The woman drove him to madness, but the physical attraction between them was still palpable after all these years. He wondered if others could sense it too. Whatever tether had existed between them as teens had not been entirely severed.

Not yet anyway.

There were still many days to contend with her before the ruse would be complete. But first, he needed to get through this one. A young laird whose name escaped Rowan sauntered back after his throw, knocking his shoulder into Rowan's as he passed and muttering, 'Luck, Seanair.'

The Gaelic word for Grandpa could not be misinterpreted, and a few other men glanced their way, interested to see what might come from the overt insult. Rowan's blood heated, and he fisted his hands by his sides again. It was obvious disrespect, and he saw Hugh's posture tighten from afar. The old Rowan would have seized the impotent dolt by the tunic and thrown him to the ground, pinning him there by the neck until he begged for mercy. Rowan rolled his neck and focused on his breathing. His daughter was here as well as his sister, and he could not be a good candidate for Susanna's betrothed if he killed a man at the first event of the games. Susanna's brothers would be here somewhere, and they would hear of his behaviour, even if they didn't witness it. He counted to ten and continued walking to the line. He would use his anger to throw the stone farther and teach the lad a lesson in humility and what it meant to be a real man.

He stared downfield at the fabric strips fluttering in the wind marked with the previous throwers' tartans. He glanced back at the lad who had passed him: a Macpherson. The orange hue in the tartan a giveaway as to its origin. His flag sat the furthest from Rowan. He stared at it for a few seconds, set his heart on matching or exceeding its distance, and exhaled a breath as he set his feet into position, careful to set them heel and toe length apart for traction. He lifted the heavy oblong stone with his right hand and tucked it under his neck, adjusting the weight until it was comfortable in his hold. The coolness of the stone against his skin settled him. His heart slowed as he twisted his body back and down to the right with his left hand high and outstretched behind him. Exhaling a final breath, he noted the silence of the crowd as they waited for his throw. He imagined the distance once more, envisioned the stone flying with ease, and turned his body with force, releasing the stone in the air along with a guttural yell of effort. He watched its flight as his body followed through on the throw. To his joy, it sailed past Macpherson's mark, sending dirt flying in the air as it landed and flipped to a stop. The crowd cheered, and little Rosa jumped to her feet as did Trice. After he raised his hand in celebration, his gaze caught Susanna's. To his surprise, she had also jumped up to cheer his throw as had many other spectators. Such praise for him was an unexpected and welcome response. His chest tightened in joy and remembrance.

The last time he had been here, Anna had been cheering for him after such a display with the hammer throw, and he had been smitten by her unbridled support of him. Such a memory complicated his feelings now, but he tried to set them aside and focus on this moment and no other. Only one other man was preparing to throw. Rowan stepped aside and allowed him the time and space to do so. With hands on his hips, Rowan watched as the stone travelled along the same arc as his own. When it stopped just short of his mark, Rowan released a breath in relief.

'Papa!' Rosa called out and clapped just before the

crowd did the same. He raised his hand in thanks and nodded to Rosa. He covered his heart with his hand and then pointed to her, so she would know he was her champion. She smiled in delight and Trice's eyes glistened with tears. Perhaps she alone knew how much this moment meant to him as she had been here when he had been a lad trying to woo Anna and win her hand all those years ago, just a mere year after Susanna had dashed his hopes and refused his proposal. Anna had been the bright light of hope for him and being here reminded him that he still had hope and a future ahead of him, even without her being here. Trice met his gaze and smiled. He nodded to her that he understood.

'Quite a throw for a *seanair*, eh?' Rowan whispered as he passed the Macpherson laird to leave the event.

The lad had no answer, and Rowan revelled in the fact that he had made his point without brutality or lowering himself to Macpherson's childishness as he might have done but years ago. Rowan had shown his strength and demanded his respect in a far different way. One that only maturity could provide. Perhaps his age could be seen as the gift it was rather than the hindrance he sometimes believed it to be.

Rosa rushed to him, and he bent down to scoop her into his arms. She hugged him fiercely, and every care in the world melted away.

'Papa! You did it! You bested them all! I knew you could do it!' She pulled back and kissed him on the cheek before looking into his eyes.

'It is because you were here,' he said, tucking her dark wavy hair behind her ear.

'Me?' she asked, scrunching her face.

'Aye. You cheered me to victory just as your mama did

the last time I came here. It is here that we met, and I knew that I would offer for her hand.'

She smiled, her eyes wistful as she took in the surroundings. 'Then this is a special place, isn't it?'

'Aye. It is.' he replied.

'Thank you for bringing me. I love it here already! Will you tell me more stories about the games? About Mama?'

Rowan's heart tightened, but he smiled away the discomfort. 'Of course, my little pitcher. Your Auntie Trice and I will fill your ears with such stories while we are here.'

'Aye,' Trice agreed. 'We will. Shall we get you some refreshment, brother?'

'I will meet you at the tables. I just need to gather some things.' He gestured behind him.

He didn't need to gather anything other than his wits. He needed a moment to recover from the rush of emotion winning and thinking of Anna thrust upon him.

'See you there, Papa!' She tugged Trice along and they headed back up the hill in search of sweeties and refreshment.

After receiving congratulations from many of the Lairds, Rowan gathered his fabric marker and tucked it into his tartan.

'Quite the start, my laird. The ladies in my section were swooning over your exchange with your daughter. You even had me a bit misty, and I have no heart as you well know.'

Rowan smiled and faced Susanna. Her gaze searched his. Words rested quietly tucked away in her eyes, and he longed to know what she wished to ask as much as he feared what the question might be. One never knew with Susanna or with any Cameron for that matter.

'Care for some refreshment?' he asked, delaying whatever it was she wished to say.

'Aye. I will walk with you. I am to meet my brothers there. I am sure they will love to hear of your victory and become reacquainted.'

He laughed. 'That I know to be untrue, but I look forward to seeing just how eager they are to become *reacquainted*, as you put it. I have a feeling it would be akin to how eager they might be to sit through a series of dress fittings or a trip to the milliner. Shall we go?' He offered her arm.

She hesitated and then accepted. 'It may be too soon, but perhaps this will help test the waters as to how well my brothers will receive you.'

Chapter Nine

By the time Rowan and Susanna reached the refreshment area, the makeshift tents and benches for seating were already full and overflowing with people as they took their fill before the next event was set to begin. It was a colourful spectacle of tartan, pageantry, music, and a bit of revelry as men and women began to fill their stomachs with ale and food as they chatted and mingled with one another.

'I hardly know where to look,' Susanna said, her gaze skipping from one person to another unable to focus on just one of the many sights and sounds around her.

'It is definitely not the forge,' Rowan muttered, a frown tugging at his lips.

'That is no look for a champion,' she teased.

'What look?'

'The scowl, my laird. While you are not required to smile, I would lose the glare. It may set people off the new charming laird guise you are trying to build.'

'Charming has never been used as a word to describe me,' he said releasing her arm and shifting on his feet.

'That I know, but it does not mean it couldn't be. I saw everyone's response to you with Rosa. You have a heart. Allow people to see it. That alone might make you charming.'

He scoffed. 'Perhaps you should take your own advice,'

he replied as he greeted Hugh and another laird she could not remember the name of. There were far too many to remember. Her sister waved at her from across the way, and she left Rowan to join Catriona and her brothers, who watched her approach with interest. Perhaps her plan was already at work. There was only one way to find out. She steeled her spine and increased her pace.

'Was Laird Campbell bothering you, sister?' Royce asked, his gaze set on Rowan rather than her as he asked the words and then sipped from his tankard.

'Nay, brother. I merely congratulated him on his win at the stone put and he offered to walk me up the hill for refreshment.'

Catriona's scrutiny was so intense Susanna had to look away at a colourful red pennant flapping from one of the tents. Her cheeks heated.

Why am I embarrassed?

She was a grown woman. She didn't have to explain herself to anyone, let alone her brothers.

'And you allowed him to?' Rolf countered in disbelief.

'Aye, I did,' Susanna answered.

All three of them focused on her.

'What?' Susanna finally asked, unable to endure more silent and confusing scrutiny.

'Did he say or do something inappropriate? If he did, I'll—' Rolf began.

She set her hand on his forearm and held his gaze. 'He escorted me up a hill. We exchanged pleasantries. Nothing more.'

'Pleasantries?' Royce scoffed. 'Rowan Campbell? He isn't capable of such. Never has been. It was a blessing when

Father commanded you to refuse him when he offered for your hand years ago.'

'Aye,' Rolf agreed. 'And a further blessing when the marriage planned for you and his brother Brandon also failed, despite his slight in refusing you. Otherwise, we would be bound by marriage to the Campbells.' Rolf feigned a shiver.

Susanna rolled her eyes. Rolf could be a touch dramatic at times. 'People can change,' she replied, the need to defend Rowan and his clan name a sudden and curious development that surprised even her.

Rolf quirked his head, his lips falling open in surprise. 'Are you defending him? Are you unwell?' he asked.

'Is everyone enjoying themselves? I cannot tell you how happy it makes me and Ewan that you are all here.' Catriona grasped the shoulders of Susanna as well as Rolf, interrupting their exchange. Her message to remember where they were and who was watching was unmistakable and well timed. Even Royce turned his scowl into a neutral indifference before he drank more ale. Once again, their sister had saved them from themselves. A skill she was quite adept at.

Susanna released a breath and sent a glance of thanks her sister's way.

Catriona winked back at her. 'Anyone up for the hammer throw? It is the next event. Setting up in the lower fields in the next quarter hour for the event at half past.'

'Perhaps the stone put champion will take part. Unless he has already pulled a muscle in his efforts,' Rolf chided. He bit into a tart and glared behind Susanna.

Her heart dropped. Rowan must be right behind her.

'I may be older than you, Cameron, but I am far from dead or elderly for that matter. Perhaps we should take part in it together. What say you, my lady?' He paused by Susanna's side, so close the fabric from their clothes touched. The proximity didn't go unnoticed. The hackles on her brothers rose as they might on a hound sensing danger.

'Seems a fine idea, does it not, brothers? You could prove to the Laird how wanting he might be.' Susanna smirked at Rowan, who frowned back at her. She bit her lip. She kept forgetting they were to be friendlier towards one another. Baiting him would be a hard habit to break.

'So little faith in me, my lady?' Rowan shook his head.

'Why would she have any faith in you, Campbell? We will not have you sniffing about our sister. She has other plans than the likes of you,' Rolf replied.

'I do, do I?' she countered, irritation ruffling her. They spoke of her as if she was not there and incapable of a thought of her own.

Royce balked and stepped closer. 'Aye. You do,' he replied. 'Campbell needs to set his sights elsewhere. I have heard the rumours, Campbell,' he stood almost toe to toe with him now. 'Eager to secure your footing as head of the clan by finding a bride to sire an heir with before your brother steals your seat as laird again?'

Rowan's jaw tightened, and Susanna pressed her elbow against his own, hoping that pressure might signal a reminder of their plan for the day, and deter him from falling into her brother's trap of baiting him into a true and horrid scene in front of most of the men and women of import in the Highlands. While it was one thing to make their meeting noticeable to people, so that their later betrothal seemed logical, it was quite another to squabble or worse in front of their peers.

The silence between the men lengthened, and neither

man seemed willing to concede to the other. Susanna's throat dried and her muscles tightened. The merriment and music played on around them, while the men stood entrenched in their own private war of wills, as they always had been.

'Papa, there you are!' Rosa burst in between the men and clutched at her father's hand. 'Auntie Trice and I have been looking for you. Come try one of the apple tarts. You must be hungry after your winnings.' She tugged on his hand once more, jostling into Susanna's side.

Susanna released a nervous chuckle and smiled at Rosa. Her timing could not have been better.

'Sorry, my lady,' the wee lass offered.

'No apology needed. Apple tarts make me excited too,' Susanna added. Her relief over the young girl interrupting what could have been a horrid exchange made her limbs tingle.

'There are plenty. Perhaps you would all like some tarts?' She smiled up at each of them, awaiting their answer.

'I will be joining you,' Catriona quipped, rubbing her belly. 'I am famished.'

'I think we shall wait, miss,' Royce replied, smiling at the girl. His ire softening. 'We will be competing in the next event.'

'Will you be competing too, Papa?' she asked, looking up to him.

Rowan paused. 'I had thought to sit that one out, but I think a bit of a proper challenge might be in order.' He sent a meaningful glare to Susanna's brothers that could not be misread.

'So, you are doing the hammer throw?' Rosa squealed. 'Another victory to be sure.' She turned to Royce and Rolf.

'Not that I wish you to do poorly, sirs' she offered to them and shifted on her feet.

Royce chuckled and smiled at her. 'Of course not, wee lass. You must cheer for your papa.'

'But I do hope you come in second or third.'

Rolf suppressed a chuckle.

'Good luck,' she offered. 'May we go get some tarts now?' she asked.

'Aye,' Rowan replied. 'Seems the perfect time for some refreshment. 'tis a good thing, I have another lass cheering me on,' he offered, sending a heavy glance to Susanna, before turning away and disappearing into the crowd.

Blast.

He was angry with her. Did she blame him? She had done little to ease the waters between him and her brothers and had remained shocked in silence as the tension between them grew. Now they were all competing against each other in the hammer throw as some test of superiority and masculinity.

It was not exactly how she had hoped their initial meeting would go, but at least they had not come to blows. She cleared her throat and smoothed her skirts. But, who knew what would happen after the hammer throw? They might wrestle over the winnings.

'You say you wish to assess your options for a husband here and the first man you land on is Campbell?' Rolf asked.

'My thoughts exactly,' Royce growled in low tones, his gaze still following what she assumed was Rowan's movements in the distance. 'Care to explain, sister?' He crossed his arms against his chest.

Her cheeks heated. 'How dare you scrutinise me?' she

hissed, angry at being spoken to as a child rather than the grown woman she was. 'I am leaving all my options open. I believe you said I could pursue my own interests in a match, or have you changed your mind on that bit as well?' She mirrored him and crossed her arms against her bosom.

Rolf and Catriona watched the exchange between her and Royce in utter silence despite how much Susanna would have delighted in some sibling interference right about now. It seemed they remembered what she did: an angry Royce was not to be trifled with. No matter how softened and changed he had been by his accident on Lismore and by falling in love with Iona, he was still Royce. He had a temper, and his tongue could be sharp and spiteful, especially if he felt threatened. Based on his reaction to Rowan, their mutual disdain for each other hadn't wavered over the last decade.

Royce still hadn't answered her.

'So, have you changed your mind?' she asked again, not caring about what his reaction might be. She was too desperate to know the truth. The idea of an arranged marriage turned her stomach. A fake betrothal was much more to her liking.

'Nay,' he relented, the anger having abated from his voice. He exhaled and rubbed the back of his neck. 'But the idea of you considering every man will take some getting used to, especially the likes of Campbell.'

The knots in her stomach loosened and a rush of air filled her lungs. Catriona and Rolf seemed equally relieved.

'Then let us enjoy some refreshment before they have been devoured,' Catriona offered, tucking her arm around Susanna's elbow before leading her away. 'What are you up to, sister?' she asked in low tones as they wove through the crowd, greeting people as she awaited Susanna's answer.

Susanna had worked out her answer to this the night before once she deduced Catriona suspected her of something nefarious, which was an accurate account of her motives.

'Finding a husband,' she answered. She congratulated herself on how real and authentic the words sounded as they fell from her lips. Practicing in front of the looking glass had helped.

'Nothing more?'

'Nay. Nothing more. Although I cannot say I am thrilled about the idea of relinquishing some of my freedoms and attempting to find a man who can respect my mind as well as my wishes.'

Catriona chuckled. 'A tall order to be sure, but I have no doubt that if anyone can find one, you can. Just do not force it. Listen to your heart.' Her amber eyes set upon Susanna and her heart skittered.

Ach. How did one do that? 'It has been some time since I have listened to my heart in such matters,' she confessed.

'I know, but that does not mean you cannot begin now. Just look at me and Ewan. It took us both a good deal of time to believe we could love and trust one another because of our past and all the disappointments that accompanied it. But the risk was worth it. I cannot imagine being without him now. And soon we shall have our own family.'

The love in her sister's voice and gaze stole Susanna's breath and she paused. 'You make it sound so easy.'

'Easy?' Catriona scoffed. She let go of Susanna's arm and shook her head before calling back to her. 'Hardly. It is the most difficult thing in the world.'

Chapter Ten

❧❧❧

Rowan ground his teeth as he approached the line for the hammer throw. Somehow, he'd been slated to go last. Perhaps because he had just won the stone put. Either way, he cursed himself for being drawn into participating in yet another event. His pride failed him more than once on past occasions, and he hoped this wouldn't serve as such a reminder again. He should have ceased while he was ahead with a victory. Despite it being merely late morn, he felt spent. So much socialising, small talk, and pretending to be agreeable wore him through. He didn't remember the Tournament being so tiresome. But he'd been younger and less battered and bruised then. Life hadn't yet had its way with him.

Unlike now.

He met Rosa's gaze across the field and remembered this was for her. Sure, he was fulfilling some ridiculous promise to Susanna, but by all accounts, Rosa's happiness in this weekend mattered most to him. He wanted her to remember it fondly. He also wanted her to be proud of him. He'd fallen short as her father many a day since Anna's death, and although he hoped she was too young to remember him falling apart and into the mad well of grief, he was no fool. She couldn't have escaped all of it. Replacing some of those horrid failings with these memories of him being a celebrated champion and respected laird would serve them both well for years to come.

'Campbell?' the older man assisting with the hammer throw called, bringing the present back into focus.

'Aye,' Rowan replied and took the heavy wooden handle from the older man. Rowan shifted it in his grip as he tested out the weight of it. It was heavier than he remembered. Yet another sign of his age. He cursed under his breath.

A small cheer of applause sounded, and he turned to greet the crowd with a wave. Although they cheered for him now, they would equally celebrate his demise. He was no fool as to the fickle nature of approval. His gaze searched the distance to see just where the furthest fabric marker rested fluttering in the swell of the breeze. The blue, green, and red Cameron tartan taunted him. Royce's throw was best, with Rolf's not far behind. Their success was an annoying complication to the situation.

Even now, both glared at him with hatred, at best disdain. He settled in a low wide stance, rocking back and forth from his heels to toes to gain traction in the moist grass that had become trodden by previous competitors. He completed two revolutions to gain speed before he set the hammer free with a wail of effort. To his relief, the hammer was gliding straight in the sky and hadn't hooked, which had impacted a handful of throwers before. It sailed past many of the markers before it dipped. He urged it on as the crowd fell into silence, watching its advance and anticipating where it might land. As the hammer hit, throwing up dirt and grass, before skidding to a stop, Rowan held his breath. It would be close. He couldn't tell where it had landed from this distance.

The lad carrying his grey and brown marker followed

the burly man in charge of the events as he jogged out to the divot where the hammer had first hit the soil. He stopped among the Cameron markers and studied the area. He pointed to a spot and the lad tucked in the Campbell fabric. It fluttered between the two Cameron markers.

Curses.

He was just shy of the win, but he'd bested one of the Camerons. At least that would offer a bit of a sting to their collective pride, which brought Rowan some temporary satisfaction. The crowd cheered his throw despite it being just short of a victory. Perhaps they favoured his unlikely comeback after so many years. No doubt all the men and women knew of his past difficulties after losing Anna. Hell, he'd temporarily lost his title, the elders deeming him incapable of ruling while he struggled with his grief.

He squared his shoulders. None of that mattered now. He was laird. He was well. And he was here with Rosa… who was now chatting with Susanna and Trice. His skin prickled as he approached them. Seeing all of them together felt odd and uncomfortable, but he knew this would be the first of many moments moving forward if he was to uphold his end of their arrangement. He sucked in a breath as he climbed the small slope, counted to five, and released the air from his lungs slowly as he approached. After all he had been through, this was a small challenge.

'Ladies,' he greeted with a nod.

'Papa!' Rosa turned and hugged his legs. 'You did well. Second best!'

He ruffled her soft hair. 'Thank you, my sweet. Lady Cameron's brother bested me this time.'

'Your brother won, my lady?' Rosa asked, craning her head up and around to see Susanna properly.

'Aye. Laird Royce Cameron, my eldest brother won, and my youngest brother earned third.'

'What is it like to have two brothers? I miss mine.'

Rowan's heart ceased beating. Her words a crushing pressure upon him and his ears buzzed. Trice squeezed his hand, anchoring him back in the present. He squeezed her hand back, grateful for the small gesture to support him.

Susanna bent down next to Rosa. 'I have no doubt you miss him greatly. I bet he watches over you even now to keep you safe.'

'Aye. Just like Mama.' She smiled.

'Aye,' Susanna continued, and dropped her voice to a whisper. 'Having two brothers is much like being in this field. While it is quite nice to always have the company, sometimes you need a bit of time to yourself. I am lucky to have a sister too. She makes me laugh. You have met her. 'tis Lady Stewart.'

'Oh! She is quite nice, and she has beautiful eyes. Like amber.'

'Aye.'

'I hope to have a brother or sister again one day,' Rosa added, reaching over to fiddle with Susanna's cloak ribbon. It slid through his daughter's fingers before resting against Susanna's cloak again.

Susanna smiled. 'And you just might,' she replied. 'The future is full of secrets that we can only dream of.'

Her words stole Rowan's breath and reverberated through him, the hope in them igniting a seed of desire for a happy future.

The future is full of secrets that we can only dream of.

He stared at her. Did she really believe those words? He'd never thought her capable of such hope, and suddenly he saw her as a woman longing for more out of her life, much like he was. Had he misjudged her? Was she more than the manipulative, distant woman he had always perceived her to be after their relationship had ended?

She stood and met Rowan's gaze. 'My laird, I shall be off. Congratulations on your placement. I hope to see you and your family later this afternoon.'

'Aye,' he replied, his voice husky and low, with a bit of a crack at the end. Nothing else came to him. He just stared at her.

'Aye, my lady,' Trice replied, eyeing him suspiciously. 'We look forward to seeing you.'

'Bye, Lady Cameron!' Rosa called to her waving as she left.

Susanna headed off and turned to send one last wave to them.

'Have you been struck dumb, brother?' Trice asked, her brow furrowed.

'Nay,' he replied, clearing his throat as his gaze continued to follow Susanna's fluid movements across the field to where her brothers were. He was still foggy after her words, his mind ambling between memories of their past and present relationship, if one could even call it such. That misty idea of hope lingered about him, but he didn't trust his mind enough to hold onto it.

At least not yet.

She poked his arm and studied his face. Mirth filled her voice. 'Wait?' she asked, dropping her voice to an even lower whisper as she moved closer. 'Are you interested in her? Do you still fancy Susanna?' Her mouth gaped open, and that look—the look of giddiness she often had as a girl when she uncovered secrets of her younger brothers lit her eyes and features, making her look a decade younger. 'After all this time?' she asked, her words high pitched and eager for an answer. 'I never would have thought it.'

He frowned at her despite the bit of heat he felt entering his neck and cheeks.

'I am right.' She covered her mouth and chuckled without waiting for any answer from him. He realised now, not answering had been his fatal error. Omission equalled agreement to his sister.

Now what was he to do.

'She is pretty, Papa,' Rosa said giggling, adding to Trice's ridiculousness. 'And nice.'

His daughter's words yanked Rowan harshly to the present. While it might suit their plan in the long term, for hints of their 'renewed' romance to become whisperings among the crowds, Rowan needed to slow his sister's expectations and thoughts on the matter until they were ready to have such notions bandied about.

He rolled his eyes at both of them, eager to dismiss their enquiry. 'I do not fancy anyone but you, my little pitcher,' he replied reaching down and tickling her to help change the subject.

She squealed in delight, and he picked her up and popped her over his shoulders in one deft movement. He needed to enjoy this time with her. She was growing up far too quickly. Soon, she would be too grown to do such things.

She leaned down, wrapped her arms around his neck, and kissed his cheek. 'Thank you for bringing me, Papa. It is such fun here!'

He leaned his cheek against hers. 'Aye. And the weekend has only begun, my sweet.'

Chapter Eleven

Susanna tapped her slipper on the floor with impatience and sighed as the hands on the mantel clock of the study at Glenhaven Castle rested neatly together on the twelve as if in prayer. Perhaps it was a prayer for her patience. The chimes rang off, and with each passing echo, her frustration from waiting alone in a cold dusty study at midnight grew. Where was the man? She had sent a note to Rowan in his chambers a half hour ago and he'd still yet to arrive. At this rate, she would throttle him if she didn't freeze first. It was bad enough he'd said scarce more than a greeting to her at the dinner this eve. What was wrong with the man? He'd been attentive and almost doting this morn at the Tournament games, but then he'd all but disappeared.

She frowned. It was much like the way she remembered their relationship had been when they were teens: an awkward and infuriating dance of closeness and distance. Not viewing Rowan as a good enough match for her, Father had commanded her to end their involvement after Rowan had proposed, and she had agreed without complaint, frustrated by his moods and inconsistency. Soon after, she had met Jeremiah, whose warmth and constancy had filled her heart. Her chest tightened at the memory of his glorious smile and rogue dimple. After her father had sent Jeremiah away to punish him for daring an attachment with her and her for loving 'below her station,' and he had died in battle, she'd had little interest in marrying or pursuing attachments of any kind.

Her Father's forced engagement to Rowan's brother Brandon during his brief reign as laird two years ago was a ridiculous farce meant to punish her for refusing to take a husband. The fact that it would also sting Rowan had been an unexpected boon for her father. The farce of an engagement had been brief, but by aiding Brandon and his men with her own soldiers to help rescue Brandon's son and now wife, Fiona, from Audric's clutches, Susanna had gained her freedom from the betrothal *and* a favour that her father had never known about. It was the calling in of that same favour Rowan had inherited when he became laird once more that had brought her to this very moment.

And in this moment, she was alone, cold, and waiting in secret to strategize another scheme to escape marriage by crafting a pretend betrothal with her first love. In short, her love life was one complicated disaster after another and showed little hope of improvement.

Blast.

The second hand inched on towards the one and she stood, no longer able to sit and wait, and desperate to warm herself. She rubbed her hands together and blew on them. She roamed through the study with its books lining the walled cases as well as the additional standing bookcases lining the inner workings of the room. It was a maze of learning. Her fingertips trailed along the spines. She'd never been much of a reader although she didn't dislike it. The outdoors, weaponry, and strategy had always intrigued her and called to her far more strongly than inked letters on parchment. Poetry and literature really hadn't won her over. Evidently, the Stewarts were far more refined creatures than the Camerons, who were known more for actions rather than words. Shelves of literature, an unholy number of texts on botany, and a smattering of what she believed to be poets sat nestled in each case amongst other more mundane topics such as history, geography, and science. There wasn't even dust on them. They must *use* them… regularly. She lifted her brow in surprise.

Who had time for such reading?

A door creaked open, and she turned to see Rowan's sharp profile in shadow as he came into the room. She'd recognise those features anywhere: his strong nose and chin along with a full forehead. After he closed the door, she watched him study the darkness, evidently looking for her. She smiled and watched him.

'I know you are here,' he said. 'I can smell the scent of your perfume. Violets, if I remember.'

She pressed her lips together and gripped her skirts. How had he remembered such?

And more importantly, why did his remembering such make her heart skitter a bit in her chest?

'Aye,' she replied evenly, releasing the hitch in her breath.

He roamed through the bookcases that lined the middle of the room in search of her, and instead of revealing herself, she remained hidden, exulting in this small game.

'Why is it so dark and cold in here?' he asked, moving through the rows, his boots landing with a subdued hush.

'I didn't dare light a candle or ask for the fire to be lit. Surely, you understand.'

'Aye. Secrecy is essential to our ruse,' he replied.

'Care to tell me why it took you so long to arrive?'

'You failed to tell me *which* study. This is the third one I have been in.'

She smirked at the chuckle in his voice. 'I had forgotten. The Stewarts are readers to be sure.'

'This castle is also a bloody labyrinth.'

She laughed aloud at that, and then covered her mouth, lest she reveal herself.

He turned the row. 'Finally,' he said approaching her.

Her breath caught. In the darkness, his eyes sparkled with light, and she could see the playfulness in his gaze. His tunic was untucked and open at the neck, his hair mussed and unruly, begging to be touched, and his entire demeanour was relaxed.

But instead of saying any of this, she uttered. 'Why have you been ignoring me since this morn?'

He balked at her sharpness, his body suddenly tense. 'What are you talking about?' he asked, opening his palms to her.

'If we are to be believed to be rekindling something, we must be seen together.' She crossed her arms against her chest.

He stepped closer, his arms falling back to his sides. 'I know that, but it cannot be rushed, can it? While we want people to talk, we do not want them to 'talk' badly of either of us, especially you. Or have you forgotten how cruel and unrelenting idle gossip, especially among women, can be?'

She didn't answer. She well remembered. While he had a point, she didn't wish to concede it just yet. She shivered.

He looked at her, concern in his gaze. 'I did not bring a coat or I would give it to you.' He reached out and rubbed her arms from shoulder to elbow, the heat from his hands sent a flush of awareness through her like whiskey. 'You are freezing, Susanna. How long have you been in here?'

'A half hour,' she whispered, some of the irritation receding. The warmth and comfort of his touch was a delicious distraction.

'Then, let's be quick, so you can get back to your chambers and warmed.'

His kindness was distracting her. What had she been angry about again?

'And what of tomorrow?' she asked.

'Aye,' he answered, still rubbing her arms absently, his body closer to her now. The motion along her arms was hypnotic, and her limbs softened to him like clay warmed when it was held and worked. 'Perhaps a planned exchange when we break our fast? Then, a chance meeting again as the events come to close in the afternoon?'

She nodded.

The door to the study creaked open. Candlelight spilled into the room, casting dancing shadows on the floor. They both stilled. Rowan pulled her closer, an instinctive gesture of protection she didn't resist. Perhaps if they made themselves smaller, they might not be noticed.

Susanna's heart pounded in her chest and in her ears. If they were discovered, her reputation would be in tatters, their plan ruined—and then her brothers would kill Rowan and scatter his body parts along Loch Linnhe. She cringed.

Perhaps meeting here had been a poor idea.

Susanna could see the person more clearly now. She almost sighed aloud in relief. *Catriona*. Her blossoming figure and distinctive amber hair were unmistakable. Even if her sister discovered them, she would take such a discovery to the grave.

Catriona selected a book with care and headed back to the door. She paused and said quietly, 'While I know not what you are up to, Susanna, best you wait ten minutes before emerging. Ewan is up making me a kettle of tea for I cannot sleep.'

Rowan stiffened against Susanna.

She squeezed his arm. 'Do not worry,' she mouthed to him.

He scowled.

When the door finally closed again and they were left alone, Rowan frowned. 'Why should we not worry?'

'Because Catriona knows only I am here, not you as well. No doubt I need to wear less violet perfume. It is too distinctive,' she fretted.

'Or we should stop planning secret encounters that put our reputations at risk.'

'*Our* reputations?' she asked.

'Aye,' he replied.

'You are a man. You have no reputation to lose, especially after...' she began and then stopped realising her error too late.

'My what?' he asked gripping her arm.

She stared up at him.

'Go ahead. Do finish. My what? Bout with insanity?' he bit off angrily.

'Aye,' she answered.

'Well, anytime you wish to release me from this ridiculous ruse of yours, say the word. I would hate to damage your pristine reputation as cold and heartless.'

She yanked her arm free from his hold, his words a barb lancing her pride. 'And miss out on your quest for vengeance?'

'I could do so on my own.'

'Doubtful.' She took a step back, but he closed the space as he advanced on her again.

'You think me incapable?'

She said nothing and merely lifted her brow, uncertain as to why she continued to bait him. She could have denied it. She believed him capable. Otherwise, she wouldn't have dared to enlist him in her scheme, but she'd rather eat a volume of poetry than tell him such now.

'Incapable, eh?' he scoffed, moving closer, so close she could see the flutter of his dark lashes move against his skin and the bright blue of his irises catch the meagre light in the shadows. 'Like you,' he hissed. 'I am capable of cruelty and revenge. Do not test me. For I may rise to your challenge.'

He gazed at her lips, and she thought he would kiss her, but he didn't. He cursed under his breath and left the study, ignoring her sister's previous warning to wait.

Susanna leaned heavily against the bookcase, resting her forehead against the cool wood of the shelves. Why did it always go this way between them?

Hot and cold with nothing in between.

The woman was impossible. Infuriating. Irritating.

And he couldn't stop thinking about her and how close he had come to almost kissing her. Rowan ran a hand brusquely through his hair and cursed as he strove down the hallway with purpose.

Who did she think she was? Telling him he was unfit or incapable. It was she who had come to him begging for his help. He had a mind to search out her brothers and reveal her absurd plan. No doubt they would then owe him and my how the roles of debt would be reversed. He froze and turned on his heel with a smile.

That was exactly what he would do. He scanned the hallway with its many chambers and tried to remember exactly what rooms the brothers would be staying in. Candlelight danced along the floors and walls from the sconces lit at friendly intervals to aid the many guests in their travels. What he really needed was a map. Glenhaven was a labyrinth.

Frowning, he set his hands on his waist. It stood to reason that all the Camerons would be on the same hallway, would it not? And as family of Lady Stewart, they most likely had the nicest of quarters to stay in, which should be closest to Lady and Laird Stewart.

Now if only he knew where their chambers were… But he had no idea.

He smiled. They couldn't be far from the study they had just been in. Lady Stewart had popped in for a book. Surely, she would peruse the study closest to her own chambers so late at night and so heavy with child. He turned around and headed back down the hall where he had come from, made another turn, and then one more before he was on the hall with the study. He paused. By that logic, Susanna's room was also somewhere near the study. Why had she failed to tell him that before or met in her chambers?

Well, perhaps not *in* her chambers. That would be inappropriate.

He grumbled in irritation. Vexed by the whole situation. While he'd never asked outright, she could have offered him the information in case they needed to discuss any matters further. Although they had also just been arguing.

The large clock in the hallway chimed the half hour, and he continued with quiet, thoughtful steps, pausing along the doors to see if he could hear any noises that might give away who was in what room. It was a poor and rather risky strategy, but what other did he have? Three doors down, he heard what he thought was a knob turning and the hesitant opening of a door. He froze, scanned the hallway for a place to hide and scurried to a small alcove he spied across the corridor, most likely meant for servants to take a quick respite before continuing with their duties, and shoved himself into it. He held his breath and pushed himself a touch deeper into the space, wincing when the moulding of the small space dug into his back.

The door closed and a collection of footfalls echoed quietly down the hallway. Then, another door squeaked open and another voice joined in. He lifted his brow. The chances of him happening upon an evening rendezvous like this were odd. He couldn't help but be grateful for his good fortune. Whatever it was would provide him information on something and someone of import. Why else was there such a surreptitious meeting in play?

He could kiss Susanna now for making him so cross. He frowned. Nay, that was too far. He focused on the murmurings as they neared trying to distinguish who was talking.

'What is this about?' a man asked, his voice weary.

'Our sister.'

Rowan smiled. The second man was Royce. His brusque unyielding tone made his voice easy to distinguish.

'Catriona?'

'Nay,' he offered. 'Susanna.'

'Ah,' the other man said. 'Come to the study. This sounds

like it shall be longer than a hallway exchange, and my wife has finally fallen asleep.'

Laird Stewart! Now things were getting interesting. Why would Royce need to speak with his brother-in-law Ewan under the cover of darkness? Rowan's interest piqued, and gooseflesh rose along his skin.

'Aye,' Royce agreed. 'We have much to discuss with you and need your help.'

We?

Rolf must be with them, even though the man hadn't spoken a word during the exchange. Rowan pressed his palms flat to the wood of the nook he hid in, straining to hear, and leaned forward waiting for more. But the conversation had ended, and the men were walking away.

Their footfalls disappeared into nothingness as they moved further down the hall away from him, and then another door squeaked open and then closed softly. Most likely they had gone into the study he and Susanna had been hiding in but minutes ago. The irony of not being caught and now being so desperate to go back into the space he was so eager to leave not long ago was not lost on him.

He stilled. If Susanna hadn't left yet, she would now be trapped and forced to listen to her brothers and their plans for her. He pressed his lips together to prevent a chuckle. *Saints be.* He would pay good coin to watch her endure that exchange without saying a word.

Rowan waited. He *had* to know what they were talking about. This could be the break he needed to create an advantage over Susanna and the Camerons. He could almost taste the thrill of finally having the advantage over a clan known for having the upper hand on everyone else.

But it would be a risk. The only way to attempt to overhear anything would be to eavesdrop outside the door, in plain sight of anyone else who might be exiting their rooms or travelling the hallways. Surely, servants still moved about the large castle, tending to the needs of all the many guests here during the Tournament, especially this hallway, since it seemed he was correct in assuming the family chambers were here.

He could be one servant bell pull away from discovery. And if discovered, his rather precarious relationship with the Cameron brothers would be even more uncertain, if it didn't turn contentious. But the risk was well worth the payoff, wasn't it?

While Hugh would say it wasn't, Rowan was ready to gamble on his chances. He eased slowly from the alcove, eager to stretch his cramped back and bunched muscles from the tiny confines of the space. He stepped out into the hallway and his body sighed in relief. He smelled the air and scanned the long corridor from one end to the other listening for noise. Nothing. So he advanced slowly, rolling his feet from heel, ball, to toe as best as he could in his boots to lessen the sound of his movements. He passed one chamber door, then another, hearing little more than snoring.

Finally, he reached the door of the study. He settled on occupying the space on the opposite side of the door. That way if it opened suddenly, he would be facing their backsides rather than their faces and go unseen. Or at least he hoped that was how it might work.

Rowan pressed his ear to the wall, and soon he was able to decipher the men's words.

'So, you understand how challenging this situation is?' asked Royce.

'Aye,' Ewan answered, his voice weary.

'We know Susanna does not wish to marry, but she must. And while we have told her she has the option to choose her husband, if she does not settle on a man soon, we will choose for her. As with all things Susanna, it is proving...difficult.'

'And?' Ewan asked.

'We wish for you to ask Catriona what she knows about Susanna's plans or report to us on anything you may over-hear between them. She has been odd as of late and prone to keeping her own secrets,' Rolf added in a lower tone.

Ewan scoffed. 'You wish for me to spy on my own wife and her sister and report back to you? Catriona is with child. I cannot cause her any further difficulty or strain. For the babe's sake and her own. Surely, this has crossed your mind?'

'Aye,' Royce answered, his voice hardening. 'We are her brothers and care for her well-being. Who Susanna chooses or does not choose may impact the clan's welfare as well as our own. Much hangs in the balance based on her choice.'

'Why? It is but one marriage.'

'There are rumours that other clans may be joining forces to overrun us to gain control of the Highlands before the British further their advance north,' Royce explained.

'Nay,' Ewan countered. 'Just idle gossip. I have heard no inkling of truth in those claims. Nor have any of my men.'

'Even so, we would be fools to ignore it,' Royce added.

'Are you calling me a fool?' Ewan countered.

'Nay,' Royce added in a softer tone. 'But we cannot af-ford to do so. Too much is at stake.'

Rowan stilled.

Violets.

He smelled violets. Glancing up, he saw Susanna watching him from her cracked chambers two rooms down from the study.

Curses.

'What are you doing?' she mouthed to him.

He scowled at her and wildly gestured for her to go back to her chambers with his hand.

She shook her head and popped her hands to her hips, returning his glare.

The talking ceased. 'Is there someone outside?' Rolf asked.

Blast.

Rowan moved away from the study door quickly, rushed into Susanna's chambers, and shut the door as quietly as he could. When she attempted to object, he covered her mouth with his hand, and pressed her against the wall behind her. 'Quiet,' he hissed near her ear. She stilled and they both waited, desperate to know if either of them had been or would be discovered. Rowan heard a door open and close, the hushed footfalls of boots in the hallway, more doors quietly opening and closing, and then…silence.

He sighed, his body relaxing. 'I will take away my hand but be quiet,' he whispered.

She nodded.

As soon as he removed her hand, she spatted out a series of hushed questions. 'What were you doing? And why were you shushing me away?'

'I was trying to overhear what your brothers were secretly meeting about with their brother-in-law at half past midnight,' he whispered. 'Then, you interrupted me.' His annoyance was returning with a vengeance. He stepped away from her and continued further into the room before he halted. 'Where is your maid?' he whispered, realising his mistake.

'Downstairs. There are not adjoining chambers in this room. You may speak freely, but quietly. I do not know how easily one can overhear conversations between rooms. But perhaps you know, since I caught *you* eavesdropping.' She crossed her arms against her chest and lifted a single eyebrow, her scorn over his actions evident.

'I did it for you,' he offered before moving deeper into the chambers. He'd leave out the part where he had been hoping to turn the tables on their arrangement and get the advantage on her family. She didn't need to know *that* bit.

She followed him into the room and headed to one of a pair of lush chairs in front of the hearth, where her evening fire still smouldered. Gesturing for him to sit opposite her, she settled in, tucking her legs beneath her, like she always did, looking like a contented cat having lapped up its fill of milk. She had removed her slippers, and his body reacted to the brief flash of her small, delicate pearly white bare feet before they disappeared under the folds of her dark dressing gown. She waited for him to begin.

He cleared his throat, moved the chair a bit closer to her, so they wouldn't have to speak too loudly, and settled into the soft cushions. The subtle fragrance of violets cocooned him, as if the room had absorbed her in the two days she had been here, and he began to relax. She ran her fingers over the dainty ribbon that held her long, woven plait of hair in place. How he wanted to pull the ribbon loose, set her bound hair free, and run his fingers through the long wavy tresses.

'Rowan?' she whispered, her brow furrowed.

Deuces.

He shook his head. *She* was making him addled. Or perhaps it was his need for touch that was making *him* addled. It had been some time since he had lain with a woman, well longer than *some time*, if he were being honest. He had not lain with a woman since Anna's death four years ago as he hadn't had many urges—until now—but he set aside that budding need and focused on a far more pressing matter…

'Rowan?' she hissed, this time with more urgency and annoyance.

'You are right,' he answered impatiently, rattling off the list of information he could surmise from his spying before she had interrupted him. 'First, your brothers have grave concerns about your well-being as well as their own and the clan's future. Second, I overheard them asking Ewan for help. They fear other clans are planning a combined attack upon them. Why they think this, I don't know. But they are trying to enlist him to spy upon your sister for information about your marriage plans. And—' he paused and took a breath before continuing'—they will marry you off if you do not select a match…and soon.'

She balked at the news and her lips parted as she stared upon him, but no words followed.

Perhaps he *could* have softened it a bit, but he wanted to be succinct and leave no room for doubt that something was afoot, as she suspected. She also had been harassing him for information, so he provided it.

Now that her eyes brightened with concern, he realised his error in his thinking. 'You wished to be wrong?' he asked, his tone softening.

She dropped her gaze from his and studied her hands, which worked the delicate lace edging her gown. 'Aye,' she answered quietly. 'I had hoped to be. They are all I have.

I do not wish to lose them. And the idea of being wed to a stranger...' her words trailed off.

Puzzled, he studied her. 'You mean despite the effort you have put in place to find the answers to their secrecy and to enlist a pretend fiancé, you deep down hoped none of it would be needed?'

She looked up at him and met his gaze. The desperation in her face matched the eve of their first meeting in the forge, and he felt as he did then: intrigued—and despite his past anger with her, he felt sorry for her. *This* was the young Susanna he had known all those years ago and cared for deeply, not the cold, detached woman she oft appeared to be to him now.

Before he could think too much upon it, he rose and knelt before her. Feeling like the young Rowan he had also once been before life had taken its hold on him and shaken out some of his hope, he grasped her hands gently in his own. The smooth, cool weight of her fingers was a contrast to the rough warmth of his own. They trembled slightly in his hold, and he squeezed them in reassurance. 'We will figure this out, you and I. I am far too deep within this intrigue to cease now,' he offered with a smile. 'Hell, Trice will have us engaged before the end of the Tournament tomorrow if we are not careful.'

She sniffed and shifted closer to him, not releasing his hands. 'And if something horrid does happen? If my brothers are killed, if I am married off to a man I do not know or like, if the clans are uniting to crush us beneath their feet, what then? Will you still help me?' Her gaze flicked up to his, the challenge in them evident and unflinching.

His stomach tightened into a knot.

Would he? Could he even promise such as laird of Clan Campbell and father to Rosa?

He squared his shoulders and risked the truth. 'If I can,' he replied.

She nodded and gave a small smile. 'At least you tell me the truth. You do not fill me with vapid platitudes and nonsense. Thank you.' She leaned forward and kissed his cheek.

The soft feathering of her warm lips against his skin and the heat and smell of her so close to him made him lean into her, turning his face just enough that his lips skimmed hers before she could fully move away.

Once their lips touched, they both stilled. He lifted a hand to cup her cheek, running his thumb along her cheekbone, eliciting a sigh from her lips. 'Kiss me,' she commanded, and for the first time this eve, he didn't question her words but gave in easily to her demand.

Still kneeling, he moved forward, holding his lips open near her own, letting the heat and desire build in him until he couldn't hold the dam of want any more. Then, he seized her mouth, letting his lips pull and linger upon her own until her mouth answered back with her own demands of him. Her palm slid up his tunic and neck before weaving into his hair. Small bursts of desire bubbled and popped beneath his skin, and he kissed her harder, deeper, claiming what he could of her in their kisses. She moved forward and her other hand slid down to untuck his tunic. While he registered the action in his mind, he didn't react but kept plundering her mouth. When her bare hand slid beneath the fabric and up his spine and back, he shuddered and pulled away.

'Susanna,' he murmured, resting his forehead against hers. 'I must go. We cannot. I should not.' His attempts at sentences and clarity were shattered somewhere along with his restraint.

'Aye,' she replied. 'I well know the limitations…' she replied between uneven breaths, 'of our arrangement. I just wanted to remember,' she finished before shifting away from him. She gently shoved him back and stood.

He sat on his haunches bewildered and confused by the sudden end to their embrace. What had just happened? He blinked back the cobwebs of lust and tried to focus on comprehending her words, but before he could rise, she was walking away from him.

Her robe slid to the floor in a liquid pool of fabric, revealing a sleeping gown so sheer that he could see the outline of her lush form in the meagre moonlight streaming in the partially open curtains. His throat dried.

She shook out her hair and let the ribbon fall to the floor before she continued walking, her body's gentle movements against the fabric arresting his attention. 'You can go,' she said coolly.

He balked. Had she just dismissed him as if he were a servant, and she was done with his services?

He cursed, rose, and tucked in his tunic.

'Christ, Susanna,' he muttered. 'You don't have to always pretend to be the cold-hearted minx everyone thinks you are and expects you to be. Remember, I knew you once or at least I thought I did.'

He closed the door behind him, perhaps a bit louder than he should have, leaving whatever illusions he had held about her being the young Susanna of his past shattered upon the floor.

Chapter Twelve

Susanna clanged the teacup on the saucer. Could one have a kiss hangover? That was sure what her pounding head, shattered nerves, and general irritation of this morn felt like. She had enjoyed their kiss last night more than she wished to admit and had wanted and needed to be fulfilled. Unfortunately, the kiss had left her wanting, which made her feel as she did now. When Rowan had ceased his attentions so abruptly, she'd felt rejected and angry, and had dismissed him. Now, she feared he might cast aside their plan altogether, and then where would she be, especially with the news he shared with her about what he overheard with her brothers.

She grumbled and rubbed her temple.

'Feeling unwell, sister?' Catriona asked as she entered the small family banquet room to break her fast.

Susanna cringed and attempted to reset her features before meeting her sister's gaze. As expected, Catriona studied her with a smirk and continued to the buffet where the morning meal was set out for the family. The guests were supposed to eat in the adjoining room, but Susanna felt she would be better able to volley the enquiries of her family rather than the rest of those attending the games, especially Rowan, so she'd sneaked into the smaller banquet room this morn.

'Merely tired,' Susanna answered, sitting up straighter in her chair and smoothing a few loose tendrils from her face.

'Aye. Not unexpected since you were up quite late.'

'Oh?' Rolf asked as he entered the room, having heard part of their exchange.

Curses.

Now she would have to answer to not one but two siblings. At least Royce was not here—yet.

'I had trouble sleeping, so I went to the study to select a book,' Susanna offered and then took a sip of her tea to hide the ridiculousness of her statement.

Rolf scoffed. 'You? The study? Gathering a book to read? Did you also find some fresh needlework that needed to be finished?' He laughed at his own joke and plunked some sausages and bread onto his plate.

Susanna rolled her eyes, trying not to rise to the bait despite the pounding of her head. 'That is why I gathered the book. To help bore me enough to fall asleep.'

Catriona sat across from her and lifted her brow. 'Did you sleep well after?' she enquired, a bit too sweetly for Susanna's taste. No doubt a further prodding for information from her younger sister would ensue later when they were alone.

At least her sister had not outed her to her brother. She mouthed 'thank you' to Catriona before biting into a chunk of bread with her favourite currant jam. As the sweet fruit hit her tongue, she sighed a bit and relaxed against the back of her chair. All she needed to do was take this day a bit at a time. She would make it through, and Rowan would keep to his word. She had to trust that he was more eager for revenge against Audric than punishing her for calling him weak.

'So, have you some contenders?' Rolf asked. He sat down

heavily, hitting his knee on the table, shaking the contents atop it. 'Sorry,' he added. 'It is lower than ours at home.'

Catriona chuckled. 'No worries, brother.' She set her gaze on Susanna.

Only then did Susanna realise he was talking to her. 'What?' she asked, confused by his enquiry.

'Contenders,' he said, cutting into his sausage. 'For a husband,' he finished and then bit into the hearty link.

Susanna's stomach dropped, her appetite evaporating with it. She set aside her bread. She shrugged her shoulders, trying to bide time. Names had to be mentioned based on the dire urgency Rowan mentioned to her from what he overheard last night.

But she couldn't lead with Rowan. That would be too obvious. But who else had she met? And why did she always forget everyone's names?

Well not everyone, just the people she had no interest in. She sighed and played with her napkin in her lap. 'Well,' she began and faltered. 'There was a man who finished third in the stone put.' Of course, his name escaped her, but he seemed a solid choice. Not too young, nor too old. 'And perhaps Laird Campbell.'

Rolf stopped chewing and swallowed, setting his knife and fork back on his plate. He assessed her, quietly. His eyes widened. 'You are serious? About Campbell?'

'What about Campbell?' Royce enquired, his tone was light, and he almost smiled as he entered the breakfast room, catching Susanna and everyone else in the room off guard. The three of them paused their conversation and watched him as he hummed, gathered a plate, and began to fill it.

Royce sat down, oblivious to their confusion, and asked.

'Where is Ewan this morn? I had hoped to see him before we set off today.'

'He is meeting with a few of his men and the servants to settle departure arrangements for everyone. I am sure you will be able to speak with him before you all head off for Loch's End,' Catriona answered. 'You are in a fine mood today,' she added.

'Aye,' he replied. 'Eager to be back home with Iona and the bairn on the way. But I am glad I came. There are many prospects here for you, sister.' His gaze settled on Susanna. 'Who have you settled upon?' He ate happily, and the knowing that she would send his good mood down the loch was unsettling.

'I have not selected *the one* yet, but there are many candidates as you mentioned. Rolf and I were just speaking of it.'

Royce swallowed and studied her, his gaze narrowing in on her. 'You were just speaking of Campbell. Are you telling me you are seriously considering the man, especially after all his—difficulties?' he added, dropping his voice, so as not to be heard outside the room.

'Aye. I am.' She paused, preparing to provide them the logic she had given Rowan early on that night in the forge that would help them agree to such a match. 'That is precisely why I am considering him. He can be handled quite easily, wouldn't you think? A man as fragile as that.'

Catriona stilled, the colour draining from her face. 'Susanna,' she whispered in disbelief. 'Surely, you would not take advantage of his past difficulties and use such weakness against him. You cannot be so cruel. He has a daughter. What of her?' She absently rubbed her swelled belly, an unconscious act of protection she probably didn't even recognise.

'Blimey,' Rolf muttered, shifting in his chair.

Royce moved the food quietly around his plate and they all sat in silence apart from the occasional scraping of a utensil across a plate, sip of tea, or squeak of a chair. Susanna's stomach curdled. Perhaps it was even too dark of a suggestion for Royce. She'd gone too far and played too risky of a hand in her game. She feared all was lost. Her pulse picked up speed and she wrung her napkin in her lap.

With his plate now empty, Royce sat back in his chair, wiped his mouth, and rested his napkin on the table. He lifted his gaze to her. 'This seems the best option for you at present?' he asked.

'Aye.'

'You would live with a marriage built on such deceit?'

'It would be not a marriage of love but of control, which you know I prefer. I could bend him to the whim of our clan and influence his decisions with ease to benefit our own interests.' The words sounded as cold and heartless as she had intended.

Catriona sucked in a breath. 'Sister,' she replied. 'Surely, you cannot be truly considering this.'

'Aye,' she countered. 'I am. I know I shall never marry for love. Father and Royce made sure of that,' she added, her words anchored in the hard steely resentment she still felt about what had happened with Jeremiah—*to* Jeremiah—because of them.

What may have been sympathy and regret flickered briefly in Royce's eyes before a muscle worked in his jaw. He held her stare. 'Then, if that is what you wish, I will support it. But I would encourage you to spend more time with him and with your thoughts about it before you officially choose such a course. Living a lie could be hard, even for someone such as you.'

His words cut her, deeply. Emotion tightened her throat, and she couldn't move. Catriona and Rolf watched her, waiting, while Royce pushed back from the table. 'Thank you for breakfast, sister. Brother, I shall see you on the field.'

He didn't acknowledge Susanna before he walked away, which was just as well. Any further words from him might have made her cry. *This* was the Royce she did not like. When they fought, they resorted to this role between them: he became like her father and she the spoiled daughter. And, as with every time it had happened before, there were no winners. And in the middle was Rolf—and now Catriona, since she had re-joined their family.

'He did not mean it,' Rolf offered, reaching his open hand across the table to her. The familiar refrain almost made her smile. This is what he always did. He tried to mend and soften whatever blows were made and tried to make her smile.

She reached across and took his hand and smiled back. 'And as you well know, he did, and that is all right, brother. Perhaps I deserved it.'

He squeezed her hand. 'Nay. That is just an old wound that never heals.'

Catriona set her hand atop theirs. 'But perhaps this could be the year it does.'

'Unless your future wee babe has the ability to unwind the past, I do not think such is possible,' Susanna teased.

Catriona shrugged. 'Perhaps not my bairn, but maybe Royce and Iona's. Seeing his wee babe in his arms next spring might change everything for him—and for you.'

'Let us hope you are right, sister,' Susanna offered, smiling upon her siblings.

Chapter Thirteen

Rowan rode through the open field and then back on the well-kept road leading up to the massive looming dark grey stone entity that was Loch's End. The trees were golden and mystical against the gothic style castle now that the first few days of November had arrived. The ethereal early morning light, dewy green grass, and crisp autumn air ignited his senses, making him even more alert and in tune with his surroundings than he already was. Even though the invitation to visit Loch's End so soon after the Tournament of Champions had surprised him, realising the invitation had come from Royce and his brother rather than Susanna had shocked him more. It had also set him on alert. High alert. So much so that Hugh had insisted on joining him for this visit, and Rowan had been grateful for the unsolicited offer. Something was off about the invitation, but Rowan didn't know what it was—yet.

His gaze scanned the horizon as the horses slowed to a canter, and he took in all the new sights and sounds of the Cameron estate. It had changed much since he visited many years ago. The Camerons didn't go around inviting just anyone into their lair, and usually there was a reason for doing so. This invitation had been vague, sudden, and without cause. Yet another reason Rowan's hackles were raised. The Camerons always had an underlying motivation for everything, and it was best to remember that.

'Seems we are not the only guests this morn,' Hugh said under his breath as they neared the barn. Rowan cut his eyes to where Hugh nodded and spied several stable boys hard at work brushing down horses that had just arrived and readying them for any future journeys. The various tartans and saddle types spoke to the variety of clansmen that had beat them to this gathering. His pulse increased at the sight of the red, navy, and green tartan on a dark stallion.

Devil's blood.

The MacDonalds.

His horse neighed and yanked on the reins to loosen Rowan's fierce grip.

'Easy, my laird,' Hugh offered. 'We don't know who it is yet.'

'I do,' he replied, his jaw tight. 'I can feel it in my bones. It's him. Audric's here.'

'Well, then, you best set to controlling your temper now. This could be a test. The Camerons may be setting you up to see just how capable or incapable you are as laird—and as their future brother-in-law.'

He scoffed. 'I don't plan to be one, so it is of no consequence.'

'Breaking your word already?' Hugh replied, patting his stallion's mane as he shifted on his hooves, eager to keep moving.

'Nay,' he replied. He'd never achieve his revenge if he messed up their scheme so early on. 'Perhaps I should be grateful for having spied his arrival now rather than in the foyer.'

'I know I am. I didn't have enough oats this morn to

hold you back from killing your mortal enemy.' Hugh stifled an exaggerated yawn and smirked.

Rowan clapped his trusted soldier and friend on the
shoulder. 'Point taken. I will not kill him…today.' He
shrugged. 'At least I do not plan to.'

'Just the words I hoped to hear, my laird.'

They continued, dismounted, and handed off their steeds
to the stable boys. Then, they headed to the main entrance,
climbing the large stone stairs two at a time. After being
greeted by several servants, who took their coats and
gloves, the men were escorted into a banquet hall, which
if memory served was where they held their large, crushing seasonal balls, one in summer and one closer to the fes-
tive season. As he scanned the room, he realised quickly
what the Cameron brothers had done, and he cursed under
his breath.

'Steady,' Hugh murmured, no doubt also realising what
the brothers had done.

They had created a 'husband market' for their sister
Susanna. Every man in the room was an eligible laird or
the father of one. And no doubt every man here was now
aware of it and in the same predicament Rowan was. Although insulted by being invited here under false pretences,
he couldn't show how he felt or merely leave. Otherwise,
he would be insulting the Camerons and have a target on
his back. And once you were in the crosshairs of the Camerons, there were few places to hide.

He shifted on his feet and commanded himself to hold
his open stance and position of power rather than crossing
his arms against his chest despite the annoyance he felt.

As always, the Camerons were scheming and had an
underlying motive for everything. They had seamlessly

created a situation in which they had the advantage. He fisted his hands by his side. He wondered if Susanna knew of what they had done and dared not warn him. His irritation with her intensified.

Until he saw her coming down the stairs. Dressed in a dark gown with her Cameron tartan draped gracefully across her torso and secured with a large brooch, she stole everyone's attention, including his. Her gaze took in her surroundings, her eyes widening and smile straining as she realised what he had: she was being made a fool.

While the men here were being offered up as some sort of husband market, she was also being shown off like a prize mare. The cords of her neck stood out as she sucked in a breath and released it. Rolf greeted her at the last stair and took her hand to help her down, whispering something in her ear. The tension in her face softened briefly before her gaze flicked over to Royce and tightened once more.

Evidently, she was just as surprised by this gathering as Rowan was, and he felt sorry for her. It offered a distraction as Royce began speaking.

'Thank you all for accepting my last-minute invitations, gentleman. My brother and I thought this the most efficient way for selecting a match for our sister, Susanna. We hope you enjoy your day on Loch's End. Please make yourself at home here and spend some time with our lovely sister. If you have need to discuss any matters with my brother or me, we will be available.' He then had the audacity to smile.

Saints be. The man had nerve. Rowan dared a glance at Susanna.

Colour rose in her neck, easing its way into the apples of her cheeks. Instead of making her look mottled and upset, the added colour made her more beautiful, and Rowan's attraction and feelings of the eve of the Tournament flickered and ignited in him once more. That had been the last time he'd seen her, and he realised he had—missed her. It was an altogether odd and unexpected feeling.

Her gaze met his and the utter agony in her face cut him to the quick. If he'd wondered if she'd had any inkling of what her brothers were planning, he had no doubt as to her ignorance of it now. Such embarrassment and anguish could not be manufactured, even in Susanna. She was capable of many things, but that emotional fabrication she was not. He thought about going to her, but the young Laird Macpherson made his way to her, unfettered by the circumstances of this gathering.

The lad had no idea what he was up against.

'Campbell,' a man called out across the room.

Every nerve and drop of blood in Rowan's body stopped and froze at the sound of Laird Audric MacDonald's voice. The room fell silent, all conversations coming to an abrupt halt as everyone's gazes rested on the two of them, despite the number of people in the room. The man had nerve calling out to him, but Audric always had nerve—and a flair for the brute drama of cruelty. In a moment, the past overtook Rowan.

The memory of Anna's death, the smell of blood, the sounds of her last exhale in his arms, and the hot rage of anger and grief he'd felt then flooded his senses. His pulse surged back at twice the pace of before. His hands rested on his leather waist belt. The old man wasn't far. His pale blue eyes, long white hair, and smirk of a smile were in this room, so close that Rowan could imagine killing him—finally. In a matter of seconds, Rowan could pull the blade from his belt, throw it, and watch it land in the brute's chest or neck.

His fingers twined around the cool worn handle easily, his mouth watering at the thought of such sweet bliss.

It would be so easy.

And it would feel so good.

Rowan could watch the old laird fall to his knees and know it was over. Finally, over.

For Anna.

For our son.

For their memories.

And the daily agony of guilt and grief he woke to each morn would cease.

His grip tightened, his breaths became shallow, and his hand slid further down the hilt, his index finger skimming the cool blade.

'Think of Rosa,' Hugh murmured low, resting his hand on Rowan's forearm.

Rowan blinked and came back to the present. Lifting his gaze, he found Susanna. Her features were tight and the soft blush of before was now darker and higher in her cheeks. The emotion in her bright blue eyes was unmistakable to anyone who knew her, and it held him transfixed. With a subtle shake of her head, some of the anger coursing through Rowan abated. She was warning him. This was a trap set by her bothers, and he'd not fall for it. Rowan breathed, counted down from five, and was able to take in his surroundings with more distance and clarity. His fingers tingled with awareness as his pulse slowed, and he could smell the subtle hints of horse, earth, men, and the remnants of a morning meal hovering in the air.

Emotion wasn't flooding his reason as it had been moments before. He took in the scene with fresh eyes. The gazes of everyone in the room were upon him and Audric as if *they* were the main attraction and event for the gathering this morn, not the announced meeting with Susanna and possible suitors to determine her future husband.

His stomach lurched.

Maybe they were. He gripped his sword anew. Anger washed over him again at the realisation that he was meant to be made a fool.

Was *this* Royce's plan all along? A way to bring him down amongst his peers and secure his hold over the clans in the Highlands while also finding a husband for Susanna. Rowan shifted on his feet and his mouth gaped open a measure before he clamped it shut and cursed under his breath.

Saints be.

He had not even considered Royce capable of such a diabolical plan. Perhaps Rowan was getting soft after being holed up in Argyll Castle and his forge the last four years since Anna's death. Either way, he had to find a way through this without losing his self-respect or standing with the clans, ruining his secret arrangement with Susanna, or ending up dead.

With Audric and the scene before him, it was a rather tall order.

But not insurmountable. He was known for his creative battle strategy. It was his greatest asset and never failed him. It was emotion that got him in trouble.

Rowan's gaze flitted back to Susanna, and she nodded to him as if she were following his logic and affirming that this *was* contrived, a test, and perhaps little more than a game to her brothers. He sent her a small smirk, and her eyes widened briefly.

Well, he would give them a show to remember.

And he would learn a few things for himself while he

was at it. He did still plan to have his revenge on Audric but it wouldn't be now.

Not yet.

Despite how he desired to taste the sweetness of such vengeance, it would have to wait for another day when not every leader in the Highlands was present.

Rowan took a heavy step forward towards Audric, and then another, the speed of his movements picking up slightly as he advanced. His hand rested on his weapon's belt, and he could hear the echo of Hugh following him close behind. Fellow lairds and their fathers parted to make way for their advance, some knew well not to interfere while others may have just been eager to see how the scene would play out. Everyone knew what Rowan had lost four years ago.

Everyone also knew that one day such vengeance against Audric would come due.

To his credit, the old man never moved as Rowan approached, not even a shift in his stance. Laird Audric MacDonald's gaze never wavered, and their intense glare between each other was locked in. Emotion tugged at Rowan, reminding him he could still take his vengeance now. He didn't need to wait. This moment could end the agony of grief and guilt that still weighed down his every step and every breath.

Think of Rosa.

Hugh's words from earlier echoed in Rowan's mind like a cadence and a motto with each step. Rowan stopped one boot length away from Audric, so close he could smell the man's stench from his ride here and what may have been dung on his boots.

'MacDonald,' Rowan replied loudly. 'Such a surprise to

see you here today. Are you looking to take a new bride?' he said, sarcasm evident in his tone.

Audric laughed. 'Nay. I desire no further shackles for this lifetime, but my son Devlin is in dire need of settling down and taking roots.'

'Oh? I had no idea you had become…reacquainted.' Rowan made an exaggerated effort to look behind and around Audric for his son Devlin. 'Is he here?' he added.

Audric's lip lifted in what almost appeared to be a snarl rather than an answer, and a quiver of pleasure rolled through Rowan making his toes and fingertips tingle. He had pricked a nerve, knowing fully Devlin was not here and that he still had no interest in returning to his father's fold at Clan MacDonald to be the next laird. Their falling out two years ago over the safety of Rowan's nephew, William, who happened to also be Audric's grandson, had never mended. In fact, Devlin had resided with his sister Fiona, his brother-in-law and then laird of Campbell, Rowan's brother Brandon, and his nephew at Argyll Castle. He had chosen to live on Campbell lands for some time before setting out on his own as a soldier to find his own path away from his abusive father and laird.

A fact everyone else in this room most likely also knew. Rowan's barb had landed well, and he could not have been happier to see Audric's anger bubbling up to the surface.

The room was stone silent. Rowan and Audric stared at one another, and no one moved.

'Perhaps you gentlemen could continue your…er…discussion, at another time?' Royce said, breaking the extended silence. His loud baritone echoed amongst the rafters. A hint of irritation clipped his words as he approached them, his boots echoed off the stone floors, matching his staccato tone.

His scheme had not worked. Not yet anyway.

Rowan almost smiled. Almost.

'Audric?' Royce added. 'Rolf and I would like to speak with you about Devlin and his…intentions. Join us in the study?'

'Aye,' Audric answered, not breaking his heavy stare with Rowan, 'Campbell and I will settle this at another time.'

'Aye,' Rowan replied, his tone menacing, 'we will.'

Audric followed Royce out of the room and into the study, where the door closed with a slam.

Susanna threaded through the crowd to Rowan, ignoring a few enquiries from some younger lads who seemed oblivious to her nature. He smirked as she approached him and offered her arm to him. 'Care for a walk in the gardens, my laird? I find I am in dire need of fresh air.'

He tucked her arm into his own and rested his hand firmly upon it.

'Shall I fetch your cloak, my lady?'

'Nay. I feel overheated and would appreciate the cool, sir.' A sight tremble escaped her lips on sir. Rowan squeezed her arm lightly.

Even for a woman with the steel nerves of Susanna, that exchange had proved a bit too much for her as it had for him.

Rowan nodded to Hugh before they departed, and his trusted soldier remained in the room, no doubt watching and taking in information as he saw it and heard it to report to Rowan later. Rowan and Susanna kept silent as they travelled through the crowd and headed to the main doors to the large, covered walkway leading to the gardens. Susanna's lady's maid and in this case chaperone, Tilly, fell in step behind them and followed at a respectable distance but was always within sight and sound of them, her gentle hum a reminder of her presence. He remembered Tilly from when he was a boy and smirked. She was a lax chaperone from what Rowan remembered, and he was grateful for it. He and Susanna had much to discuss, and Tilly could be trusted, no matter what she heard.

Rowan sucked in the cool, crisp air as it hit his face and almost lifted his cheeks to the sun like a child grateful for deliverance. And he was. He had faced down the man who had killed his wife and son and resisted the urge to slaughter him like an animal in a group of his peers. Three years ago, he might have stabbed the man right then and there in front of everyone and accepted his fate. Today, he had approached the situation with as clear of a head as he could and had not risen to the bait.

Rowan guided Susanna along the manicured path of stone and all the lush green shrubbery around it. Most of the flowers had died out long ago with autumn upon them and winter approaching. He stared out along the cool, still waters of the dark loch. His pulse slowed to the rhythmic sway of the material of Susanna's gown brushing against his legs and the shift of her body into his with each step forward.

'Anna would be proud of you,' she said quietly.

Rowan's steps faltered before he settled back in the steady cadence.

Are you?

The thought popped into his head unbidden, and he frowned. Why did he care whether Susanna was proud of him? He hadn't kept his cool for her—well, he had partly for her because of their agreement but mostly he'd done it for Rosa and the clan. He couldn't cause them further havoc. And it wasn't the right moment to take his revenge. His revenge would be a private rather than public act. He needed to kill the man alone.

Hell, he dreamed of it.

She stopped and faced him. 'I swear to you that I didn't know what they were up to this morn until I came down those stairs. When I realised why everyone was there and saw Audric and then you, I—' she paused'—I knew it was too late to do anything. And I was embarrassed.'

Rowan nodded. 'Aye. I know. Your surprise was evident.'

'Royce told me to dress nicely as we would be having company, and I was to greet them, but he said nothing of me being shown off like a filly at market.' She released Rowan's arm and rubbed her own absently, the colour rising high in her cheeks again. 'You would think after what happened to Catriona at the Grassmarket, he would have some awareness of what it looked like to everyone, but it seems not. What a fool,' she muttered, looking away and out along the meadow.

'If it is of any consolation, I think I was the main attraction today, not you,' he offered.

'You?' She faced him, narrowing her gaze.

'Aye. Imagine what a scene me killing the man that murdered my wife and son would be in front of all the most respected and powerful men of the area. And with such an event, he would have grounds as well as the opportunity, as would the other clan leaders, to make a move to challenge our reign over our people and perhaps conquer us all together and divide up the spoils.'

'And why would my brother do that? He has enough to contend with based on what you and I have both overheard in the last few weeks.'

He came closer and squeezed her shoulders. 'That is exactly it. It is because of his worries that he is being so extreme.'

Susanna shook her head. 'I don't follow your meaning.'

His hands dropped away in exasperation. Surely, she could see what he could, but perhaps the fact that Royce was her brother kept her from seeing him as the strategist Rowan always had.

'Your brother is not daft, Susanna. If he is worrying about maintaining his hold over the Highlands, what better way to do that than to absorb another clan with vast resources and land, such as my own. And if he is being threatened by another laird, he could offer them a shared portion of it as an olive branch to convert their relationship into a strong alliance.'

She stilled, her realisation of the danger of the situation settled in her now pale cheeks, the colour draining away as he spoke.

Rowan paced, walking away from her and staring far off into the loch. 'But why now?' he wondered aloud. 'If anything, I should be seen as far stronger to him than before. At the Tournament, I bested men far younger as well as those far wiser, and I have been seen by the masses as fit and capable. I am no longer the crumbling, grief-stricken man of years ago that was stripped of his title. It makes little sense.'

An unladylike curse yanked Rowan from his study of a pair of starlings chasing one another across the sky.

'It is my doing,' she said.

Rowan stilled, his blood chilling with Susanna's words. He turned slowly to find she was right behind him, close enough to touch. 'Your doing?' he asked.

'Aye,' she added with a sigh. 'Although I never imagined *this* would happen.'

'Explain,' he replied, resting his arms along his waist belt.

'I may have told my brothers of my interest in you as a husband too prematurely while we were at the Tournament. They wondered why I was spending any time with you at all, and I told them it was in an effort to help further our cause. I did not think they would react in such a way.'

'And?' he prodded, taking a step closer. Why this woman always had to swing between vexing him and driving him wild with desire, he didn't know. Minutes ago he'd wanted to kiss her, now—now he wasn't sure what he wanted except for answers.

'I told them you were weak and that I could control you because of your—past illness, and that I felt I could influence you to do as I and they might wish you to, much like we spoke of that first night in the forge. It was a way to make my interest and time spent with you at the Tournament believable. It was simply strategy to support our ruse, like we had agreed.' To her credit, her bright blue eyes held his and didn't drop away.

'And is that what you truly believe about me now?' he asked, his words sharp and menacing. Somehow before when she'd said it in the forge that night weeks ago, the idea of her perceiving him as weak had not bothered him, for he hadn't cared about her opinion or cared enough to challenge or correct her. But now, what she truly thought of him mattered, and he had to know the truth of it to move forward.

She didn't answer but sniffed and swallowed.

'Well, do you, Susanna? I have a right to know if you truly believe me to be the weak broken man that you told them I am. Is it part of the ruse or not?' he asked again, stepping closer to her, needing to know her answer more than he wished to admit. What she thought of him mattered. They were in this hellish agreement together, and he needed to know just how much of a fool he had been and whether she could be trusted at all. He loomed over her petite form, his pulse and breathing rate increasing as he waited. She shivered slightly, but Rowan didn't know if it was from the cold, from him, or both.

'I used to,' she answered, holding her gaze.

'Used to?' he countered, her honesty a surprise.

'Aye. When I first came to see you in the forge that night, I thought you were weaker and could be manipulated easily.'

'And now you do not?'

'Nay. I realised it is restraint, not the weakness I first believed, that I see in you now. And that—that is true power.'

He feared he might blow over with the first soft breeze. Whatever he believed she might say, he hadn't been prepared for those words. He turned away from her and walked off the garden path and into the lush meadow, needing the air and space to allow his body and nerves to settle. This was turning into a far different day than he expected.

And he didn't know if he wished to kiss Susanna or flee from her and the words she had spoken. While his gut told him it was the truth of how he felt, it brought up the array of guilt, shame, and pride he often felt when he thought of where he had been years ago after the death of Anna and his son and where he was now as a restored laird and father to Rosa.

He felt pinned in a vice, unable to wiggle free and unable to shed the past. Perhaps he was never meant to. If he forgot how lost he had become, it might happen again, and he never wished to return to that place of grief and madness ever.

A soft breeze blew, and he smelled a hint of violet in the air and smiled despite himself. The grass rustled next to him as Susanna approached.

'Tilly will be none too happy with you dragging that gown through the heavy dew this morn,' he said, still staring out at the loch. 'I was pleased to see you are still under her care.'

Susanna chuckled. 'She is oft displeased with me, so this shall be no different. And aye, I am lucky to have her.' She settled in quietly next to him, looking out. 'I meant what I said,' she said quietly. 'You are changed.'

He shifted on his feet, the discomfort growing in his gut. 'I am not, Susanna. I am the same man on the brink of madness.' He faced her, taking in the lovely full bloom of her in the wake of the soft light kissing along the edges of her face. Even after the strain of the morn, she was beautiful.

She stepped towards him, her heavy gown sliding over the tip of his boot. 'You do not seem so to me.' Her gaze raked over his face, and she studied him. 'I remember you then.'

His chest tightened under her expectations. 'You see what I show you.'

'Then what do you hide from me?' she asked.

He stared out and inhaled some steadying breaths through his nose. He focused on a large tree on the edge of the loch, leaning heavily over the water, struggling to hold its roots, much like him. 'Every day, I wake with the same rage in me. The anger has not passed or lessened. But each morn I greet and acknowledge that rage within me just as I acknowledge the hope and light and goodness of my daughter and the other blessings in my life. And each day, I choose that light over the anger, rage, and darkness, but it is always there. Close, ready to be set free, like a trapped wolf with its snapping jowls eying its prey before it has freed itself from its irons.'

Her hand wrapped around the clenched fist at his side, her fingers working to open his hand, each one sliding along his own slowly, until she wove her cool petite fingers through them. His breath caught at the intimate contact as if she had pressed her full body along his own and he shuddered but still dared not meet her gaze.

'When Jeremiah died, I retreated from everyone and let my rage soar. I cut down everything and everyone in my wake, and it felt…so good,' she began. 'I did not eat or sleep, but the anger and rage fuelled me until I was a shell of who I was and collapsed one day. I slept for days and then tried to live again. But it was so hard…' she paused. '…Pretending that the world was a place I wished to be in without him was a farce, so I focused on controlling everything and everyone else. I annihilated everyone in my path who would not bend to my will.'

Gooseflesh rose along his skin. How many of those thoughts had he also had? How many of those feelings had he also struggled with?

They were kindred spirits in their loss, and her vulnerability in sharing such with him surprised him as much as it unnerved him. Perhaps she had changed too. The Susanna of old had never been comfortable with speaking of her emotions. She hid them well much like she often hid within her cloak.

'I can honestly say,' she said turning to him, her eyes glistening with unshed tears as their gazes met, 'that if the man who slew Jeremiah on that battlefield had stood before me this morn, I would have cut him from throat to navel.' A tear slid down her cheek as her voice broke. 'The fact that you did not makes you a far better person than me. I want you to know that.'

Without thinking, he leaned closer, wiping away her tear, his thumb lingering along her soft, warm cheek. He kissed her gently on the other cheek and she trembled against him. 'Don't think I didn't imagine it,' he said with a chuckle. 'I just didn't wish to mess up your lovely carpets.'

She half choked on a sob as she laughed, and he felt a thrill in comforting her and in having her so close. It was a feeling he had not had in such a long time that he stilled, not sure whether he should trust it or not.

When she turned her lips to his and kissed him in a soft feathering whisper of a caress, he responded in kind, his mouth lingering over hers.

A cough sounded from behind them.

They both stilled and stepped back to create some semblance of distance between them. Rowan was startled to remember where he was after being forcefully yanked back to the present.

Devil's blood. He had forgotten they were in public. He risked a glance behind them expecting to see Tilly sending a chilling look of disapproval upon them both. Instantly, his shoulders dropped in relief when he saw only Hugh.

'Hugh,' Rowan said clearing his throat.

Susanna muttered under her breath and turned to face the

man as well. She smoothed her gown and set a forced smile to her lips. 'Are you enjoying the view from the gardens?' she asked loudly, so she could be heard by anyone else passing by.

Hugh pressed his lips together to smother a smirk. 'Aye, my lady. 'tis a fine view from here.'

Rowan frowned at him, fully aware of his friend's meaning since he had interrupted his kiss with Susanna.

Hugh cleared his throat. 'Shall we return, my laird?'

'Aye,' Rowan replied without hesitation 'I believe Lady Cameron and I have concluded our—erm—discussions for today, have we not?' *Curses.* He sounded like a dolt.

She set a glare on him in reply. 'I suppose so, my laird. For now.'

Rowan swallowed hard and heat rose along his throat. He offered his arm to guide her, and they began the small climb back up the sloping hillside.

'Have them ready the horses for us,' Rowan called to Hugh, a touch too loudly.

Hugh nodded. 'Already done. We can depart when you are ready.'

Of course, they were. Hugh often knew Rowan better than he knew himself and was able to anticipate many of his needs.

'You will leave without incident?' she asked under her breath as they walked.

'Aye. For now. When shall we meet next?'

'Here at the Holiday Ball, my laird. When your overt wooing is to truly begin. Although there may be whisperings of that beginning today,' she added, scanning the area around them.

'Aye. I blame myself. It was reckless to be out here alone with only your maid. Where did Tilly go?' he asked.

Susanna shrugged. 'I do not know.'

'We must be more careful. Otherwise, you may be found compromised and we may be truly stuck with one another,' he teased with a whisper as they reached the edge of the garden path again.

'There you are, my lady,' Tilly exclaimed. 'Mr. Hugh and I have been all about looking for ye.'

'I am fine, Tilly,' Susanna began, exasperated, leaving Rowan's jest unanswered.

As they walked away, a winkling of wonder stirred in Rowan's gut. Could Susanna have changed too?

He frowned and headed to the stables reflecting on what he'd admitted to her: she saw what he allowed her to see, and he hadn't really changed. Perhaps she did the same and only showed him the bits she had wanted to this morn and hadn't really changed either.

Or had she?

While he wanted to believe Susanna might truly care for him, he stilled as he remembered what she had said to him that first night in the forge: *'It is either you or my family, and as you well know, I will always choose them.'*

And he knew deep down that her words were true.

Chapter Fourteen

Susanna paced in her chambers.

'Ye will wear a hole in this very floor, my lady, if ye are not careful,' said Tilly, glancing up from where she was re-organising Susanna's wardrobe. That single grey eyebrow zeroed in on Susanna as Tilly shifted gowns about on their hangers.

'I can only hope so,' Susanna replied, making her steps louder. 'That way my brothers' prize mare will be injured and unable to be brought out to market again.'

'My lady,' said Tilly with an edge of sympathy and what may have been understanding in her voice, which set Susanna on edge. Kindness simply wouldn't do right now. Tilly set aside a lush goldenrod gown on Susanna's bed for her to consider.

'Throw it out,' Susanna sniped, desperate to cling to her anger to avoid the tears that might replace it. 'I despise yellow.'

Tilly sighed and patiently placed the gown on the tee-tering pile of rejected dresses on the bench seat near the large windows overlooking the meadows. 'Ye seem to de-spise them all today, my lady, but ye must wear something special for the upcoming Holiday Ball here at Loch's End, especially if ye hope to marry before the year is through.'

'Must I?' She cast a wicked smile at her maid. 'Perhaps I shall only wear a cloak with nothing beneath and shock them all. That will put an end to this marriage nonsense. Would it not?'

Her maid gasped and muttered something unintelligible under her breath before returning to the wardrobe. Susanna knew she was being a brat among other things, but she was so angry. Nothing would abate her anger until she could unleash it upon her brothers after the stunt they pulled this morn. And she couldn't do that until the last of their guests departed. Many of them lingered well into the afternoon, taking advantage of the time to meet with her brothers and offer terms for a possible union with her.

She wanted to scream and then retch all over the pile of glorious rainbow-coloured gowns Tilly had sorted through. Not only had her brothers treated her like livestock to be bartered over at a market rather than a person, they had set a trap that had almost ended in Rowan's humiliation as well.

She cursed. All because she had told them why she had set her attentions upon Rowan, in order to protect her own plan to discover their ridiculous secrets. *Ach*. It had all worked against her. Even in her exchange with Rowan today when she told him she believed he had changed, she'd revealed more than she'd wished to about losing Jeremiah, making herself vulnerable to him.

She shuddered. She had even cried. And she hated being vulnerable to anyone, even her family. To know she had revealed such feelings and intimacies with him of all people, especially after their past...

Blast.

She wrung her hands.

Then, he had been so—gentle with her. And his kiss had set her toes tingling, which made it worse. Then Hugh caught them kissing. She huffed in frustration and put her head in her hands. She was losing control of the situation. If her brothers would just tell her the truth, she could abandon her plan, create some distance between her and Rowan, and get back to her real life rather than this false one.

Rowan.

She touched her fingertips to her lips, remembering the tender touch of his own there, and the way their hands had fit together as sweetly as they had when they were young. All of it was making her addled and unfocused. She pulled the pins from her hair, letting her long locks fall free. Sighing in relief, she massaged her scalp. She could always think better when her hair wasn't bound. As she began pacing once more, Tilly released an exaggerated sigh, which Susanna ignored.

'Shall we speak of ye and Rowan?' she asked lightly.

'Oh, Tilly, please. I beg you. Nay.'

'Do not "Oh, Tilly" me, my lass. Ye are playing with fire, ye are, just like when ye were young. Ye two have always been, well, reckless with one another.'

Had they?

'What do you mean?' she asked, pausing her steps.

She shrugged and held up a lavender gown to Susanna.

Susanna made a fake retching noise in reply, and Tilly placed it on the discarded pile of gowns, rolled her eyes, and continued. 'What I mean is ye have an intense connection. Always have. Be careful. He is still recovering from losing his wife, is he not?'

'Aye.'

'And ye are still mourning yer Jeremiah, despite the time that has passed.'

'Aye. But I still do not understand?'

'Grief and loneliness can create a heady combination, especially when ye mix in the history of a past courtship. Do not get lost in it. That is all.'

Susanna scoffed and glanced away, her pulse picking up a bit of speed over her maid's warning. 'That is ridiculous, Tilly. You have nothing to worry over,' Susanna responded, perhaps too quickly and with too much certainty, as Tilly cut her a quizzical look.

'That, my dear, is *exactly* what I mean. Do not be so dismissive of it as a possibility. Be careful. I saw the way ye two were looking at each other.' She made a tsking sound and shook her head.

Before Susanna could counter Tilly's reply, the sounds of horses departing outside interrupted her, and she rushed to the window to look out. Three more men were leaving by horse. *Praise be.* While she didn't know if they were the last of their guests from this morn, she hoped they were. Heavy footfalls up the stairs and a loud knock at her chamber door confirmed they had been. If Royce thought he could give her a piece of his mind right now, he was mistaken. Susanna rushed to the door, ignoring Tilly's protests to wait.

Flinging the door open, Susanna saw Rolf standing with his fisted hand high in the air, preparing to knock again. His eyes were wide and pleading.

'I'm sorry,' he spat out softly before she could utter a sound, deflating her anger before she'd had a chance to expel it, much like her younger brother always did.

Her shoulders sagged, and she leaned on the door. 'Come in,' she replied.

Tilly nodded to them and departed through Susanna's chambers to leave them to their discussion.

Susanna and Rolf settled onto the large settee.

'For?' Susanna prompted, tucking her legs beneath her, and leaning her elbow on the back of the plush lavender fabric lining the couch. She refused to make this too easy for him. Not after all she'd been through today.

He stared back at her blankly, the strains of the day evident in his rumpled tunic and rather harried expression, both unusual for her carefree brother.

'You said you were sorry,' she explained. 'What are you sorry for? Treating me like I was a sheep at market? Not telling me you were planning to do so? Not having a backbone and standing up to our brother? Putting Rowan in a position where he might kill Audric and lose everything?'

Rolf squirmed with each question, his discomfort growing. Once she ceased her questions, he scrubbed a hand through his hair, ruffling it like he often did as a boy when he was thinking. Then he ran his hand down his face with a sigh. 'Everything?' he said almost like a question of his own rather than an answer to hers.

'Everything?' she mimicked him.

'Aye,' he replied with more certainty as he sat up straighter and faced her, setting his elbow on the back of the settee as well. 'You know what he is like, Susanna.'

She scoffed. 'Aye. And?'

'And despite how he *has* changed since Lismore and marrying Iona, he can still be this force—this immovable and oft unreasonable boulder one cannot persuade or shift about some things. This is one of them.'

She chuckled. 'Aye, I also know that. But this morn? Rolf, why did you not warn me? Not one single word from you. I was humiliated.' Tears heated the back of her eyes, despite herself, which angered her more. Why was she so emotional today?

Blast.

Her brother was her beacon of safety, that was why. His betrayal cut deeply. Far more deeply than Royce's.

He reached out and squeezed her forearm. 'I should have. I couldn't find the words to tell you, and I also hoped—' he let go of her arm and rubbed the back of his neck '—I had hoped Royce would come to his senses about the whole endeavour—and about Campbell. But since you put that idea in his head about Rowan being weak and conquerable, Royce can think of little else.'

'What?' she recoiled. 'This is somehow my fault?'

He shook his head. 'Nay. I am not saying that. But you said the words that triggered this plan of his.'

She waited.

He continued. 'He said today would serve multiple purposes. One, to see who wanted to be in a union with us by marrying you.' He continued counting on his fingers. 'Two, how well Campbell was by whether he would rise to the bait of Audric being here or not. And three, if he attacked Audric, we would know just how weak he was and could formulate a plan to overtake his clan with you as his bride.'

The words hung in the air. Rancid sounds and syllables she wished to open the window to let out. But she couldn't unhear them. Rowan had been right on all counts about what her brothers had done to her and him, and it pained her. Deeply.

'Why did you not stand up to him? Tell him what a fool-hardy plan this was?'

'As I explained, Susanna, you know Royce. He cannot back down once his hackles are up. And right now, with everything so…' he paused, searching for the right words, and then continued, '…delicate, he will listen to no one. I have tried.'

She clutched his hand in his lap. 'And what is this thing that makes me suddenly marrying so necessary and everything else so "delicate", as you say? Tell me, brother. I can help.'

He squeezed her hand and then pulled it away. 'Nay. You cannot. And I cannot tell you. You must trust us.'

'After today, you want for me to trust you both?' she scoffed. 'What happened to Royce no longer keeping secrets as he promised when he returned from Lismore? And about the two of us, you and me, *never* keeping secrets from each other, ever?'

'Susanna,' he replied, the agony evident in his tone and strained jaw. 'I know it is an unreasonable request, but we are in a precarious position, and caution is our best option over the coming months. The future of our family and the clan's future are at stake. We cannot afford a misstep.' He kissed her cheek, rose from his seat, and headed to the door.

'Brother, just tell me. You leaving me in the shadows of the situation may cause the very misstep you fear.' She pleaded with him one last time, the desperation making her voice high and almost shrill.

Although Rolf's steps briefly faltered, he didn't stop. He left the room. Susanna groaned in frustration, pounding the pillow on the settee until she was too weary to continue.

Chapter Fifteen

'You are late,' Rowan complained, emerging from behind his favourite pairing of trees in the rowan grove.

'And you are becoming predictable,' she countered, lowering her cloak hood, and swinging around the trunk of the tree just across from where he had hidden himself. Her hair was loose and swayed out around her in an arc. For a moment she seemed a young lass to him, sending a ripple of memory through him. The carefree action made him long for something else he didn't wish to name, so he batted it away.

'Because I continue to be irritated by having to wait for you?' he said, gesturing to the same boulder they had met at before to formulate their initial strategy, which needed some adjustments based on how the gathering at Loch's End had played out.

She made a face at him as she followed him. 'Nay. You disguised yourself behind the same pairing of trees. Why?'

He stiffened. Was he so predictable? Had he hidden behind the same trees each time they met here?

He cursed himself. Surely not. Today would be challenging on its own, but managing Susanna's snipes would make it even worse. He sent her a withering look to let her know he was not to be trifled with today.

'You are no fun, Rowan Campbell. It is a glorious morn, and I had a blissful ride here. What is there to grouse about so early?'

Evidently his withering look was not what it used to be. 'It is a glorious morn, but we have lost some of it because someone—' he replied.

She cut him off and lifted her palm. 'Because I was late. Blah, blah, blah. Let us begin, so we can get this meeting concluded.' She sat upon the boulder, settling herself too close to him.

He shifted away.

'I do not bite,' she teased.

Not yet.

He ignored her and unrolled the parchment. Together they placed rocks upon the corners to keep it flat. She leaned over it, reading the newest additions and findings to their scheme. Her hair slipped from underneath the hood of her dark cloak and over her shoulder, blocking his view. He reached his hand out to move it aside and found his fingertips lingering along the silken strands. Her gaze met his.

'Can you not tie back your hair? I cannot see,' he griped.

'My, you are in a mood today, my laird. I have never heard anyone so angry about my hair before.' She leaned back with a smirk and gathered her hair quickly, twisting it into a knot at the nape of her neck. The swift and graceful movements seized his attention, and he could not look away. Her hands fell, resting in her lap, and she studied him with concern. 'Something is wrong. What is it?'

'Nothing I wish to discuss with you,' he replied, his words sharper than he intended.

When she recoiled slightly, he softened. 'I did not sleep well,' he added in a lower voice and glanced back to the parchment, running a smooth palm over it. While a vast understatement, it was true.

It was just not the whole truth.

But she did not need to know it.

'Then I wish you better sleep this eve. For now, let us talk about our revised plan. What have you learned? Then I will share my own findings and see what we can piece together.'

'You share first,' he countered, unable to simply agree with her suggestion.

'I can do that,' she replied, watching him with caution. 'Seems whatever is plaguing my brothers has something to do with Royce's time on Lismore. I have heard them talking about someone named Webster. They have also traded a parcel of land to someone that also knew Webster.' She reached down her bodice, and Rowan could not help but follow her hand's movements, spying a flicker of creamy flesh and the rounded curve of a breast before she retrieved what lay hidden there. He swallowed hard and cleared his throat.

Susanna cut him a disapproving glance. 'It is the best hiding place. Do not judge.'

'Not judging. Just surprised.'

'Anna never hid anything in her bosom?' she enquired.

Why was she talking to him about this? They needed to focus. 'I've not time for this trifle. What did you learn?' he replied sharply.

She balked and shifted away from him. 'Your tone leaves something to be desired today. Shall I go, and we will meet another day? I have enough rebuke from Royce. I need not more from you.'

He closed his eyes, rubbed his brow, and sucked in a breath before opening his eyes and meeting her gaze. 'Nay. My apologies. Continue.'

She situated herself again on the boulder, and unfurled the small, rolled note on the parchment, holding it flat with her hand. 'The man's name is Chisholm. He selected a fine plot of land on the loch where one could easily dock. I made a small sketch of it here from memory. I spied it on my brother's desk before he could roll it back up. Seems suspicious, does it not? To give a man one does not know easy access to a port location such as that?'

'You made this from memory?' He leaned forward, impressed by the detail in her sketching.

She smiled. 'I mastered the art of reading upside down when I was a girl in my father's study, and I have a fine memory for visuals.'

'Good to know. I will be wary of what documents I have out if you ever darken my study door.' He smoothed his hand along the small parchment. The warmth from where it had been hidden sent a flush of desire through him, but he dashed it away. He had no time for such distractions today of all days.

'I believe the man may be planning a visit before the new year.'

'Oh?' he stilled. 'Why?'

She shrugged. 'I cannot say, but my brothers are nervous about the idea of him coming. Even Royce.'

Rowan leaned back, releasing the parchment, and it curled back up. 'Hugh said he overheard some of the other men discussing how the British are redistributing their soldiers along the Borderlands and that supply channels are being strained. Perhaps Royce wishes to get supplies from this man?'

'From Lismore? Not much is there, from what Iona has relayed to me.'

'What of neighbouring isles?'

'I cannot say, but I can find out. Iona is eager for a distraction these days with the bairn on the way making her so queasy.' She smiled. 'Royce is hoping for a son, of course, while I hope for a girl.'

A bairn. *A son.* Rowan's gut tightened. He ignored her comment, focusing on the task at hand. Only that would get him through the remaining hours of today. 'Anything else?'

'Nay,' she replied quietly. 'You?'

'The men have noticed Royce has spent time and manpower fortifying his border walls on all sides.'

'All?'

'Aye. As if he believes he has no allies and may be forced to defend his own lands alone. It is intriguing, is it not?'

'Aye. And frightening. Why would he think such? We have more alliances than anyone.'

'Makes you wonder what he believes would change that, does it not?'

'I cannot think of anything.'

Rowan sat silently. He had thought of one, but he could not say it. It was too reprehensible to utter aloud.

She leaned towards him. 'But you have thought of something. I can see it in your eyes. What is it?'

He shook his head. 'It is not possible.'

'What? Tell me. We are in this together, are we not?'

'That they have turned on us. All of us. And have secured favour with the British. Future protections in exchange for…' He couldn't finish the rest of it, but she would know what he meant.

She balked and leaned towards him. 'How dare you,' she hissed, her voice low and husky, her hands fisted. Her features flushed with anger, just as he expected they might. He would have been just as insulted.

Yet he wanted to tell her his thoughts. He didn't want to hide them from her.

He lifted his palms in supplication. 'I know, Susanna. I do not believe it either. But you asked what might cause your brothers to fear losing their alliances in the Highlands, and that is the only thing that came to mind.'

She sat back on the boulder and stared out into the grove. 'Despite all, I cannot believe either of them would manage any such arrangement. Ever.'

'I hope you are right, for there would be no turning back. Your clan would be outcasts if they pursued such a precarious route.'

'I know that. So would they. There must be another reason we cannot see yet. I cannot help but feel we are running out of time.'

'Why?'

'My gut, as illogical as it sounds for me to say it aloud.' She stared down her hands, studying the palms.

'I have made more than one decision based on instinct. And it has never failed me.' He watched her until she looked at him. 'Trust it.'

She lifted her brow and turned her body to fully face him. 'Then I shall do that now. What is wrong with you today? My gut tells me it is far more than you not sleeping well as you say.'

Deuces.

Why did she always turn him on himself? And in such an exquisite manner. It was irritating. He frowned at her, hoping it might quell her questioning. She merely lifted a brow in challenge. 'I have nowhere to be at present. Tell me. Some people say I can on occasion be a good listener.'

Did he dare?

They sat in companionable silence, neither of them pushing or prodding. Taking his own advice on trusting his gut, Rowan finally spoke.

'It is four years today…when I lost them. Anna and our son.'

He felt parched after such an admission, his mouth dry and his voice brittle as if the words had fought and crawled their way out of his throat against his will.

Perhaps they had.

She released a rather unladylike curse, and he couldn't help but chuckle.

'I am sorry, Rowan. I should have remembered before I sent you a note to meet today.'

He shook his head. 'Nay. There is no reason for you to remember. It is just a day to everyone else, but to me it is a day I can never forget. And the hours of each anniversary drag on painfully long.' He took a rock and scratched against the larger boulder. 'I merely pray to survive it each time it rolls back around.' The words felt easier now. He reminded himself that she understood his loss in her own way and that she would not judge him. Not about this, at least.

She set her hand around his own, which held the small rock. 'Truly. I am sorry. We can end our meeting. We can do this another time.'

'Nay,' he said, gripping her hand in his. 'We must make our plans for the Holiday Ball coming up at Loch's End so we can begin this pretend courtship of ours and prevent you having a horrid engagement to some other sot. I also wish to plan how I shall effectively end Audric. I have some ideas…many ideas.' He squeezed her hand and let go.

It almost felt like they were becoming friends, if nothing else, which was such an odd thing. Loss was binding them to one another in a way that their affection for each other in the past never had.

'Then let us discuss the Holiday Ball,' she said with a tone of resignation. 'I do despise such affairs, but I know this one is essential to our plan for this fake attachment of ours. How do you plan to woo me, my laird?'

'Dancing,' he said with a smile, setting the rock aside.

'Dancing?' she echoed. 'Is dancing not a normal part of the balls? How will this seem like you courting me?'

'You shall dance with no one else.' He gifted her another devilish smile.

She scoffed. 'No one else? How will that be possible?'

'I will continue to ask, and you will refuse anyone else who sets their attentions on you.'

'That would be rude.'

'Nay. That would be classic Susanna. Cold to those who mean nothing to her, fiercely loyal to those who do.'

'I see now what you are suggesting and where you are going with this, but how do I not offend any other suitors in the process? I do not wish to make more enemies for us to manage, and you lairds are a rather arrogant and delicate lot prone to having your pride pricked rather easily.' She lifted a brow at him and smirked.

'Simply show your interest in me first in a way that shall cast no doubt as to your intentions, so you will not appear to be misleading any other men with undue attentions that evening.'

'Again, how do I do that?'

'Shower *me* with your attention. It shall be easy.' He smiled at her, and she groaned.

'It will be difficult if you are so—arrogant.'

He ignored her complaint and continued. 'Oh, and you must wear a blue gown.'

She shifted and looked away. 'Can it not be another colour?'

'It could, but blue is the most stunning on you as it brings out your eyes.' He paused. 'Why can it not be blue? Do you dislike it? Now that I think on it, I cannot remember you wearing blue in quite some time.'

'It is because I choose not to.'

'Why?'

'It was Jeremiah's favourite colour on me. I have not worn it since he died,' she said softly. 'Everyone knows this. I am surprised you do not.'

'Perhaps I missed that part of our reacquaintance,' he muttered, unsure why she would believe he knew one whit about her fashion choices. 'But now that I do know this, you *must* wear blue. It will signal you have moved on. It will show everyone how serious you are about a betrothal. Your brothers and others will see the significance, and our ruse will be more than believable.' Excitement rushed through him.

'I do not know, Rowan.' Her voice was fragile now.

It was his turn to convince and support her as she just had for him. 'You can do this, Susanna. For your family, for your clan, and for yourself,' he added. 'It may even help you to heal and release some of your grief.'

She bit her lip and sat quietly. Too quietly for his liking. He moved closer to her. 'Think of all the other things you have done and survived. This will be a small thing once you commit to it.'

'Will it? It feels like a betrayal, even though it is only a dress colour.' She played with the ribbon of her cloak.

'Trice often tells me the only betrayal to those we have lost is to not live.'

Susanna narrowed her gaze at him.

Rowan shrugged. 'Some days I believe it. Other days it rings more of horse dung.'

She snorted. 'You, my laird, just said *dung* like you were five years old.'

'I did. And you laughed. I win.'

'Fine,' she relented. 'I will think upon your suggestion. Nothing more, mind you.'

He nodded. 'Fair. At the Holiday Ball, you may or may not wear blue, but you will commit to dancing with me?'

'Aye. As much as I can stand,' she agreed.

'Now, we must discuss Audric.' His body tightened instantly as he said the man's name. 'I have thought upon my revenge after we unearth this secret of yours.'

'And?'

'You will secure me an invitation to visit you at Loch's End a suitable time after the Holiday Ball, when our official "attachment" has begun. I will visit while he is there, and he will simply…vanish.'

'Vanish?' she asked. 'You have lost me. One cannot vanish a laird.'

'Nay. But I can drug him, bring him back to Argyll Castle, and have some time with him before he is dispatched from this world.'

'Your family approves?'

'They will not know.'

She shook her head. 'Aye. They will know. They are not daft.'

'In the forge I can. No one is allowed in when I work late at night. It is my sanctuary and has all the tools I may need to serve my purposes.'

'And that would give you peace?' she asked with a raised brow.

'Peace? Nay. I am merely trying to stop the agony of my grief and grant some justice to my wife and son. Peace is a dream I gave up long ago.'

'Killing him in such a way will not haunt you?'

'Not more than my memories of that day.'

'You have never told me all of it,' she replied, a question in her voice.

He studied her. Perhaps if he told her all, she would have a better understanding of why Audric's death was necessary. It was a risk to share such with her, but she had just shared with him more about Jeremiah. Perhaps she could understand. Perhaps he could dare trust her in this budding friendship of theirs.

'The attack was sudden.' He began settling into the scene in his mind. 'One moment, Anna and I were asleep. The next, guards were shouting, maids were screaming, and the clash of weapons filled the night air.' He took a breath as his pulse increased. 'They had stormed the castle from within, breaching our walls using a hidden tunnel that only the family knew about, or so we thought. Brandon had secreted Fiona in through that very tunnel to continue their affair once her father, Audric, had forbidden it to continue, but we didn't know that. Fiona's maid had overheard the exchange. As you may have expected, that maid told Audric to earn his favour.'

Susanna sucked in a breath. 'I had heard bits of this as rumour, but I didn't know if any of it was true.'

He nodded. 'As with most gossip, there are some parts that are true.' He paused. 'Once the walls were breached, the castle was swarming with MacDonald soldiers, and we all took up arms to protect our home and those we loved. Even my Anna.' He smiled at the memory of her fierceness. 'She never wavered in her efforts. While I went off to gather Rosa and ensure our daughter's safety, she stayed in our chamber, sword in hand, to protect our wee son.

'I fought my way to Rosa one soldier at a time and reached her as a MacDonald soldier had just breached her door. I was able to rescue her and her maid in time, but when I returned to gather Anna...' His voice broke.

Susanna reached out and took his hand. 'You do not have to continue if you do not wish to.'

'Nay. You need to understand. I *need* you to understand,' he replied, the urgency to finish driving him on. 'Audric was at the doorway of our chamber when I reached it. His sword was bloodied and drawn, and Anna had crumpled to the floor behind him, with our son in her arms.'

His chest tightened, his pulse raged, and the smell of the death and bloodshed of that day seized him, turning his stomach. Sickness threatened.

'I attacked him,' Rowan added. 'A rage fuelled me, but when I heard Anna call out to me, I shoved him off and rushed to her. As I cradled her and our son in my arms, I knew it was too late and that she had little time left. Our son—' he shuddered '—was already gone from this world. Anna left me soon after to join him.'

'And Audric?' she asked.

'Little did I know it, but he had remained at the door,

watching her die in my arms. When I cried out in agony, he said that now I would know and understand sons would pay for the sins of their fathers—always.'

Susanna stilled, her mouth dropping open. 'I… I cannot fathom it. What did he even mean?'

'That my son's death and my suffering from losing him as well as Anna and so many others that day was revenge for what my father, grandfathers, and great-grandfathers before me had exacted on his clan in the Glencoe Massacre decades before.'

'And so you will continue that cycle of revenge and kill him?'

'Aye. I will,'

'But, Rowan,' she began.

He gripped her forearm. 'Nay. We had an agreement, Susanna. You know this was part of it. Do not act as if this was not what I had in mind. If you try to back out, I swear I will—'

She yanked her arm out of his hold. 'Do not be so dramatic,' she countered. 'I just want you to think upon the risks if you are caught, that is all. You have a daughter and clan counting on you. What you do impacts them all. And killing him will not bring your family back.'

'I know well my role in this,' he scowled, refusing to address the rest of her statement. He stood abruptly, rolled up his parchment, and tucked it in his waist belt. 'See to it that you do not forget yours.'

He'd had enough of this meeting and Susanna scrutinising him and his decisions. She couldn't know what he'd been through. Not really. No one could. Why she didn't have more of an understanding after all he had just shared with her, he didn't know. Why had he even tried to make her understand?

He left her, headed off through the hillside, and kicked at the ground in frustration, sending up a tuft of grass and a loose stone. It didn't matter if she understood or not. He just needed her to help him take out his revenge on Audric. Nothing else mattered.

As he started down through the grove, glancing up at the position of the sun, he cursed. It wasn't even midday. Several more hours remained before this horrid day would be through.

Chapter Sixteen

'Stop yer fidgeting,' Tilly instructed and swatted at Susanna's hands as she adjusted her gown for the one hundredth time.

'I am not so sure, Tilly. I do not think it suits me, and the bodice is far too tight.' Music and merriment echoed up into Susanna's chambers, but she could not get herself excited about this year's Holiday Ball. The more she looked about her room, the more perfect it seemed. 'I could just stay here for the evening.'

'Nay. The gown fits ye as it should and isn't hanging off ye like the other ones ye have. Ye look glorious. The blue was a fine idea. Ye will be the belle of the ball.'

Susanna rolled her eyes and sagged forward. While she wasn't normally prone to such insecurity, tonight her nerves fluttered and bubbled, and every flaw she had stared back at her from the standing mirror. Her bound-up hair was too limp, her breasts too small, her waist too narrow, and her skin too pale. And while the gown was a gorgeous sapphire blue, she did not do it justice. She feared it may well look better on its hanger than upon her. Even if she was trying to appear ready for marriage and a future engagement, who would want her? She was older and not the typical lass lairds were eager to bind themselves to.

As Rowan and her brothers were quick to point out, she could be a tad stubborn, difficult, wilful—and now she just looked, well, odd.

'I do not think I should go,' Susanna said quietly.

Tilly paused and took her hand. 'I know the significance of ye wearing this dress colour this eve, wee girl. And I am so proud of ye for trying to move on, to heal, to live yer life. Jeremiah would have wanted this for ye. We all do.'

Jeremiah.

She stared back in the mirror and almost smiled. He would have loved this dress. He would have teased her to no end about how much he'd wish to get it off her, and she would have laughed. He would have joined in with that deep, throaty laughter of his, and she would have felt like the most beautiful woman in the world.

Which was the opposite of how she felt now. Her heart sank. 'I do not think I can do it.'

Tilly crossed her arms against her chest. 'And what shall I tell him, then, when ye do not show?'

'Who?'

'Ye know exactly who. Laird Campbell. I am no fool.' She began folding the other shifts Susanna had not selected for the eve and set them aside. 'While I am not sure what ye are about, I know ye are up to something together. And I saw ye in the garden that morn.' She slid her gaze to Susanna and then went about her folding.

Susanna began to utter a rebuttal, but Tilly put her hand on hers. 'I do not need to know the details of anything. I just want ye to remember that ye will be disappointing people if ye don't go. Yer brothers will be there. Lady Cameron is there, no doubt longing for more familiar faces at her first ball as grand as this. Yer sister and her new husband will be there, and Laird Campbell—as well as any other suitors. If ye do not go, there will also be talk. Most likely ugly talk. Ye know how some of those ladies can be.' She went and put the shifts away in her wardrobe, leaving Susanna with her reflection.

And her conscience.

'You win, Tilly. You have persuaded me, but I will not have any fun. You cannot make me enjoy it.' She blew out a breath, popped her hands to her hips, and pulled back her shoulders. She could do this.

She was wrong. She could *not* do this. Susanna stood at the top of the large staircase that led down to the main entrance of Loch's End. Her brothers flanked each side of the doors, greeting the guests at the expansive and ornately decorated entryway as they arrived. Her sister Catriona and sister-in-law Iona stood beside them, exactly where she should be—instead of hovering behind the large wooden railing at the top of the stairs, hoping no one would see her.

She sucked in a breath. *Rowan.*

He walked through the door and greeted Royce as coolly and calmly as if the man had not set him up for absolute ruin weeks ago. They were almost a matched pair standing hand in hand. They were similar in height and stature, with Royce perhaps a hair taller and more muscular. But Rowan had an underlying ferocity and emotional intensity her brother lacked. He also seemed to have developed far more patience. He cut an impressive figure with his dark fitted coat, Campbell plaid and kilt, and crisp tunic. A shining silver brooch winked at her from his shoulder, and she wondered if he had made it himself.

His gaze clicked up as he neared the staircase. When he

saw her, he stilled, stopped cold as if he had been arrested by the sight of her. She flushed and bit her lower lip, fighting the urge to wring her hands.

Why had she allowed Tilly to talk her into this?

Rowan's heated stare softened, and he smiled up at her. 'Good evening, my lady. You look enchanting this evening.'

Enchanting?

Her throat dried, her heart picking up speed. She clutched the railing for dear life.

Her family looked up towards her, and soon all their gazes were locked on her. Iona clapped her hands together, turning to Royce. 'I told you she would come, and she is perfection.'

Royce kissed his wife's cheek. 'Aye. But not as perfect as you.'

She batted his shoulder. 'You say that because you must and I am carrying your child, but I love to hear it anyway.' Then she kissed him back.

'Join us, sister,' Rolf called out to her, waving her down the stairs encouragingly.

Susanna faltered. Uncertainty weighed down her feet. It was one thing to be greeted warmly by her family and Rowan, who were charged with approving of her. It was quite another to wade into the swamp of lairds and ladies below. They would smell her fear and be primed to devour her. Perhaps it was not too late to cry off and disappear into her chambers with a megrim. To her surprise, Rowan started up the stairs to her, his gaze full of appreciation—and what looked to be desire. Surely not. Everything she did irritated him, and he plagued her. Only their bargain held them together, and even that was precarious.

'My lady,' he said, offering his arm. 'Smile,' he whispered when his back was to everyone else. 'I am here,' he added. His blue eyes were strong and steady, and held the world. 'You are not alone.' Susanna's heart squeezed in gratitude as she slid her arm through his and finally smiled. If he could play his part as the doting suitor, then she could settle into her role as a woman eager to secure a powerful match this eve.

She lifted her chin, pulled back her shoulders, and nodded to him.

'There we are,' he murmured. He turned, leading her down the stairs. 'May I have the first dance?' he asked her, loud enough for her family and most everyone in the nearby room to hear.

'Aye, my laird,' replied, pleased there was no tremble in her voice.

Susanna smiled at her family as he guided her past them. To her vast relief, her brothers held their tongues and did not chastise her for not greeting guests as they arrived or challenge Rowan for stealing her away with such brazenness. As they entered the thick of the crowd, he cooed in her ear, low and husky. 'Keep smiling,' he encouraged her. 'We are nearly there.'

Fine music echoed in from the outer ballroom. Susanna swallowed back the acid rising in her throat as the overt stares began. Men and women alike gaped at her as she walked past, and she forced herself to meet every gaze and acknowledge them with a nod.

Enchanting, she reminded herself. *Be enchanting.*

Soon they were on the dance floor. He guided her along with an unexpected grace, their feet gliding along to one of her favourite reels. She smiled. 'I had forgotten you were so skilled, my laird.'

He lifted his brow in challenge.

'On the dance floor,' she added, a mock frown on her lips.

'I believe there is much about me—and us—that you have forgotten,' he said, his words heavy with meaning.

She didn't answer, but allowed herself to relax in his hold, some of the space between them disappearing as she did so.

'All eyes are upon you,' he whispered close to her ear. 'Just as we had hoped. No one can be in doubt of your intention to secure a husband now. Not with the way you look tonight.'

'Am I enchanting?' she teased, using his earlier words against him.

'Aye,' he said, his voice dropping lower. 'You look beautiful. Every lady here wishes that she were you or that she could kill you and steal that gown from your bones. Every man here not related to you wants to ravish you.'

Her breath caught in her throat.

Even you?

But she would not ask it, for either answer would strike terror through her. To be desired by Rowan would be just as dangerous as being repelled by her.

'And we are happy about this because…?' she asked.

'You will be the talk of the ball, whether good or bad, and no one will be unaware of your intention to marry and my intentions towards you, no matter how false.'

'Which suits part of our plan perfectly, but what of getting more information? Of discovering what my brothers fear?'

Rowan pulled back from her, his smile falling into a bit of a scowl. 'We will have to do what we both despise: socialise.'

Dread prickled along her skin.

'I know,' he said with a sigh.

'Did you not tell me when we met last that it was essential we dance together all eve? To show our affections for one another and to make our engagement later believable?'

'Aye,' he replied, looking over her shoulder as he spun her out and then back to him with an ease and delicacy that surprised her. 'But Hugh reminded me of the flaw in such a plan.'

'Flaw?'

'Staying together would limit the amount of information we could gather. Splitting up, mixing with the other guests here, will allow us to linger, eavesdrop, and whatever else seems reasonable. Then we can share what we have learned and hopefully have some more meaningful information to piece together than what scant information we have gathered as of now.'

Drat.

She couldn't fault the logic behind his words, but mingling? It was akin to driving thistles under her fingernails.

'All night?' she asked, her voice forlorn.

He chuckled. 'Nay. That would be more than anyone could bear.' He squeezed her hand and ran his thumb along her own. 'One hour. Then we gather again. Perhaps at the refreshment table? Or out of doors for fresh air?'

'Definitely out of doors, but not too far within the gardens. There must be nothing unseemly,' she added in a hushed tone. She hoped he would remember what had happened during their last foray into 'gathering fresh air.' He'd nearly kissed the life out of her, and they were lucky not to have been seen by anyone but Hugh and Tilly. Such risks they could not take now.

He smirked. 'Understood.' The reel came to an end, and they separated and joined in the crowd's applause. As the next jovial chords began, Rowan bowed and took his leave. 'Have fun,' he murmured, 'and be nice.' Young Laird Macpherson swooped in, almost knocking into Rowan in his hasty and haphazard approach to Susanna.

'My lady,' Laird Macpherson said, his gaze raking over her face and then down to her bosom in a rather indelicate fashion that told of a man undisciplined by youth. 'You look beautiful this eve.'

'Thank you, my laird. Are you enjoying yourself?' she asked, intrigued by his confidence. He was wide-eyed with floppy chestnut hair. He also had an easy smile, and the promise of a nice stature once he grew into his body. He was much like a sloppy puppy eager in his approval and devotion, but uncertain as to how to show such affections.

'Aye. And I would enjoy myself even more if you would join me. This reel is one of my favourites. May I?' he asked, extending his open palm to her in invitation.

Susanna watched Rowan walking away and being approached by a young lass who happened to 'drop' her handkerchief just as he walked by. He paused, picked it up, and returned it to her, unable to escape the woman's attentions. Susanna valiantly did not roll her eyes and set her gaze back on Macpherson, his face open and expectant...hopeful. She remembered what such young hope and desire felt like. His smile widened.

This was part of their game, and she and Rowan both had to play it if they were to uncover the secrets that threatened her family *and* keep them safe *and* prevent her from being forced into a marriage with someone like this young colt. Susanna slid her arm around Macpherson's, pleased to feel the slight flex of his muscle beneath, and smiled. 'Aye. Of course, my laird.' Playing with him for a bit might be fun, but then she remembered Rowan had *also* commanded her to be nice. She quirked her lips and sighed.

Blast.

It would be a trying hour.

Chapter Seventeen

'Well, that hour was horrendous. Is there no easier way?' Susanna pouted at Rowan and bent her head down as she readjusted her bodice, pulling it back up slightly. A long wavy tress fell from its pins and skimmed along her creamy skin.

She was an utter vision in blue, especially in this mix of soft moonlight and the tender flames of the torches lighting the garden path outside where they stood. Although Rowan hadn't known Jeremiah well, he was a wise man. Susanna was bewitching this eve, and their plan of making her appear a ready and willing participant in securing a husband had been a success. People could talk of little else, and every man in that room had trouble taking their eyes off her.

And *he* needed to stand guard, lest he act on his body's endless awareness of her beauty this eve. Their attachment was a ruse, nothing more.

Rowan watched her and frowned, distracted by the continued tugging and tucking on her bodice and sleeves. 'What are you doing?' he asked.

'Moving my gown back to its rightful location.'

Had it been in the wrong location? He flushed, suddenly determining her insinuation. 'Susanna, when I said be fun and kind, I did not intend for you to—' He gestured towards her bosom but said no more.

'Do not be a dolt,' she replied, blowing the hair out of her vision as she continued to struggle with the gown's material. 'If you did not already know, gowns as heavy as this pull down as the evening goes on, especially with all the dancing. And despite how I might wish it, I am not as—ample—up top as others, so it is even more prone to slide and stretch.'

He stared at her. What was she talking about? She was perfection. And her breasts, from what he could remember and see of them now, were just the right size to cup in his palm, which was ideal for him. For any man, really. His throat dried.

He scowled at himself. He *was* being a dolt. He needed to refocus his efforts, or he would have an entirely different problem at hand. Even now his body throbbed in all the right places in response to just this conversation and his mind's suggestive imaginings.

She paused. 'What? Why are you making that horrid face at me? Just because I do not have huge breasts does not make me a beast.'

He shook his head. *Devil's blood.* 'What? I am not—' he began and then stopped. He ran his hand through his hair in frustration. He couldn't even recall what they were supposed to be talking about.

He sighed and closed his eyes, willing some of the blood to flow back to his brain so he could have a coherent thought. After counting down from ten, he looked back up.

She was scrutinising him and had her hands on her hips. 'Please tell me you learned something to make the last hour worth such agony?'

The familiar sound of Tilly's humming nearby reminded him that they needed to drop their voices a touch to not be overheard. He edged closer to Susanna, tilting his head so she would follow his lead and come nearer as well. They hovered together at the edge of a tall hedge, and Rowan realised his error as soon as the familiar hint of violets arrested his senses.

His body kicked up a small revolt again, and he shifted on his feet.

Not now.

He forced himself into warrior mode, setting his emotions and body on shutdown with his mind alert, or at least he really tried to. His body was too far attuned to her to pretend she was not there, her bosom rising and falling within his gaze as she breathed.

Deuces.

He clutched the hedge, letting the prick of a broken limb in his palm focus his energy elsewhere as much as possible. 'Lady Menzies was quite talkative.'

'I noted she was quite a close talker,' Susanna added, lifting a brow at him.

'Aye. But nothing to be worried about. She was adamant that any attachment we formed would be temporary and for pleasure alone.' He smirked.

Susanna frowned. 'And? Did you agree to such an attachment?'

He sighed. 'How could I when I have you as my betrothed, beloved?' His sarcasm hit its mark, and Susanna pinched his side. Hard.

'Ow,' he groused. She'd always known exactly where to pinch him so it hurt the most. He rubbed the spot. 'Lady Menzies made a friendly and adult offer of companionship that I might have agreed to if I knew I wouldn't end up dead. Lady Menzies's affairs are short-lived. Word has it Laird Menzies is quite a jealous man who adores his wife.'

Susanna chuckled, her breath a whisper along his cheek. 'Aye. I have heard he believes they bewitch her. He does not believe she is the pursuer. Poor sod.'

Poor sod indeed. Rowan was starting to feel quite bewitched himself. He blinked away his desire. 'She also told me your brothers have been in talks with her husband about securing his fortifications along the border he shares with the MacDonalds.'

'Hmm.' She stilled, staring off in the distance. 'The young colt Macpherson told me the same. He was trying to show me that my brothers approve of him, since they have been working hand in hand to get portions of the border walls re-established.'

'Did he provide a reason?'

'Nay. I think he was busy investigating my too-small bosom,' she countered, glaring at him.

'I never said—' he started, but she cut him off with a raise of her hand.

'Too late,' she said.

'Uh,' he replied, vexed by her persistence on the matter. 'What else?'

'I intercepted a note from Royce's study earlier today. Just let me remove this rock,' she muttered, tugging her slipper off to shake the stone out. Tipping slightly, she clutched his shoulder, and he steadied her by holding her waist. The smooth, firm feel of her beneath his hold, along with the unexpected view down her bodice of the slight curve of her breast and its darkened nipple, threatened to bring him to his knees.

Focus.

'Got it,' she said in triumph before replacing her shoe. Then she pulled a note from her bosom. Unfolding it, she handed it to him. 'Here is the note from my brother's desk. It means little to me, but perhaps it will mean more to you.' The parchment was warm to his touch, another reminder of where it had been…nestled. This was going to be a very long night. Shaking off his distraction, he studied it. When he realised what it was, his desire buckled.

'This is a battle plan,' he said.

Her eyes widened, and she peered over his shoulder. 'It does not look like one.'

'Well, it is. I am certain of it.'

'Why would my brothers be drawing up a battle plan? Do they think they will be attacked? Or are they planning to attack?'

'I cannot tell. To be honest, what is here would serve both purposes. It is focused on protecting the castle from outside as well as within. As if it would be done in two phases if need be.'

It was a worst-case scenario if the outer fortifications fell, and they were forced to fight inside for their lives and for those they loved. The sight of it chilled him to his bones. The attack on his family at Argyll Castle four years ago had been too similar. The MacDonalds had used the secret entrance to their castle to try to overrun his soldiers by surprise and they'd almost succeeded.

Susanna's hand closed around his own and the parchment. 'You are trembling. Rowan, can you hear me?'

When he turned to Susanna, he saw her face overlapping Anna's, and he blinked rapidly to dismiss the horror of his memories. What if Susanna died as Anna did? He thrust the thought away. 'We need to know what this is about. Now,' Rowan said. 'Waiting may not be an option.'

'We cannot simply barge in and ask,' Susanna replied. 'They do not know I took this from them in the study. We will reveal ourselves if we do so.'

'Would you rather reveal yourself or be dead?'

She balked, her hand falling away from his own.

'There is no need to be dramatic or cruel.'

'I am being neither. I am reacting to what I see on this page.' Rowan stared at her and saw his own agony and fear reflected in her eyes. He cursed himself. Losing his temper or his reason wouldn't help them.

And they were at a ball. What could he do right this moment?

Nothing.

He tamped back his emotion and handed her the paper. 'You need to return this to Royce's study immediately. Your brothers will be alarmed if they find it missing. Once you have done that, you can tell me more of what you have discovered, and I will do the same. Although I cannot imagine it holds more significance than this.'

She watched him with scepticism. 'I will return the paper. Then you will explain to me what this—' she drew an exaggerated circle around him to emphasise her point before continuing '—reaction was all about. It cannot just have been from that paper. It is only ink and tree pulp.'

He gestured for her to go without agreeing to her terms. He didn't need to explain himself to anyone. And she'd never understand. Not completely.

The night had cooled since they had first stepped out, and even Rowan felt chilled as they wove back through the winding paths of the garden to the castle. Tilly still trailed behind them. The woman had the patience of a saint and ought to be canonised.

'My jacket?' he offered, beginning to shrug it off.

'Nay. It will only lead to more questions from my brothers. I would rather remain chilled.'

As they crossed the threshold of the doorway and into the warmer ballroom, Royce called out. 'Sister. I was wondering where you had been off to. I'd like a word.'

'Royce,' Rowan offered in greeting.

'Campbell,' Royce replied with a nod and a scathing glare of disdain that could not be missed.

'My laird, thank you for the walk. Aye, brother, what do you need?' she asked as he led her away.

To their keen luck, he appeared to be taking her to the study. Rowan frowned. Or he was taking her there because he had already discovered the paper was missing and believed she might have it?

Either way, she would be interrogated. Either about why she was with him or why she had taken the map. Rowan did not envy her in the slightest. He spied the refreshments table, gathered up a full glass of wine, and threw it back with fervour. He reached for another.

'Campbell.'

Devil's blood. He set the wine back on the table. He'd suddenly lost his taste for drink.

The sound of Laird Audric MacDonald's voice did that to a man, especially him.

How had Rowan not seen him here already? Doing a quick visual sweep of the area behind the man yielded nothing other than the watchful gaze of Rolf from far across the room.

There was something he was missing of great importance regarding the Cameron brothers and this plan of theirs. Why was Audric always around? Were they forming an alliance? One to unseat him as laird? Rowan's gut churned with unease. Even the Camerons would not be so desperate, would they? Audric couldn't be trusted. No alliance with him was true. If anything, it would leave them more exposed as they would have their guard down and believe he could be trusted.

'Something on your mind, lad?' he asked with an arrogant smirk. 'Seems we never settled that discussion from before.'

'Oh? And here I thought we had no need to communicate further.' Rowan's spine tightened, and he stepped forward, an instinctive move to show the old man he held no power over him.

'Perhaps not yet, but in future we may need to renegotiate our boundary walls. I have some old maps that say you are encroaching on what is mine. But I will let Devlin bring up such matters with you. I am far too old to care.' He took a long draw from his tankard.

Rowan released a low, hearty laugh before his lips fell into a tight scowl. Narrowing his gaze and baring his teeth, he said, 'Do not attempt to provoke me, Audric. You will regret it. I have special plans for you, and one day you will know what they are. You should fear them. For they will be slow, lingering, and full of agony—for you.'

'Oh? After all this time?' Audric said with a shake of his head. 'I doubt it. You are not man enough, Campbell. You could not save your family then, and I doubt you shall be able to save your new lass now.' His gaze cut to Royce's study and then back to him. 'Oh? You do not know?' He chuckled and covered his mouth to recover. 'Then I can hardly wait for you to find out.'

Rowan grabbed the old man by the tunic, lifting his feet from the floor just slightly. 'Do not test me. I can end you. Here. Now. Gutting you may ruin these lovely floors of theirs for a time, but it would be worth it.' His voice shook, and his body vibrated with rage.

'Gentlemen,' Rolf intervened, placing a firm palm on each of their chests. 'This is a celebration, not a battlefield. If you must—settle your differences elsewhere. Do not make me remove you by force.' His voice was firm with an edge that caught Rowan's attention. Rolf was usually the most subdued of the siblings, but Rowan recognised the familiar steely Cameron resolve in the man's tone. Cameron soldiers were also closing ranks around them as quietly and swiftly as one could manage at a ball. Rowan caught their subtle movements in his peripheral vision.

Cursing, he released Audric roughly and stepped back. He had fallen into MacDonald's trap. All gazes were upon them, and the dancing had stopped. Evidently, the possible bloodbath between them was far more interesting than continuing into the next reel even though the musicians still played.

'Royce wishes to speak with you, my laird,' Rolf offered.

Rowan looked up, but realised the younger Cameron was speaking to Audric, not him.

'One day, we will settle what is between us,' Audric offered. 'But I suppose it shall not be today?' He released a dramatic sigh as if disappointed.

Steady. Think of Rosa.

Rowan said nothing but glared at the man as he left, watching him disappear down the corridor, passing several rooms before being guided into the study. There in the darkened shadows just beyond that chamber, Rowan's gaze met Susanna's unexpectedly, and a surge of relief, desire, and longing crushed him. She mouthed to him and pointed to the other end of the hallway indicating that he should meet her there. He wove through the crowd as the dancing picked back up. Some people still stared he passed, which was no surprise, but some of their words were. He gritted his teeth and ignored them, focusing on the task at hand: getting away from Audric and to Susanna. Somehow in all of this, she had become a beacon of safety for him. The irony was not lost on him.

His world had been turned on end, all because of Susanna Cameron's late-night visit to his forge. She walked down the hallway ahead of him, and he followed at a discreet distance. He rounded a corner and paused, staring at an empty hallway. Where had she gone?

A hallway door creaked open, and she waved to him. *Deuces.* They would be trapped in another room together. He shook his head. He was out of patience, among other things. She waved him on again, her eyes pleading this time. Something was wrong. Against his better judgement, he tucked himself into the room, which turned out to be a small alcove beneath the stairs.

'Could we not have met in a larger space?' Rowan complained. 'This is not even meant for one person, let alone two.' The smell, heat, and feel of her was consuming him, and with his defences already worn down after yet another encounter with Audric, his body was surging, responding with speed to his desire for her this eve.

He pushed his body as far against the wall of the small room as he could, attempting to create distance between their bodies. He failed. She was still touching him, and his body could not be fooled otherwise. 'Shh,' she countered, pressing a finger to his lips. 'Listen.'

Rowan fell silent, and her hand dropped away. 'We are out of time,' she said breathlessly. 'My brothers have decided upon a match for me already. One that they say it is imperative I agree to. They say I may no longer choose.'

'And?' he asked.

'Of course, I refused. But now they plan on ignoring my desires and forcing me into it anyway.'

'Why? What has created such urgency?'

'I do not know. That is why we are in here. They will not tell me who I am to marry, but that it has been decided.'

He stared at her quizzically.

She glanced away and fiddled with her gown sleeves. 'You can hear quite well from this vantage point.'

He smirked. 'Their study, you mean?' he whispered.

'Aye.'

'Is this how you have gained some of your information?'

'Aye.'

He nodded. 'I am impressed. Have you tried every chamber along this hall?' he asked, anticipating her answer.

'Aye, I have.' she said.

'I cannot fault your strategy. 'tis a fine one.' He smiled at her. Only Susanna would have tried every room near the study for the best advantage to eavesdrop.

She smirked back at him. 'And now we shall discern who they plan to shackle me to. Or at least to make the attempt.' She leaned her ear against the wall closest to the study, which caused her to be pressed side to side with him. When she shifted to get closer, he slid his arm around her waist to make it more comfortable for her, and she smiled.

'That is better,' she whispered.

Perhaps for her, but not for him. His body shifted into a higher gear of alertness. She smelled of violets, wine, and something sweet. The warmth of her pressed alongside him felt like a drug, making his muscles relax against her own.

Then he could hear the murmurings of voices, and he pressed his ear to the wall and closed his eyes. Although it was hard to discern the voices at first due to the music from the ball, finally Rowan could hear some of what was said, but not all. He concentrated and slowed his breathing, and soon it became easier.

'I have spoken to my son,' Audric said. 'He is not yet enthusiastic about the plan, but with the proper incentives, I know he can be persuaded to come around to my position on things.'

'And what additional incentives would be necessary?' Royce countered, an edge of annoyance in his voice.

Audric made a dramatic pause. 'Some additional land, perhaps an extension of our shared border wall, and a promise of a yearly payment of resources.'

'What *specifics* might that include, my laird?' Rolf added, his voice low.

'Hmm… I venture one hundred acres and a ten per cent share of your yield of goods for trade would suffice.'

Rolf cursed.

Royce took longer to respond. 'We will half that request. Fifty acres and five per cent of our yield of goods while our sister lives. If anything happens to her under your son's care or your own during her marriage, our arrangement will end.'

Rowan stiffened, his chest tingling, and met Susanna's gaze. Her eyes were wide and wild with disbelief. He had not imagined the words or their intention. Her brothers meant to marry her off to Devlin, and she would be the daughter-in-law to the devil himself, Audric MacDonald. Well, he'd not allow it. He clutched her hand, and she held it fiercely as they continued to listen to the exchange.

'Then we are agreed,' Audric replied, the sound of a chair scraping. 'Draw up the agreement. If it is sound, we will announce the arrangement. I want them married by the end of the year.' Audric paused and added, 'Be sure that sister of yours is in line. Any disobedience will not be tolerated.'

'And you, my laird,' Royce called out, his boots resonating on the floor. 'Your disobedience or your son's will also not be tolerated, and our sister will be well cared for. If not, you will answer to us—personally.'

Chapter Eighteen

Susanna clutched Rowan's hand. She shook her head and stared at him. A scream and a sob duelled at the base of her throat, and tears of rage rather than sadness threatened. How could they do such? Her own brothers trading her off to the MacDonalds? What could she have done to elicit such a punishment, and what did they fear so much that they would risk her life and well-being to secure an alliance with him?

She stared ahead but saw nothing but a blurry figure. Her ears buzzed, and she struggled to hear anything at all. Rowan cupped her face with his hands and pulled her close to his ear, murmuring to her. She could not decipher the words, but the feel of him brought her back from the fear and disbelief threatening to devour her from within. Her family was her world, and yet they were ready to sacrifice her? Why?

A shaky hiccup sounded in her throat, and Rowan's cheek pressed against her own.

'Breathe,' he murmured, his warm breath skimming her cheek. She sucked in one trembling breath and then another. She gripped his wrists, clinging for solid ground and safety. She felt like she was floating, and blackness edged in on her narrowing vision.

'Aye,' his voice cooed. 'Good. One more.'

Another shaky breath in and out, and the blackness ringing her vision began to recede.

'You are safe, Suze. I won't let anything happen to you. You will not marry into that family. And he will never—' he growled '—touch you. I swear it. I will die first.'

She believed him.

Suddenly, she was that young lass Susanna in the rowan grove all those years ago. Her father had reprimanded her and made her feel like she was less than nothing for standing up for herself. Rowan had made her feel safe, protected, and beautiful. Just like he did now, when she felt her world as she knew it was splintering in two.

Perhaps he was still the boy in the grove who loved her.

She crushed her mouth to his and kissed him fiercely, desperate to find out. He stilled under her touch at first, and then his hands fell away from her cheeks. She let go of his wrists and wove her fingers through the hair at the nape of his neck before plundering his mouth again with a heated kiss, her teeth tugging at his lip. His hesitation was palpable, but she knew the moment his dam of uncertainty broke. He groaned, took control of their kiss, and squeezed her waist, pulling her body flush with his, even closer than they already were in the confined space. And she felt alive, so alive, for the first time—since Jeremiah.

She answered his demands and tucked herself into the folds of his body, her legs twining with his as his lips trailed along her neck. She gasped, and she felt his lips curve into a smile along her throat.

'I still remember,' he murmured. Confidence laced his words.

She smirked. 'Well, I remember too,' she whispered,

sliding her hand under his plaid and between his legs, feeling the full length of him harden and shudder against her. She stroked him with the base of her palm before closing her hand around him.

'Deuces,' he said through gritted teeth. 'Aye. You do.'

While they had never fully consummated their love affair when they were young, they had always been passionate with one another. It seemed time had not changed their bodies' memories of one another or their mutual attraction. If anything, it had become more intense. They were adults who knew how to make each other's body sing under their touch.

'Susanna,' he murmured, pulling his lips away after some effort. 'We are in little more than a closet. There are hundreds of people on the other side of this door.'

'And?' she replied. 'I can be quiet,' she teased, running her fingertips over his length once more.

He shuddered, and the muscle in his jaw tightened as he gripped her wrist to cease her movements. 'I do not wish to take advantage,' he whispered, his tone serious and concerned. 'You have had a shock and—we are not truly betrothed. We are pretending, remember?'

'Aye,' she replied, wondering deep down if really *they* were the ones lying to themselves. What she felt now didn't seem like they were pretending. It seemed real, true, and she didn't want it to stop, no matter the words he spoke, no matter where they were.

No matter if it was to be only this once.

'Aye?' he asked, his brow furrowed, not knowing what she meant.

'Aye,' she replied, her voice low and husky. She freed her hand from his and held his gaze as she lifted the heavy fabric of her skirts. Then she slid her bare leg slowly over the rough wool of his kilt, until it coiled around his bare thigh and calf. The flesh-on-flesh contact made his eyes close, and he rested his head back against the wall, his Adam's apple bobbing as he swallowed.

'Susanna,' he murmured, his voice a low growl of satisfaction.

'Aye, my laird?' she replied, leaning against his chest, allowing her bodice to gape open. The air hit her flesh, making her skin pebble with anticipation.

His hooded gaze met hers, the desire evident in his eyes. He gifted her a sultry smile and leaned forward, his lips barely touching her neck, sending trills of sensation all throughout her body. Lazily his lips travelled along her collarbone and then drifted down her chest. He seized her breast in his mouth. His lips worked her nipple until it was so sensitive that the skim of his teeth against it almost made her cry out in pleasure. She bit her lip instead and moved restlessly against him.

'Not yet,' he murmured, holding her waist gently, his scruff scraping along her breast.

Why was the most impatient man ever being so patient? She shifted against him, the ache for him increasing.

Not used to waiting for anything she desired, she reached beneath his kilt and took hold of him, revelling in the power she felt as he stilled and cursed against her chest.

She smiled as he tugged up her skirts, having broken his resolve to tarry.

He lifted his head and met her gaze as he positioned himself. Then, with one swift and certain movement, he was inside her.

Rowan held Susanna's waist tighter and roughly seized

her mouth with his lips. What other choice did he have to quiet their lovemaking and hide them from the ladies and lairds on the other side of these walls?

Her lips clashed against his and were as soft and warm as he remembered. Her form was as toned and muscular as when she was a young lass on the cusp of womanhood, but now—now he could feel the fullness of her hips and breasts against him as she pulled him closer. His body tightened and surged with need, a base and hungry need he scarce allowed himself to feel any more as he slid in and out of her warm body. Her urgent response fuelled his desire even more. *Saints be.* He was cresting soon, and so was she, by the tight feel of her core around him. And they were in a bloody closet.

Imagine what would have happened if they weren't confined by space, time, and a castle full of people. She gasped in his mouth and shuddered as she climaxed. Soon he did the same, clinging to her.

They leaned heavily against each other, holding one another upright as best they could.

'My laird,' she murmured with inflection, her voice relaxed and purring with contentment.

'Aye, my lady,' he panted out. 'I agree.'

He slid down the wall with Susanna alongside him, until they rested in a tangled mesh of limbs, flesh, and fabric.

'I do not think I can stand,' she chuckled.

'Then let us sit,' he murmured in her ear, relishing this sweetness in her that he knew he would never have again, for he'd never let this happen again. Despite the fact that it had been more beautiful than he'd thought possible. After Anna had died, he never believed he'd feel anything close to such a connection again, but he had—with her.

It sent his heart pounding and his mind into confusion, but he closed his eyes as she leaned her head into the crook of his neck and sighed.

All of that would matter later.

But for now, all that mattered was this, the sound of her soft breaths, the feeling of her gentle heartbeat against his chest, and this quiet contentment.

Chapter Nineteen

Everything around her was warm and lush, her body as languid and relaxed as a summer loch, and she eased her eyes open. It was dark, and her limbs were heavy with sleep. She shifted and stilled. Someone was holding her; she eased back, trying not to panic.

Rowan?

Rowan.

She cringed and clutched her forehead with a curse as a flood of memories came back to her. They had been hiding in this small closet to eavesdrop when they'd heard of Audric and her brothers' plan to marry her off to Devlin. She and Rowan had kissed, and then— She curled her toes in her shoes and smiled. She tried to feel some sense of shame about it, especially with it happening in a closet, of all places, but she couldn't. What had happened between them had been lovely. More lovely than she ever thought she would feel with a man after losing Jeremiah. She could not begrudge what she and Rowan had shared so freely and without expectation with one another. It was as if a chapter that had been left undone between them for so long had been written—and written quite well.

'Where has she disappeared to?' Royce asked, his voice drawing Susanna from her daydreams to wakefulness.

Without the music and noise from the crowd of the ball, it was quite easy to hear the conversation.

'Perhaps she has deduced your plans and run from here. I couldn't blame her. There must be a better solution, brother. *She. Is. Our. Sister.* And that family—Audric—I have been patient and gone along with your schemes, but *this*—it is too much.' Rolf cursed, and Susanna's mouth gaped open. She had never heard him use such language before. Her younger brother was angry. Very angry.

She shifted her ear closer to the wall, and Rowan stretched his arm across her waist, gripping her hip. The possessive yet gentle action made her smile. Her pulse increased, her body remembering the pleasure his touch had brought her hours before. Her leg cramped, and she flinched, stretching it as best she could so she wouldn't cry out. The movement jarred Rowan. His eyes opened into small slits, and he squinted. Then they widened once and then twice before he opened his mouth to speak.

She pressed a fingertip to his lips and shook her head, pointing to the study next door that the closet wall shared. He frowned but closed his mouth, leaning back against the wall again. 'It is the only plan I can think of that can protect them both. And I cannot sacrifice one for the other.' Royce's voice wavered.

'He may never know, and then this will never be a problem. We may be making it more of a problem than it might ever be.'

'You think no one on that island will ever speak of it? I never should have gone there. It is my fault, and I know that. I was stubborn and arrogant to believe that I deserved to know the truth. That I knew better than Father. They knew it was best to let it rest and stay hidden, but I was determined to uncover it. And to think, originally, I was relieved to have discovered the truth. And now—now it plagues me to think one day, all will know, and our clan's livelihood and our family's lives will be at stake.'

Rowan's body shifted, his features alert and his brow raised.

Susanna held her breath, reached for his hand, and held it, desperate to know what her brothers said next. This could be it. This could be all that she had been waiting to find out.

'Who would benefit from telling him?' Rolf asked, his voice dropping low.

'Chisholm,' Royce's answered.

Rolf sighed. 'We have already dealt with him. He is pleased with his arrangement.'

'And when he wants more? Or one of his family members discovers the secret and wishes to make a deal with Audric instead?' Royce asked.

Blast.

Susanna squeezed Rowan's hand. Audric was part of this secret? No wonder her brothers had been appeasing him and willing to marry her off to his son, whether Devlin wished to marry her or not. But what could he have on her family? They didn't deal with the MacDonalds unless necessary, one of the few of her father's rules she agreed with.

Rowan's scowl deepened, and his grip around her hand tightened. He pressed his ear closer to the panelling. Susanna nibbled her lip and waited.

'No one will know that Catriona is his daughter unless we tell them,' Rolf said, his voice almost inaudible.

'How many times have I told you never to speak of it

in this house?' Royce growled, slamming down his fist to the table and rattling the contents on it.

'I cannot talk to you when you are like this,' Rolf argued.

'Like what?' he countered, his anger building.

'Like Father. You are obsessed and making aggressive decisions based on fear and the need to outmanoeuvre them, whoever they might be, before they make the first move against you. I am going to bed. Hopefully, when I wake tomorrow, Susanna will have returned. I cannot bear to think she is gone for good, and that we have lost yet another sister. Wasn't losing Catriona for almost a decade enough of a price to pay for our father's fear?'

'Perhaps he knew what was best for all of us.'

Rolf scoffed. 'You cannot mean that. The life she lived. What she was subjected to? She is still our flesh and blood, even if it is only half. Do you not care?'

'We have much to lose, Rolf,' Royce said in a quieter tone. 'If Susanna is bound to them by an alliance of marriage, if something does come out, he will be unable to strike out against us.'

'And Susanna? What of the cost to her?' Rolf's voice broke.

'She is strong. She can—'

'Nay, brother. It is a betrayal she will not survive. Nor will I.'

The door of the study slammed shut, sending a vibration through the wall and against their ears.

Susanna stared blankly ahead.

Catriona was Audric's daughter?

How was that even possible? Susanna had watched her mother carry her youngest sister and saw her moments after she had given birth to her. And if Father knew—what had happened to Mother? Had something horrendous happened to her? Or had she chosen to be with a man as cruel as Audric and shamed her husband?

None of it made sense.

Susanna's mind fought the information, and she sat dumbfounded. They had to be wrong. It all had to be untrue. It was madness. Utter madness.

Rowan's touch along her cheek startled her, and she flinched, gripping his hand. Their gazes locked. In his eyes, there was sympathy and—something else she couldn't name. He pulled her into his arms. She knew she should, but she did not resist his comfort. She leaned into his embrace, buried her head in his rumpled tunic, and wept.

Rowan's mind raced as he held Susanna. His hand smoothed over her hair, and he murmured words of comfort to her as loudly as he dared. They were still hiding in a closet, after all. The absurdity of being in such a situation and hearing the news she had long desired, but it being as horrible as it was, made it almost unfathomable. He couldn't imagine her thoughts and feelings right now. Part of him felt conflicted with the sympathy he felt for her and her family's position if what they heard was indeed true. The other part of him felt a cool, calm peace. As if this was supposed to happen, especially after their evening together. They had risked vulnerability with one another, and now he and Susanna could face this new chaos together. They had a common enemy now, and they could strike Audric down. The Camerons and Campbells could join forces and end Audric for good. It would be in both of their best interests, and it would end this farce of her having to marry Devlin. He smirked. While he now found he liked Devlin, the lad was no match for Susanna. She would raze him to the ground. What she needed was a man like him.

He stilled. Did he need a woman like her?

Part of him believed he did. She challenged him, pushed him, and spoke her mind. She was strong, intelligent, and unholy beautiful. He played with the end of a wavy tress, running it between his fingers. Who said this fake betrothal plan of theirs couldn't become a real one? But could he trust her? His hand stilled, resting along the smooth nape of her neck. Trust? Of that, he wasn't so sure. She was a Cameron, and her family had always been her priority. She had not been shy about reminding him of it. He didn't know if that could ever change. And he couldn't bind himself to a woman who didn't put her family first, Rosa included. The wee girl deserved the world.

By the time Susanna's tears had subsided, and she gave a last sniffle into his sleeve, the house was quiet, achingly so. 'Perhaps we should try to sneak out while we can?' he offered.

Susanna lifted her head. Her eyes were bright and glassy and her nose a bit puffy, but she was gorgeous. If anything, seeing her so vulnerable and soft made his heart ache. 'Aye,' she replied with a bit of a croak, and began untangling herself from him as they both struggled to stand after being in such a cramped position for hours.

He gained his footing first and winced as his left foot tingled. He rolled his ankle. 'My foot fell asleep,' he murmured.

She chuckled. 'And I have lost half of my hair pins.'

He studied her half up, half down hair and nodded. 'Aye.

And your—' he began, gesturing to her bodice, which was far too low and awkwardly twisted to one side. She began tugging and twisting it until she had it close to where it was when he first saw her this eve at the top of the staircase. That moment seemed a lifetime ago. As if they had gone into a cave in that closet and emerged a year later. He felt like a different man and her a different woman. And perhaps after all that had happened between them and all that they had learned in those hours, they were.

He gripped the doorknob and turned it slowly before peeking out into the hallway. It was dark but for the flicker of a sconce lit in the hallway. He stepped out and waved her on to follow. She squeezed his arm and shook her head. 'Follow me,' she whispered.

He rolled his eyes at her need to lead but pressed himself back against the wall until she exited.

'My exact steps,' she added. 'This floor creaks.'

So perhaps there *was* a reason for her to lead. Such things like floor creaks he wouldn't know, and every squeak or groan would echo in this silence. He closed the door, released the knob, and fell in step behind her, matching her stride for stride despite how much shorter hers was than his. They made it down the hallway without incident and turned a corner. Voices sounded from the outer room, and Susanna flattened herself to the wall. Rowan followed suit, holding his breath so he could listen.

Fortunately, the young lasses, most likely maids, were too far away to distinguish, which meant Susanna and Rowan could continue. Soon they were out the back door and into the chilly night air of the garden. Rowan took a deep breath. Being able to move freely and take in some air after being cramped for hours in such a small space was bliss. Susanna stood beside him with a similar smile of relief.

'What an evening,' she said, shaking her head.

'Aye. There is much to take in.'

'Perhaps too much,' she replied, rubbing her forehead. 'My mind races, but my thoughts are incoherent. I do not know what I think about anything now.'

'Much has happened. That is expected.' He fisted his hand by his side. It was the most neutral answer he could give. He needed to give her time, despite how eager he was to discuss their plans to end Audric. His mouth watered in anticipation.

'I will leave you to your thoughts and to rest. It has been a trying evening,' he said, risking a small kiss to her cheek, revelling in the sweet smell of violets that still clung to her skin. 'When you are ready to move forward, send word.' He squeezed her hand briefly before letting go.

'Move forward?' she asked, tilting her head, her eyes glittering in the moonlight.

He stilled. 'With killing Audric,' he whispered.

She shook her head. 'We cannot move forward with that now. Our plans must change. To kill him would put my sister and family in danger.'

Was she addled? 'Nay. To allow him to *live* would put you in danger. Did we not hear the same words?' He moved closer to her, his blood pulsing through his body, disbelief roaring through him. 'And we had an agreement. Do you plan to go back on your word now? Now that we are so many weeks into this plan?' He stood over her.

She squared her shoulders and met his gaze. 'You will force me into nothing. You were repaying a debt to *me* by helping me unearth this secret, and so we have.'

'And your betrothal to Devlin? You will just marry him to appease your brothers and to keep your clan safe by insuring such an alliance?' Outrage caused his volume to increase.

She gripped his forearm. 'Lower your voice, my laird. I will do what I must do to protect my family. I will contact you when I have decided on my next course of action, not before.'

He stepped closer, his disbelief rising like bile in his gut. 'And what happened between us this eve? Did that mean nothing?'

She dropped her hand from his and studied him, as if calculating her next words with care. 'I believe it served both of our—needs in that moment. It does not have to *mean* anything.'

He scoffed. This was the Susanna he knew. The one he warned himself about. Perhaps he had only imagined this woman as having feelings and care for someone other than herself and her beloved family. 'And just when I thought you had changed. You are just the same cold and calculating Cameron you have always been.'

Her face hardened. 'And you are still the emotional, impulsive man you have always been. Just spouting off words and doing things without thought of the consequences to others.'

'Then I shall take my leave of you and our agreement, but know this. I will have my justice as you promised, with or without your blessing.'

'Even if it ruins us?' she challenged him, her gaze pleading.

'Aye,' he growled. 'Even if it burns you bloody Camerons to the ground.'

Chapter Twenty

Susanna watched Rowan stalk away, his rigid and angry gait a harsh end to their evening together. She scarcely knew what had happened. This eve was a blur of emotion and crushing fatigue and confusion weighed her down. As he disappeared through the garden, her body felt heavy. She hadn't wanted it to end this way between them, but perhaps it was meant to. This was what always happened between them, wasn't it? They were fire and ice. Heat and passion followed by distance and discord. Why could they never find the middle ground and fight alongside one another rather than with each other?

It didn't matter.

She had far greater matters to tend to now that she knew what her brothers had been keeping from her and what their worries were. If this was just about Catriona, why had they not brought her into their circle and allowed her to help her sister? Susanna would ask them that very question—tomorrow. For now, she was too tired to do much other than wearily climb the stairs, shrug out of her gown, and crawl into her bed. She made her way through the castle, skilfully avoiding all of the squeaks and creaks as she went in case her brothers or others were up. She opened her chamber door, entered the room, and closed the door. She relaxed against it with a sigh and took a deep breath. The smell of musk and shave cream stilled her.

She was not alone.

'Although I am beyond relieved you are back, where in hell's name did you disappear to for hours?' A candle flickered to life near the settee, casting shadows on her younger brother's face.

Rolf.

Her body sagged forward in relief followed swiftly by outrage. 'You are a fine one to lecture me upon anything. Perhaps I merely wished to have some brief moments of joy before you and Royce barter me off to Audric and his son like livestock to keep your secret safe.'

His eyes widened and she smiled, enjoying being one step ahead after feeling behind in their game of secrecy for so long. She plucked off her shoes and tossed them on the rug. She joined him on the settee and rubbed her toes, almost sighing aloud at the relief of being back in her own room and off her feet.

His rebuttal died on his lips as he scrutinised her. 'We will discuss how you know any of that in a moment. What happened to you? You look…' He was kind enough not to finish the sentence.

She held up her palm. 'Do not change the subject at hand. I am fine, except for this business with Catriona being Audric's daughter, you both lying to us about it, and making me feel a fool looking for a husband when you already had other plans for me.'

'We never intended—' he began.

'What did you intend, then? Beyond the lying and deception?' She leaned her head back and pulled the remaining pins from her hair, letting them fall haphazardly to the floor.

He said nothing, so she lifted her head. 'Although I do appreciate that you at least stood up for me. Tried to reason with Royce because you feared I might perish in the clutches of Audric and his son.'

'How do you know all of this?' he sputtered.

'Eavesdropping,' she said smiling sweetly at him. 'I am quite good at it.'

'Why am I not surprised?' His tone reeked of exasperation.

'You are annoyed because I learned the truth you were hiding from me?' she snapped back.

'Aye. Who else knows?'

She pressed her lips together.

'Susanna,' he said, his voice low with warning.

'Campbell,' she replied, lifting her chin a notch.

'How?'

'We found out together.'

'You were both eavesdropping?'

'Aye.'

Her brother scrutinised her once more. 'Did he do this to you?' he asked, pointing to her rumpled gown and mussed hair.

'Only because I asked him to,' she replied with a wink.

Rolf cringed, his face souring. 'You are my sister. Not only should you never tell me such things, but it is a disrespect to you.'

'And you are a virgin, I suppose? My chaste brother, Rolf?'

He blushed, the colour rising high in cheeks. 'That is different,' he muttered.

'Because you are a man?' She laughed. 'We are adults. I am beholden to no one yet, so I may make my own choices.'

He clutched her hand. 'Susanna, this is no game. It is serious. All of it.'

She squeezed his hand. 'I know that. And I wish to speak to you and Royce tomorrow. You *will* include me in your plans moving forward.'

'I will ask him,' Rolf replied, letting go of her hand.

'You misunderstand me. It is not a request, brother. I *will* be joining you.'

After a long bath and even longer sleep, the next morn, Susanna dressed and went to Royce's study.

Royce's frown told her Rolf had briefed him on last night's events. All of them, by the depth of his scowl. Susanna sent Rolf an accusing glare, and he just shrugged back. So much for not revealing everything to her brothers.

'Sit,' Royce commanded.

Susanna closed the door and settled in across from him and next to Rolf. It felt as if she were a wee girl being brought to Father's study for a punishment. She was in no mood for it.

'Have you summoned me to apologise?' she asked, crossing her legs and sitting up taller in her chair.

'Susanna,' Rolf warned under his breath.

She ignored him. She was weary—of everything. The secrets, the aloneness, and the dread of whatever might happen next that she couldn't control. Speaking her mind was well overdue with her eldest brother and laird.

Royce leaned his head forward. 'Excuse me?' he said, pretending to have not heard her.

'You heard me. I am waiting.'

Rolf sighed. Susanna glanced over to see him shaking his head and then rubbing his temple. 'Cease,' he murmured.

'I will not,' she answered aloud. 'I am bone weary of doing your will, doing Father's will, and trying to be compliant. What has it served me? You are to marry me off after making me promises that you would do nothing of the sort. And then to keep me and Catriona out of learning the truth of who her real father is? I can still hardly believe it. If I had not heard you say it aloud from this room, I wouldn't.'

Royce rested his arms on the desk, interlacing his fingers. 'And how did you happen to be in a position to be eavesdropping?'

'That is of no matter.'

'It is of great matter,' he mocked her.

She sat with her mouth clamped shut.

He waited her out for some time before giving up. 'And what do you plan to do with such information?' he finally asked.

'I have thought upon it, and I think we should tell her. If she knows, she can be mindful and take care, and Ewan must also know. He cannot protect her properly otherwise.'

'We will protect her, without either of them knowing.'

Susanna scoffed. 'Even you cannot be so arrogant, Royce, as to believe that you and you alone can protect them.'

When he did not reply, she continued. 'They have a babe on the way. You cannot leave them in the dark about such an important matter. What if Audric discovers the truth and retaliates?' She gripped the chair. 'If roles were reversed, you would want to know so you could protect Iona and your bairn, would you not?'

He leaned back in his chair. Her words had landed where she had hoped they would: on his heart. Iona and his bairn were the most important part of his life. Finding her and building his own family with her had changed him.

Or at least, Susanna thought it had.

'I am not trying to put them in greater danger, but in less,' he finally replied.

'Telling them *is* a way to protect them. The only way, as far as I can see. Especially if you fear the truth may reach Audric and his clan in ways you may not suspect.' She pressed her nail into her fingertip, finally asking the other question she wished to know the answer to. 'Do you understand how such a thing happened? I cannot imagine Mother would have…' She dropped her gaze.

'We have not been able to unearth how, but we have guesses. I wish to think upon none of them.' His voice was low and subdued, a mirror of what she felt.

'And Father? Did he know?'

'Aye. It was why he left her there, according to Webster. She is the woman I went in search of on Lismore, although before I met her, I believed her to be a man.'

'Left her there? What are you talking about, brother?' Susanna's pulse increased, and she moved forward in her chair, glancing at Rolf.

The sadness in Rolf's gaze told her it was true, and Susanna's stomach made a sickening flip. He reached out and took her hand in his own. 'It seems,' Rolf began, 'that Father knew she was on Lismore for quite some time. He paid Webster. She was charged with caring for Catriona, but as we all know, that *care* was less than ideal.'

Susanna's eyes welled, and her throat tightened. She swallowed back the agony of such a thought. 'He left her? He left his daughter on a strange island alone? Left us all to grieve her? How could anyone…?' she began, but a sob escaped her, and tears fell down her cheeks.

Rolf clutched her hands tightly.

'I fear I may be sick,' she murmured, leaning forward.

Rolf let go of her hand, rose from his chair, and rubbed her back as she grasped her knees. Susanna tried to still the churning in her stomach and the sickness roiling there.

'He believed he was protecting us all in the best way he could.' Royce's voice was distant and stoic, as if he did not believe his own words.

'There had to be a better way,' she muttered, lifting her face. She wiped back her tears with her sleeve. 'All that happened to her and us could have been prevented.'

'Aye. It could have,' Rolf added quietly. 'But it cannot be unwound now. And telling her. It will break her heart.'

'Has her heart not already been broken?' Susanna asked quietly. 'Isn't building a future on truth important for us and for her family? Now more than ever?'

'But we still do not know all of the truth,' Royce countered. 'We do not know what happened between Audric and our mother, why Father did what he did, and if we really know all the impacts revealing such a truth will bring about, especially with the Highlands being in such a delicate state politically. It could bring us and the MacDonalds or even more clans into a war.'

'Over Catriona?'

'Possibly. But most likely, it will be over the deception,' Royce added. 'Audric is a vindictive man. His only children, Fiona and Devlin, have all but abandoned him for the Campbells. He may try to convince Catriona to come to his clan—or worse, exact retribution.'

'How?' she asked.

'By stealing his grandchild once he or she is born,' Rolf added quietly.

'A child for a child,' she murmured, a tremor in her voice as she shivered. 'Is that what you fear?'

'Aye,' Royce replied, his voice heavy and cryptic. 'To my very bones.'

'Then why are you doing things to bring him closer to us? This sham of an engagement to Devlin? Giving him more land and resources? I do not follow your logic, brother.'

'If we have an alliance of marriage with us *before* he discovers the truth, he will be less likely to retaliate.'

'Less likely?' she asked.

'With Audric, there is no hundred per cent certainty of anything. He has little left to lose, and he is aging.' Royce stood from his chair and paced.

'There must be another solution,' she replied.

'Killing him would only make matters worse,' Royce added.

'What if someone else killed him?' she said quietly.

Rolf and Royce stared at her.

'Laird Campbell. You know he wishes to take revenge on him. You have all but set up the conflict with these gatherings of yours, which have included invitations to them both. You know how close they have come to attacking one another.'

'Nay, Susanna. That was not our intention, not really. To create discord between them was a way to further our cause and alliance to get Audric to trust us, nothing more. We cannot kill him. At least not yet. I believe he holds part of the answers. We cannot kill him, nor can anyone else, until we have those answers.'

'That might be a problem,' she added and blew out a breath.

'Why?'

'Because I already promised Rowan I would help him kill the man.'

Chapter Twenty-One

Rowan wiped sweat from his brow and then continued shaping the heated metal with his forging hammer. Finally, it was softening and turning into something other than a hunk of—well—nothing. The reverberation through his arm as he fashioned the metal on the anvil eased some of the tension coiled tightly in his body. Over the last few days, he'd found himself working extra hours in the forge. His obsession with killing Audric was consuming him, and memories of his tryst with Susanna were a close second. Between the spirals of rage and desire, he was wrecked and could focus on nothing but the physical labour that might bring both of those thoughts to an end—even if it was only temporary.

He had to find a way to exact his revenge on Audric and banish his mind from further thoughts and hopes about Susanna. She had made her choice, her family, and he had made his, exacting his justice for his wife and son. There was no middle ground. He could wait no longer. Audric had to die. Justice was far overdue.

'Late hours, even for you,' Hugh said as he entered the forge, letting the barn door slide closed behind him.

Rowan looked up. He had no idea what day it was, let alone what time. He did not answer his friend. 'I need no lecture from you,' he muttered, grabbing tongs to flip the metal slab on the anvil.

'Well, you need something, my laird. The soldiers are talking, and your family is worried about you, especially Trice. She has mentioned calling back Brandon early from his trip up north with Fiona and wee William. Daniel agrees with her.'

'As usual, Trice frets with no cause, and her husband Daniel is too soft with her. There is no need to bring back my baby brother and his family from their travels.'

'Oh, no?' Hugh crossed his arms against his chest. 'When was the last time you ate? Or spent some extended time with your daughter?'

He set aside the tongs. 'This morn.'

Hugh pressed his lips together and shook his head. 'Nay. You have not eaten this morn, and Rosa has not seen you since the day prior.'

'Are you following me? You have no other pressing matters to attend to than my eating habits?' He glowered at Hugh.

'You are my prime duty, as you well know, with Brandon away. So is your welfare, my laird. And aye, I am concerned. You are losing your way.'

'You have no right to speak to me in such a manner.' He tugged off his leather apron and threw it on the large workbench.

'As your friend, I believe it is a requirement. As your most trusted soldier, it is my duty to ensure you are able and willing to lead our clan. Both demand I speak the truth to you.' He approached, his gaze softening, and he rested his hands on his waist belt. 'What happened the night of the Holiday Ball at Loch's End last week? When you returned, you were a different man.'

'What didn't happen?' he spat out as he ran a hand through his hair.

Hugh waited in silence.

Rowan continued, knowing full well that Hugh would wait in silence for days for him to speak. It was one of his friend's most admirable and irritating qualities. 'Susanna and I discovered her brother's secrets, and we also—' He did not finish, hoping Hugh would deduce his meaning.

Hugh's brow lifted in surprise. He nodded, a smirk flashing briefly before his features returned to their usual neutral position. 'Well, that is an interesting, but not unexpected, turn of events. And it explains your—current state.'

'Which is what?' he challenged.

'You are not yourself. Since this ruse with Susanna began two months ago, you have been partly energised but also distracted, bent on this revenge against Audric. Now that you two have…reunited—' he paused, choosing his words with care '—and discovered whatever it is that set you off course a week ago, you are—'

'I am what?' he asked, closing in on Hugh, daring him to speak his mind.

'Obsessed, irritable, and distracted. It is an odd combination. While it is similar to how you were after Anna's death, it is somehow different.' He said the words with objectivity rather than censure, and it yanked out the foundation of Rowan's temper.

Mostly because he knew it was the truth.

While Rowan didn't feel the same grief and rage he felt when Anna and their son died, he felt an agony of disappointment over not having Susanna's help to exact his revenge on Audric as he'd planned, but also an anger at himself for being vulnerable with Susanna and for believing she might have changed. He'd thought maybe, just maybe, when they had made love and been hidden in that closet for hours, that they were being given some new chance and beginning with one another. That she could walk alongside him on this path to healing from the past by helping him kill Audric, but also that she might choose to be a part of his future.

He cursed and sat down on the bench with a hard thud, scrubbing his hand through his rather dirty hair, and was aware of his own stench. He needed a bath. Perhaps Hugh was right.

'I was a fool,' he said.

Hugh sat down next to him on the bench. 'About?'

'Everything relating to Susanna, and I hate myself for it. Much like I did when we were teens and I believed she cared for me, for us. All she cares about is her family and keeping the Camerons as the most powerful clan in the Highlands. There is nothing else in her heart.'

Hugh's silence egged him on.

'She has gone back on our agreement. She will *not* assist me with killing Audric and finally getting the justice Anna and our son deserve, because it no longer suits her plans,' Rowan continued.

'While I still do not wish for you to kill Audric for a variety of reasons, I am curious to know why the Camerons now wish to protect him. Seems out of character even for them. Although I did find it curious that he has been invited to Loch's End more than once recently.'

'I shall share this with you as long as you agree to tell no one. Not even your horse.'

Hugh scoffed. 'It shall not leave my lips, although you know even if I told Clover, she would tell no one. She is a horse.'

Rowan lifted a brow at him, and Hugh relented. 'Fine,' he muttered. 'I will tell no one, not even Clover.'

Rowan inched closer to him, dropping his voice further. 'You know Susanna's long-lost younger sister, Violet, who we now know as Catriona?'

'Aye.'

'Well, evidently she is actually Audric's daughter. She is really their half sister.'

Hugh's mouth fell open in shock, and he sat a full minute in silence as he took in Rowan's words. 'I do not understand,' he finally offered. 'How could that be? And why?'

'We had the same questions. None of which we have answers for. I can only relay that Susanna's brothers fear that Audric or someone else in his clan will learn of this information and retaliate.'

'But wouldn't they *want* to kill Audric then? Would that not provide greater protection for them? I do not follow their reasoning.'

Rowan shrugged. 'Nor do I. There must be more to the situation than I understand. Susanna said she did not wish to kill him because it would put them in more danger.' He scrubbed a hand down his face. 'The brothers have arranged for Susanna to marry Devlin and provide a dowry of land and resources to the MacDonalds upon their union. None of it makes any sense to me at all.'

'While I have come to believe Devlin is a good man, to marry your sister into that family by choice?' he shook his head. 'You're right, there must be more to the story,' Hugh added. 'Something that puts them in grave danger, since they are making such extreme choices.'

'Which is why I am so frustrated and irritated. I cannot reason it out in my mind, and I am crushed by the outcome of it all.'

'Have you not just asked Susanna what else she has found out?'

'Nay. I cannot bring myself to do so.'

'Because of your pride?'

'That is part of it,' Rowan answered truthfully. 'She has rejected me, after all.'

'And the rest of it?' Hugh met his gaze.

Rowan sighed. 'Because I do not trust myself around her. I cannot make good decisions. My emotions rule me in her presence, which we both know leads to nothing good.' He looked down at his palms, rubbing the dark smudges of coal into the lines there, wishing they held some answers for him.

'So, your plan is to work yourself into exhaustion by hiding in here and hammering out your anger and frustration?' Hugh asked.

'That was the gist of it,' Rowan answered, almost smiling at Hugh's deduction and its accuracy.

'And your plan now?'

'To meet with Susanna and figure out what the hell is going on.'

'Might I suggest a bath first?'

He sniffed himself and coughed. 'Aye. I will bathe, take a meal, and see my daughter. Then I will see to Susanna.'

'I will have the horses readied and travel with you.'

'Aye. Give me three hours, and we can depart.'

'When Tilly told me you were here at Loch's End, I did not believe her at first.'

Rowan's body tensed at the sound of Susanna's voice as

she entered the parlour, where she had kept him waiting for almost a full hour. During that period, he'd had much time to think about and much practice in mulling over his words and what he wished to say. Perhaps too much time. When she came in and dared sit right next to him on the small settee, her gown pressing in against his trews, her violet scent assaulting his senses, every well-planned-out sentence and remark fell into a black abyss.

'I do not give up so easily on the idea of us,' he said. 'And I will collect on my arrangement with you.'

Her blue eyes assessed him, cool, icy, and without emotion. A flash of their coupling in the alcove in this very hallway flashed through his mind. Could she be so unaffected? Was only he thinking of that intimate memory between them now? His body hummed at her proximity and the memory of what they had shared. He picked up her wrist gently. A rapid pulse thrummed under his thumb. He caressed it in smooth circles.

'So, you are not as unaffected as you seem. At least I know you are human,' he said before setting her hand in the folds of her gown and releasing it.

She glared at him. 'What would you prefer I do, my laird? Swoon at your feet? I am not the type, as you well know.'

'I do.' He sat back in the settee. The anger that flashed back up in her abated his own.

'And?' she asked, sitting up straighter.

'And nothing.'

'Then why are you here?' she asked, her irritation growing, which pleased him.

He stretched out his arm on the back of the settee behind her, allowing his fingers to play with the end of her plait that rested there. He toyed with the silken strands. He could play the game as well as she. 'To ensure my part of the agreement of our bargain is fulfilled. I assume you have enlightened your brothers as to our farce and your part of the agreement. That you have promised your help in Audric's death.' He ceased moving and set his full attention on her response.

She shifted, her vexation reflected in her stiff, brittle movements. She leaned closer and dropped her voice. 'I have told them of our arrangement, and they forbid my further involvement in it. Causing Audric's demise may well cause our own, and I cannot have that.'

'You cannot have that?' he scoffed. 'And what of me? What of your promises to me? Of what I want? Of what I need?' Emotion edged into his voice.

'I am asking you to set that aside until we can see another solution, Rowan. For the sake of my family and clan, I ask you to be patient.'

'Until when? Until you are wed to his son? Until he kills more innocent people on a whim? Until when exactly?' he challenged her.

'Killing him will not bring them back,' she said quietly. 'So much time has passed that a bit longer will not matter. And it could protect my sister and her family. They have a bairn on the way. You know that.'

'A bit longer will not matter, you say?' he scoffed. 'You cannot understand. I thought you could that day when you spoke of Jeremiah with such affection and vulnerability, but you cannot. You are a woman.'

She recoiled, her anger piqued. 'I cannot understand your pride because I am a woman? I think I can. I do.'

Something roared deep within him, fracturing the reserve and patience he had been fiercely clinging to. His voice dropped so low that he almost did not recognise it. 'Nay. You cannot. It was my sworn duty, my vow as a man, father, and husband, to protect my wife and my son. My child. I failed in that. I failed utterly. They died because *I*—*I* could not protect them.' He stood, pointing to his chest. 'That was no one else's job but mine. That failure is a cross I bear every day. It rests so heavily upon my chest that some days I cannot breathe. Some days I do not wish to live. It is Rosa that brings me back to now. She helps me live. And as of late, if I am honest with myself, you did too.'

Chapter Twenty-Two

Susanna could only gape up at him. She gripped the soft fabric of the settee, frozen at the sight of Rowan, Laird of Campbell, standing before her, confessing his grief and at the same time his unexpected devotion to her. *Her*. After all these years, could he truly care for her or grow to love her? Could she trust what might be blossoming between them?

Did she dare?

She tried to clear her throat, but it was scratchy and dry as if she had swallowed a tuft of wool, and no words would come to her. At least none that made sense. Her heart screamed to get up, go to him, and hug him. To physically *show* him that she did care for him. But her mind commanded her to stay still, to not reveal her feelings, to keep them close at hand, lest she be hurt. In case his words now were untrue and in case he did not respond well to what words did finally come to her.

'It does not matter now,' she said.

He shook his head. 'What does not matter now?'

'How you feel or how I feel. I have agreed to marry Devlin and to assist my brothers in their plan to protect my sister and the clan. I can no longer help you with Audric. If anything, I must try to protect him—from you.'

He stalked to her and pulled her up beside him, holding her by the elbows. His gaze was intent. 'You will betray me?'

She settled into his hold, having missed his touch far more than she wished to admit even to herself. 'If that is what I must do to protect my family.'

'After all I risked for you to uphold my end of our agreement? After all we shared with one another these past weeks? Did it mean nothing?'

It meant more than nothing, but it didn't mean everything. He wanted all of her and all from her, and she couldn't give him that. Her family would always be a part of her, an incredibly important part, and she couldn't give them up. She wouldn't.

Not even for him.

Not even for the sweetness that he had awakened in her. Not even for the promise of something more.

'And what of you? Could you give up your vengeance? And let go of the past? For me?' she challenged him. Rowan could never give up his vengeance, his need to avenge his wife and son, and his grief over the past. He held on to his grief tightly. He was possessive of his loss.

He loosened his hold on her, uncertain how to continue. 'I cannot merely forget the past. It is a part of who I am. Anna, my son…'

'I am asking you to face the past, not forget it.' She gripped his tunic, the heat from him a reminder of what his flesh felt like on her own. Her body buzzed.

'I do face it. Every. Single. Day. It is what I think of the first and last moments of each day. How dare you suggest I do not face it?'

'Then why can you not say his name?' she whispered, knowing well she was treading on very dangerous ground.

'Whose name?' he asked, confused.

'Your son's. When we speak of him and your wife, you always call her by name, but never your son, as if you cannot bear it…'

He tried to pull away and wrapped his hands around her own to loosen her grip on his tunic, but she held on tightly. 'Do not speak to me of him…' His voice wavered.

'Rowan,' she whispered.

But he looked away and closed his eyes.

'What was his name? I do not even know it,' she murmured. 'Honour his memory,' she pleaded. 'Say his name aloud when you speak of him.'

With an anguished growl, Rowan pulled himself away from her hold, and she staggered back. 'I will say his name,' he began, his breathing laboured and his voice harsh, 'when I have avenged his death, and I deserve to say it. I will do that on my own, no matter the consequences to you or anyone. I have waited for my justice long enough. So have they. I will wait no longer. Best you prepare for the outcome, whatever it might be.'

He held her gaze for a moment before turning sharply on his heel, exiting the room, and slamming the parlour door behind him. Although he was not the broken, bedraggled man of two years ago, overcome by grief and floundering his way back to reality, he was losing himself. Guilt wriggled its way in, and she remembered that night in the forge. She knew what she'd promised him by offering to assist him in his revenge against Audric. She'd known well the pit of grief she might drive him back into by offering her help to fulfil his wishes—and the obsession to fulfil that wish that would follow once their farce had begun. Grief was a delicate tether. She knew that more than anyone.

And she had thrust him down into the well of sorrow, severing that tether in two, and offering him no way out. She remembered his words from that night in the forge:

'For revenge against Audric, I can and will do anything. I will hold you to your promise, Susanna. Nothing will stand in my way of finally ending him. Not even you.'

A shiver went up her spine, making her hands tingle. She had awakened the grief in Rowan all right, just when her family was most in danger, without even knowing it, and now there was no stopping him. The ripples of damage from what he would do were unfathomable. She had not felt so helpless since she lost Jeremiah. But she would not wallow in her grief as she'd done then. She would try to make things right somehow.

She rushed from the parlour and out to the barn in hopes of stopping Rowan and interceding. He was riding off along the road, his back to her. Hugh intercepted her.

'You must leave him be,' Hugh commanded, his features tight and his hold upon her arms even tighter.

'I cannot,' she argued.

'You must. He will not listen to reason. Not now.'

'Hugh, if he follows through with his plan…' she pleaded.

'There is nothing that you can do, but I will try to reason with him before he destroys himself and his future. Now go,' he said, releasing her. 'I need to be not far behind him.'

She nodded and watched him jump onto his mount and gallop off in pursuit of Rowan, kicking up dirt behind him. All Susanna could do was watch and hope somehow both of their clans wouldn't be left in a smouldering pile of ruin. And blame herself. She had set all of this in motion, had she not? Perhaps some secrets were better left alone. Nothing good had come from unearthing this one, nor from Royce's uncovering of the truth of why Father had written about Lismore in his journals.

She stood staring dumbly after Rowan and Hugh, noting the stillness that followed. A cold, wet nose hit her palm, followed by a slobbery kiss, yanking her back to the present. She looked down to see Jack, Iona's beloved hound, smiling up at her with his joyful eyes and wagging tail.

'I could not help but overhear,' Iona offered as she approached her from the meadows. 'I was walking with Jack.'

Susanna turned, relieved to see her sister-in-law, and greeted her with a warm hug. 'You have divine timing. I am glad you are here. May I join you? I have no wish to go back inside and face the interrogation from my brothers.'

Iona smiled and hooked her arm through Susanna's. 'As long as you do not mind the extra company Royce has assigned me,' she whispered, nodding to the soldier following at a distance. 'We are always up for company on our walks, are we not, Jack?'

The pup barked and snapped his jowls in the air before dashing down the drive, only to circle back and join them moments later, falling in step beside Iona. His devotion to her was unmatched, except for Royce, of course.

'Love is a precarious creature,' Iona offered. 'Royce and I had a similar sparring before we finally relented to one another. Neither of us wished to yield too much for fear of losing ourselves in one another. If I was to guess, I believe that is what you and Laird Campbell are doing now.' She smirked at her.

'How did you…?' Susanna asked, heat easing up her neck and cheeks.

'You have been happier and softer since he has been

around.' Iona chuckled. 'That is a fine marker for love, is it not?'

'I do not know if it is or could be love or not,' she began, savouring the cool air and sweet smell of the trees and the breeze despite the crispness of winter fast approaching. 'We knew each other when we were young. And after losing Jeremiah, I do not know if I can fully love again.'

Iona listened quietly and offered a soft smile of encouragement.

'And it is of no matter now anyway,' Susanna added. 'Royce has selected my match for *the good of the clan.*' Her last words weighed heavily on her. As much as she was willing to marry Devlin for the sake of the clan's future, it did not mean she wanted to. Especially now that she knew her feelings for Rowan were like his own for her. They might have had something, but now—it did not matter. There was no way forward for them, especially with him hell-bent on killing Audric.

Far too much was at stake, and their affections for each other were of little consequence.

Weren't they?

'Do not dismiss it all so quickly. Royce's mind can be changed. But he must be open to hearing your words. Allow him some time.'

'You know him well.' Susanna laughed.

'With each day, I discover more about him. It shall be the same for you and Rowan, I think—with time.'

Susanna sighed. 'That is the thing. We do not have that luxury, and we are at odds over an issue that is of great importance to both of us.'

'And you are both stubborn and will not yield?'

'Aye.'

'It was the same with Royce and me, and look at us now. Married and with a babe on the way. Why can it not be the same for you and Rowan?' she asked with a hopeful smile.

'While I hear your words, I just do not believe it possible for us. 'tis best I let go of such hope. It will only lead to disappointment. And we have far greater issues weighing on us at present.'

'Oh?' Iona stopped and faced her.

Susanna blanched. Why had she said that? 'Nothing to worry you over,' she added a bit too late.

'For all of your cunning, you do not lie well,' Iona said with a smirk. 'Now, tell me what these great issues are, or I shall march us into Royce's study and wrest it from him anyway.' She crossed her arms against her chest.

'Then we are off to your husband's study, I fear.' She reached out and took Iona's hand in her own. 'Follow me. I dare not utter a word of it to you, especially out here. And especially without Royce knowing first.'

Chapter Twenty-Three

'If you wish to aid me in my endeavour, then stay. If not—'
Rowan shot Hugh a glare '—leave. I have plans to make.'
Rowan yanked open a drawer of maps, riffled through
them to find the one he needed, and spread it out on the
table in his study.

Hugh handed him one large ledger and then another in
silence to help Rowan anchor the map and keep it from
rolling in on itself. Each time, his knowing gaze chipped
away at Rowan's resolve.

'And what would you have me do?' he answered Hugh's
unspoken question.

Hugh shrugged. 'I have not said a word.'

'You are speaking with your silence, as usual. It is infuriating. Especially when I have my revenge to plan out and
wish to enjoy it.' He slammed the drawer closed.

Hugh shut the door to the chamber quietly and sat on
one of the bench seats, leaning forward and resting his elbows on his knees, linking his hands together. 'And what
of Rosa? And the clan?'

Each question jabbed into Rowan's resolve, leaving him
pained and uncertain. He sat across from Hugh. 'And what
of Rosa and the clan if I *don't* do this? How can I be a father and laird if I let Audric go unpunished for his brutal-

ity? If I waste even more time than I already have waiting for the perfect opportunity for justice?'

'What if it is not your justice to impart? Have you thought of that?'

Rowan balked. 'How could it not be? He murdered my wife and my son, and countless other men and women died that day because of him and his unwarranted attack upon us. Do you not remember?'

Hugh lifted his brow in challenge, his jaw tight. 'You know well I remember. You were not the only one to lose someone that day. Do not insult me with such questions, my laird.'

'Aye. That was not fair of me. I know you remember. You fought by my side.'

Hugh's posture relaxed.

'But whose claim for justice is it, then? And how can I ever be released of this agony, this crushing shame,' he said, his throat tightening with emotion, 'if I do not finally kill him?'

'Trust me. That agony will never leave you, no matter what you do,' Hugh offered. 'It has never left me despite how I believed it would if I killed enough British soldiers. It is within you, and you must make peace with it, or it will consume you. Until recently, I thought you had come to peace with it.'

Rowan shook his head. 'Perhaps I have pretended well. Too well. I can say what I know you all wish to hear from me. And the discipline and structure I have set upon myself have helped to keep the hounds of present in charge, but recently, I feel the other wolf within me rising back up, begging to be heard. Begging to exact its wishes to wipe Audric from this earth, pressing the other, more rational

part of me back. I can taste it. My mouth waters for such revenge.' He fisted his hands and let his eyes close. His heart
pounded in his ears. 'I fear the wolf may win this time.'

'Not if you focus on the present. On Rosa. On the future. On your family.'

Rowan sucked in air through his nose and exhaled out
his mouth, counting as he went, until his pulse slowed and
he could think more clearly. He opened his eyes. Hugh
stared upon him with empathy.

'Before my gran died, she told me a story that I'll share
with you.' Hugh shifted on the bench, and his features relaxed, as they always did when he spoke of his family.

Rowan nodded to encourage him to continue.

'It was about an old man, beaten down by age as well
as time. He was kind, helpful, and never turned his back
on anyone in need. One day a younger man, lost and uncertain, clutching a small bag, came upon his hut. The old
man offered him food, water, and shelter, and the younger
man was grateful, but all the while he would not set down
his bag. Not anywhere. Always he was holding it, watching over it, and protecting it as if it were gold. The old man
was curious and asked him of its contents. The young man,
suspicious of the old man despite his generosity, hid the
bag behind him, telling him it was none of his concern.

'The next day the old man provided the younger man
directions as to how he could reach his destination, but
he warned him that some of the mountain passes were
dangerous, and he would have to use both hands to help
navigate them.

'The younger man ignored the man's warnings, intent
on holding on to his prized possession rather than putting it
in a satchel upon his back or leaving it behind all together.'

'Let me guess,' Rowan interrupted. 'He perished because he wouldn't let go of whatever he was holding on to.'

Hugh smiled. 'Aye.'

'And your message for me in this is to let it go?'

'As overly simple as it sounds, aye, that is my message to you,' Hugh replied. 'You cannot hold on to two worlds so tightly. One hand cannot cling to the past while the other clutches for the future.'

'Your gran laid all of this upon you as a lad?'

'It was an odd tale to tell a boy so young, but she knew what hatred was in my heart after I lost my parents and sister in that attack from the British. Perhaps she knew I needed to hear it to survive. I held on to my rage tightly for a long time. It wasn't until I let loose of it that I started to live.'

'You make it seem so simple.' Rowan shook his head.

'It is one of the most difficult things I have ever done.'

'Such encouragement,' Rowan scoffed, rubbing the back of his neck.

'But you are strong enough. You have come out of this grief and rage before. You have been on the precipice of sanity and come back from making decisions that could have ended badly for you and your family. Think of the rescue of Fiona and wee William two years ago. You could have let them perish so you could have your revenge against Audric, but you chose to save them instead. You pushed through that rage and put them first. You chose the present over the past. Hope over revenge. You can do it again. And you can choose your future. You can choose to be a strong leader, to be a good father, and to be the laird you want to be. Who do you want to be to your daughter, to your son, to Anna? Make the present you want, Rowan.

Do not be enslaved by the past. Let go of it.' He clapped Rowan on the back and rose. 'I will leave you to decide.'

'You sure know how to lay a burden on a man, Hugh.'

'It is not a burden to be able to choose. Think of all of those who can't, my laird. Those whose choices were made for them or those who no longer have voices to share in this world. We are two of the lucky ones. Do not forget that.'

Hugh's final words before he walked away landed hard. Rowan's gut tightened with the knowledge that his friend was right. He was alive, he still had choices to make, and he could choose to live a life without this deep-seated desire for revenge. But how? How did he let it go? How did he just move on, step fully into the present, and seek out life as hungrily as he used to before he lost so much? He gripped his neck and groaned.

Saints be.

He didn't know.

But maybe that was what he was meant to find out. While he didn't know *how* to do it, he knew where he needed to start. He pulled himself up and began the walk he needed to take. The one he had put off for too long. He needed to see his son: Keir. Setting one foot in front of the other, he climbed across the meadow to the site of Anna's and Keir's graves. It was a glorious afternoon for such a walk. The sun was high in the bright blue sky, and the crisp breeze of late autumn rustled the leaves that remained. Next August, the ridge would be awash with shades of lilac, lavender, and deep purple as the heather took over the mountainside.

Anna would have loved it. It was one of the many reasons he had chosen this spot for her and their son. Even though it wasn't nestled next to the other family plots, he knew she would have approved. He smiled when he saw how well-tended the plots were. The slate stones were clear of debris and overgrowth, and small trinkets rested upon the stones.

Trice.

His heart tugged in gratitude. It had to be her tending them with such care. He stilled when he saw a tiny wooden horse atop Keir's gravestone. Rowan knelt to pick it up, and a swell of emotion overcame him as he turned it in his fingers. He had whittled this very horse for Rosa last month, and she had cherished it so. To know she had brought it here and gifted it to her baby brother stole his breath. Trice was doing what he should have been doing: bringing Rosa here to see her mother and brother when she asked.

Why hadn't he been the one to do such?

It ought to have been him.

He cursed.

Sucking in a breath, Rowan realised for the first time how selfish and oblivious he had been to everything and everyone but his own grief. Even now, when he thought he had been getting better, he was still stuck. Rosa had lost her mother and brother, yet she charged fiercely through the world with joy. She had not been waylaid by such grief. She had not even wanted to bother her father with a request to see her mother and brother at their graves.

Rowan had been holding on to his grief and loss for so long that he had not even seen what his daughter was going through. He had not been there for her. Not really. He had not been there for his family or his clan as he should have been.

He pressed one palm on Anna's gravestone while resting the other on Keir's, the smooth, cool stone beneath his flesh soothing. 'I am so sorry, Anna,' Rowan whispered. 'I have failed you even when I thought I was better. I should have been here. Seen you. Brought our daughter. Visited our son. Visited—Keir.' His son's name came out in a tremble. He had not said Keir's name aloud since the day of his death. It sounded foreign and yet precious on Rowan's lips, so he said it aloud again, and again, and again, until the knot of grief in him loosened a whisper.

He felt along his neck, clutching the lopsided and rather ugly-looking brooch he had fashioned for Anna all those years ago to make something special for her. The one that she had worn without fail every day after he had gifted it to her despite its appearance, and that he had worn on a cord of leather ever since the day she died. 'I know, my love,' he whispered with a small smile as his eyes welled. 'It is time. Past time.' He pulled a blade from his waist belt and cut the leather cord around his neck. He pressed a kiss to the brooch and placed it gently on Anna's gravestone.

'Keir, I promise to be a better man,' he said, running a palm over the smooth stone. 'To be the father and laird that you would have been proud of. Starting today. This moment. I promise you.'

How long Rowan knelt before them, praying, talking to them, and listening to the wind, he couldn't say, but dusk was beginning to turn over day to night when he began his walk back to the castle. And while he wasn't cured and he wasn't whole quite yet, he felt lighter. He opened both of his hands as he walked, letting go of the fierce anger of the past while welcoming in the sweet hope of the present.

Chapter Twenty-Four

Susanna paced the parlour at Loch's End, her gaze sweeping from the mantel clock to the window overlooking the front drive and back to the mirror on the opposite wall. The last two weeks had been a fretful whirl of worry and frustration for Susanna. Not only had she mulled over the conversation she had had with Rowan a thousand times and found her replies wanting and at fault each time, she had no idea how to mend what she had done. While she had a right to ask him to choose her and the present, she had no right to ask him to let go of the love in his heart for Anna or his son. One could never let go of those in their heart.

But she'd been angry at him for not giving in to her demands of putting off his revenge in order to protect her family. If she were honest with herself, she was also hurt because whether she wished to admit it or not, she was beginning to fall in love with him, just as Iona suspected. She had begun to long for him and for a future she dared not hope or dream of. At the first sign of trouble, she had bolted like a wild horse and retreated, unable to drum up her courage to ask for another chance with him.

But it was of no matter now, was it?

She would marry Devlin to enhance their standing with Audric and the MacDonalds, and today they would be telling Catriona the truth about her parentage and unfurl all the secrets they had been keeping from her. Susanna's stomach curdled.

Susanna had been dreading this day since the afternoon she and Iona had walked into Royce's study and her brother had shared the truth of what was truly happening with his wife. With each day, the dread had grown, building on itself day in and day out.

A carriage came to a halt outside the large windows. Soon Catriona's sweet, joyful voice echoed as she walked through the entryway of the Loch's End, followed by her husband Ewan's low baritone. Rolf greeted them, and Susanna thought she might be ill. As much as she had demanded Catriona be told what her brothers had discovered about her disappearance to Lismore and her true lineage, now that the moment to tell her was here, Susanna wanted to run to the stables, hop on Midnight, and flee from Loch's End at a gallop.

As their footfalls signalled their approach, she stood up and clutched her hands behind her, forcing a smile. Royce emerged from his study down the hallway and greeted them warmly before following them into the parlour, where Susanna stood, waiting with a full spread of tea and offerings to tempt them. Not that anyone would feel like eating after the news was shared.

'Sister.' Susanna rushed to her Catriona and wrapped her a tight, warm hug.

Catriona tensed for a moment before she settled into it. 'What a warm greeting,' she murmured, hugging her back. She pulled away and clutched Susanna's forearms. 'Is everything well? You seem—not yourself. Tired.' Catriona's gaze assessed Susanna's face, and heat eased up from Susanna's chest. Her heart raced.

'I have not been sleeping well, but it will pass. Do not concern yourself,' she rushed out. 'You look well.' And they did. She was glowing, and so was Ewan. She clung to that and shoved away the knowledge that their news would most likely shatter some of that glow.

'Join us. Would you like some refreshment after your journey?'

Catriona and Ewan's gazes met briefly before they sat together on one of the settees. Ewan clutched Catriona's hand in his own. Whether it was out of instinct or doting over his wife's present state didn't matter. Susanna was grateful for his support. His being here would soften the blow to Catriona. Or at least, Susanna hoped it would. Royce closed the door after they and Rolf had settled in and chose a seat across from all of them.

'Thank you for coming to see us this morn,' Royce began. A muscle ticked in his jaw. 'We need to speak with you, share some news. It may be upsetting, but we all felt it was necessary to tell you, especially Susanna.'

'Are you unwell?' Catriona asked, leaning forward with concern.

'Nay,' Susanna replied quickly. 'I am well. We all are.'

Catriona settled into the cushions, releasing a sigh of relief.

'It is about my trip to Lismore,' Royce began, leaning back in his seat further, 'and you.'

'Me?'

'Aye. You were the reason for my trip last June to Lismore. I was reading Father's journals, and there was a reference to Lismore, someone named Webster, and you. I also found odd accounting in the ledgers, so as a means to discover the truth, Athol and I went there without telling anyone. I had tried to keep such knowledge to myself and Rolf for I didn't wish to hurt you by what we discovered.'

'And now?' Ewan asked, his brow raised questioningly.

'Circumstances have changed. We feel we must tell you what we discovered as well as what we still do not know so you can take precautions if need be and protect yourselves.'

'What do you mean precautions?' Catriona asked, clutching her abdomen instinctively.

Ewan rested his hand on her knee. 'Let us hear them out.'

She nodded to him and refocused her attentions on Royce. Susanna squirmed in her seat, the anxiety building. Rolf leaned forward, resting his elbows on his knees.

'Father…' Royce began and released a breath, staring down at his boots briefly before he lifted his head and continued. 'He knew you were on Lismore. He left you there on purpose under the care of others.'

She balked. 'He knowingly left me there? And under whose care?'

Ewan tightened his hold on her and awaited the answer.

'Aye. He did. He sent money to a woman named Webster and her family to care for you.'

She gasped. 'Webster? I remember her. I worked for her family. They were not horrid, but they were not kind. I don't remember them ever caring for me, though.'

'Why would your father—hell, why would any father do such to their child?' Ewan asked, anger brewing in his tone.

Royce faltered, and Susanna stepped in. 'While on Lismore, Royce found out the reason,' Susanna replied. 'Laird Cameron was not your father.'

Ewan scoffed. 'You must be joking? If Laird Cameron was not her father, who was?'

Catriona stared at them all, wide-eyed and confused.

'Laird Audric MacDonald,' Royce said.

Silence fell over everyone.

Ewan scanned their faces, staring around the room. He paled. 'You are serious? This is no joke?'

'We would never do anything so cruel, especially after we have just got you back into our lives after all this time,' Rolf added with a weak smile that faded away. He looked upon Catriona with soft eyes. 'I am sorry, sister. I cannot imagine what a shock this must be.'

'It is beyond a shock,' she sputtered out. 'How long have you known?' Her gaze landed on Susanna.

'Only two weeks, sister. Once I found out, I begged them to tell you the truth. I wanted you to know in case—'

'In case of what?' Ewan asked, his posture rigid.

'There is a chance Audric or someone within his clan may discover this and take measures against us or you.'

'Curses. Just say what you think may happen. All this vagueness is wearing. What do you think the man capable of?' Ewan asked, exasperated and angry. 'I cannot protect my wife and child without an understanding of everything. If you do not wish to say it with everyone present, then let us meet separately. But I will not have you withholding information from me, Royce. I will know everything to its finest detail. This is my wife's and child's well-being we are speaking of!'

Catriona squeezed Ewan's forearm, and he faced her, lifting a hand to caress her cheek. 'You will be safe,' he said. 'I swear it.'

'I know,' she replied, pressing a hand over his own. But

there was no mistaking the tremble in her voice. It made Susanna's stomach churn.

Susanna clutched the arm on the settee for courage. Before she lost her nerve, she spat out what Royce and Rolf had tiptoed around.

'What we fear is that Audric will be angry and driven to retaliation.' Her words were rushed and breathless, but she continued. 'And that he will take your child, once he or she is born, as his own.'

Ewan and Catriona stared at her, seemingly shocked into silence. Susanna felt the glare from Royce upon her back, but she ignored it. She had had her fill of secrets and the dangers that accompanied them. Her sister would know everything she did, no matter how Royce and Rolf felt about it.

'Saints be,' Ewan muttered, running a hand through his hair before grabbing the back of his neck.

Catriona's features hardened. 'I dare him to try. I will cut him to the bone if he does.'

Susanna couldn't help but smirk at her sister's gumption. 'He will have to go through all of us, sister, to get to you and your bairn. Even if he tries, he will be felled by all of us first, so that shall not happen.'

'She is right,' Ewan added, turning to his wife once more. 'There is an army of protectors for you here and at Glenhaven.'

'Is there any chance all of this information is wrong?' she asked. 'That I am not his daughter?'

'I have found and read more of Father's journals since I returned from Lismore,' Royce answered. 'I also thought about how your colouring is far closer to that of his other children, Devlin and Fiona, than ours. It seems irrefutable, as much as it sickens me to say it.'

'Aye. They are fair of hair and eye colour as I am. Funny how I never thought upon how different my colouring is from your own. Did Mother know about Father leaving me on Lismore?' Catriona asked quietly.

'We cannot say for certain as of yet,' Rolf replied. 'But we are still looking.'

'I would like to think she didn't,' Susanna added.

'So would I,' said Royce. 'It is hard enough to accept what Father did.'

'It is hard enough to think upon how I came to be here, then, if I am not my father's child.' She worried her hands in her lap, unable to meet anyone's gaze. 'Did Audric force himself upon our mother? Or did she choose such an affair? Or was this something else entirely we do not understand?'

'Catriona,' Ewan said quietly. 'Please do not think upon such things. It will only upset you and the babe.'

She shook her head at him and looked at everyone. 'It may seem odd, but I feel I must know myself before I can bring this child into the world. You will tell me when you discover the truth. No matter night or day, I want you to send word to me. I must know.'

'Of course,' Royce began. 'If it is that important—'

'Nay, brother,' she interrupted him. 'Do not patronise me. I have had enough uncertainty in my life. I will not accept more.'

The upset and desperation in her sister's voice was Susanna's undoing. She'd been such a fool. She had commanded Rowan to let go of his vengeance as if such a thing would be so easy, railing at him for holding on to the past. Yet after one conversation with Catriona about the danger she and her babe were in, she wanted to kill Audric Mac-Donald herself.

'I must step out for a moment,' Susanna said, quickly forcing a smile and exiting the room before the sob of anger, frustration, and sadness gathering in her throat escaped. The last thing she wished to do was upset her sister further. After closing the parlour door as softly as she could, she dashed out the entryway of the castle, hugging her arms to her body and half falling down the large stairs outside the front door. At the bottom, she collided with Iona, who steadied her with a firm grip on her upper arm.

'Susanna? What has happened?' Iona asked, her eyes searching for an answer.

Blast.

Just when Susanna thought she had escaped and wouldn't make a scene in front of her family. 'I just—' she stammered, fighting off the sob valiantly before it finally burst free. 'I just needed some air,' she choked out.

'Come with me,' Iona murmured, wrapping her arm around Susanna's shoulders and guiding her back down the walkway from Loch's End. 'Jack and I were thinking about extending our walk this morn, so join us, won't you?' Jack barked in the background and gave chase to a bird that dared settle in the grass nearby.

Susanna cried against her sister-in-law's shoulder as they walked down the rolling walkway and past the gardens, allowing herself to be guided along without question, weeping as she walked. What a sight she must have been. For the first time in a long time, she didn't have enough energy to care what anyone else who happened by them might think. She had had enough of pretending to be strong. She had had enough of a great deal many things.

The afternoon sky was grey, the kind of grey that signalled the end of autumn and the onset of winter. Fewer animals were out in search of food, and the leaves on the trees hardly moved. The air was warm but hinted at a chill this eve, and the smell of animals hit her nose. Glancing forward, she saw they were at the old barn that Iona and Royce were converting into a healing centre of sorts.

'I was going to save this as a surprise for you,' Iona said, her voice whimsical and full of mischief, 'but I think now is the perfect time.'

'What are you talking about?' Susanna sniffed, wiping her eyes with the bell of her sleeve.

Iona tugged her closer. 'Follow me and find out.'

'But I am in no mood for—' Susanna countered.

Iona ignored her and kept talking. 'Wait here. I will bring her to you.'

'Bring her?' Susanna countered, continuing to wipe her tear-stained cheeks, intrigued, and concerned for what might happen next.

The barn door opened and then squeaked closed. Unable to wait, Susanna went inside. She gasped. What she saw was incredible. The old barn had been transformed into a true sanctuary. And within the large pens, fashioned from old wood and wires, she saw animals. All in various stages of recovery.

Logan, one of the youngest of the stable boys, rushed up to them, holding a bird gently in his hands. 'Lady Iona! Lady Susanna!' he called, 'I believe he is ready to fly!'

Iona clapped her hands together. 'What perfect timing! We shall set our sweet friend free, and then you can show Lady Susanna Little Midnight.' She winked at the boy.

Logan laughed at their shared secret. 'Aye, my lady.' He rushed ahead and out of the barn. Susanna followed them, getting caught up in their joy, despite her mood. Soon they were out of doors, standing in a small half circle. Susanna saw the bird clearly in the full light and gasped. 'Is this not the peregrine falcon you found along the shore?' she asked the young boy.

'Aye, he is. Had an injured wing a few months ago, but look at him now.'

'No doubt due to your care, Logan.' Susanna smiled, and the boy beamed with pride.

'And Lady Iona's. She taught me how to help him heal and grow stronger.'

'Now is the hardest part, Logan,' Iona said, bending down close to the bird, and running a finger over the shiny feathers along the falcon's back. 'You must help him remember he is strong enough to fly on his own. Set him down on the ground, and then we will wait.'

'How long?' Logan asked, doing exactly as Iona told him too.

'As long as it takes,' Iona replied. 'He must be confident and trust in himself to take that first step, even though he doesn't know if he can fly or not.'

Susanna shivered as she stared down upon the beautiful falcon that took a step here and there, stretching out its wings, wobbling and with hesitation, only to close them again. No doubt the bird was as uncertain as she as to its next steps. Minutes ticked by, and falcon grew more confident. It flapped its wings in succession a few times and hopped along. Then in one swift movement, he turned his head back to them briefly, stretched out its wings to as full as she'd ever seen, and flapped them once and then twice, lifting him off the ground in one glorious motion. Before Susanna could take another breath, he was in the air, moving away from them, rising higher and higher until he was above the treetops.

'Do you think he will ever come back?' Logan asked quietly, wiping his nose with his sleeve with a sniff. 'I'll miss him.'

Iona bent down and kissed his head before ruffling his hair. 'I think he'll be back one day, but if not, every time you see a falcon in the sky, you can know you made a difference for him. You helped him fly again, even when he thought he couldn't.'

Susanna's eyes welled. 'That was beautiful,' she whispered.

Iona squeezed her in a side hug. 'I think she is ready for her surprise, Logan. Don't you?'

'Aye,' he replied and hustled back into the barn. 'I shall ready her.'

'We will be in shortly,' she replied. After he had left them, she faced Susanna. 'Now, tell me what has you so upset. I have never seen you thus.'

Susanna sighed. 'We met with Catriona and Ewan.'

'I knew of the meeting today. But this seems like something more, if I can speak so frankly with you.'

Susanna nodded. She shouldn't have been surprised by Iona deducing such. The woman had instincts and intuition far beyond what most people possessed. 'It is far more. I am lost. The more I try to control things, and help protect my family, the more out of control things have become, and the more defeated I feel.'

'What do you mean?'

'I was so desperate to determine what the secret was that my brothers were keeping from me and Catriona, and why they were so desperate to have me married and protected, that I created my own plan to unearth them—with Laird Campbell.'

Iona watched her silently, and Susanna continued, emotion tightening her throat once more. 'I called in a favour he owed me and made him pretend to be my fiancé to keep Devlin and the others away—and in return, I promised him I would help him kill Audric, so he could finally have his vengeance against him for the loss of his wife and son.'

Iona gasped.

'Do not worry.' Susanna clutched her hand. 'I have told him I would no longer assist him with his plans, for Catriona's sake. But now that we have learned the secret, things are far worse. Our family is in danger, I am at odds with my brothers for my lying to them, and Rowan…hates me. And I cannot say I blame him. I have made a fine mess of things.'

'Why do you say that?' Iona asked.

'I was wrong,' Susanna murmured. 'I commanded Rowan to let go of his vengeance as if such a thing would be so easy. I railed at him for holding on to the past, and yet after one conversation with Catriona about the danger she and her babe are in because of the man and his past actions with my mother, I want to kill Audric myself. I feel like such a fool. And worst of all—' she continued, her voice shaking '—I miss Rowan terribly, and it is too late. I have ruined any hope of a future between us.'

'You must let go and stop trying to control everything,' Iona replied, squeezing Susanna's hand. 'I learned the same lesson not so long ago. I worked so hard to create a safe world for myself that I was not living. And the illusion I had constructed wasn't real. Not really. I'll wager you are doing much the same. Let go and live your life in the present for you and no one else.'

'How?'

Logan emerged from the barn, cradling a small rucksack with great care, and Iona nodded. 'One step at a time, and I would recommend she be your first one.'

'She?' Susanna stared as the rucksack squirmed in Logan's hold.

'This is Little Midnight,' Logan said, smiling. 'Found her weak and hungry and all alone. She was the runt, I think, but she has spirit.' He held out the satchel to Susanna.

'We hoped you might help care for her and keep her as your own if you like. She was dark just like your horse, so we named her Little Midnight.' Iona gestured towards the small mewling kitten. The wee cat was so dark that Susanna could hardly see her face until the kitten turned to her and opened her bright blue eyes.

'She is a beauty,' Susanna cooed, running her finger over the small pink nose. The kitten tentatively licked Susanna's finger with its scratchy tongue.

'Will you keep her, my lady?' Logan smiled.

'Only if you will help me. Teach me how to care for her properly.'

'I can do that.'

'Then I shall do my best,' Susanna replied with a smile, cuddling the soft bundle close to her chest.

'And that, sister, shall be exactly enough,' said Iona.

Chapter Twenty-Five

Rowan sat in the grass, setting his knife to work on the newest creation he had decided upon for wee Rosa. She played along the hillside with Poppy, her new wolfhound, gifted to her from Catriona and Ewan from the Stewarts' newest litter. Rosa's laughter and joy travelled down to him, and Rowan paused, looking up to wave at her. She tossed a stick but instead of chasing it Poppy barked and ran after her until she stumbled into a rolling ball of fur, sending Rosa into another fit of giggles. Rowan smiled, grateful for his daughter and for this beautiful autumn day, a warm one for this time of year. He was also beyond grateful for this new trajectory he had set his life upon since he'd spoken with Hugh. Spending time with his daughter was now an essential and joyous part of Rowan's day, and he cherished his adventures with her over the last two weeks.

After each day was spent and he'd continued to let go of his anguished hold on the past, his grief, and his quest for vengeance against Audric, a part of Rowan that had not been quiet in some time was now at peace, and a new part of him had awakened. Finally, the wolf within him was at bay—for good. His time in the forge had lessened as he sought to make his amends and peace in other ways. He visited Anna's and Keir's graves regularly, spoke to them, and spoke to Rosa about them. He'd brought his love for them back into the light, and with it he had brought part of himself back into the light as well.

He couldn't help but also think of Susanna as he worked. He had forced her hand by accusing her of putting the needs of her family ahead of his own, when he had done the very same by placing his vengeance for his own family ahead of the current safety of her own. He knew the safety of Catriona and her bairn mattered more now, as his Anna and Keir were already lost. Nothing could be done to bring them back, but Catriona and her bairn could still be protected, and setting aside his grief to help was the right thing to do.

He just wished he hadn't lost Susanna in the process of realising his own folly. Now he had lost her twice. Both times because he had allowed his emotion and impulsiveness to rule him without restraint.

'What are you making me, Papa?' Rosa asked, rushing down the hill towards him, rescuing him from his brooding.

Rowan hid the blade and wood behind his back with one arm while he caught her in his other and hugged her to his side.

'It is a secret,' he teased, pressing a kiss to her cheek.

'I love you,' she said softly. 'I am glad you are happy now.' She gazed into his eyes and patted his cheek with her wee soft hand before kissing it. She laughed and scrunched up her face. 'Your cheeks are scratchy again, Papa.'

'Aye.' He laughed, making a note to shave later.

Poppy rushed down to them and barked, dropping a stick in front of Rosa's feet.

'I'll be back,' she told him. She picked up the stick, threw it, and ran up the hill after Poppy.

Rowan watched her and smiled, knowing just what his new creation would be. His blade slid into the soft wood and continued making a tiny copy of Poppy, whom his daughter adored. He was so engrossed in his work that he didn't hear his sister Trice until her shadow blocked his sunlight. Shading his eyes, he gazed up at her.

'You two look like you are having a fine afternoon with one another,' she said, smiling down at him.

'Join me,' Rowan said, patting the grass next to him. 'I'd like to speak with you.'

His sister bit her lower lip, her uncertainty evident.

'Please, Trice,' he said softer. He wanted to make amends, and now seemed as good of a time as any.

She hesitated a beat more but relented and sat down next to him. For a moment, he was transported back to when they were children sitting upon this same meadow, playing side by side. A deep longing for such simplicity overcame him, and he sighed. While the simplicity of youth might well be over, he still had much joy to embrace. He knew that now. He had more ahead of him than behind him.

He plucked two blades of grass and wound them into a small budded flower, or at least, he attempted to. He laughed and gave it to her. 'Sorry it is not nearly as good as the ones I used to make. For you, Trice.'

She took it from him, twirled it in her fingertips, and smiled. 'How many hours did we spend along this hillside, you, Brandon, and I?'

'Too many for Father's liking, I am sure.' Rowan set aside his blade and twig and leaned back on his hands as he watched Rosa. He took a moment to gather his nerve and began the speech he had been practicing in his mind over the last week. It was long overdue.

'I am sorry, Trice,' he began and met her gaze.

She furrowed her brow and pulled her long plait around her shoulder, running her fingers over the end. 'What for?'

He smiled at her sister's sweet, nervous gesture. 'For not being here since Anna and Keir died. For not being a good brother, or laird, or father to Rosa.'

Her fingertips stilled.

'You took up all the duties I was too lost or sick to remember to do. Or too grief-stricken to think about doing—especially how you cared for Rosa. Talking to her about her mother and brother when I couldn't. Taking her to their graves when I could not bear to do so. It is more than anyone should have had to do. Yet you did all those things and more without complaint.'

'Brother,' she began, but he interrupted her.

'Please let me finish,' he said. 'Otherwise, I may lose my courage.'

She pressed her lips together and nodded, her eyes shining with unshed tears.

He swallowed hard and continued. 'I was so lost in grief and vengeance that I could not move forward. Even when I thought I was better and functioning in my day-to-day life these last two years, I really wasn't. I've been in a fog. I was not *here*. Not really. But I want to be now.'

'I have seen the change in you these last two weeks.'

'You have?' he asked, encouraged.

'Aye. Even Rosa has spoken to me of it. She is pleased to have her father back. Each afternoon she rushes in to tell me of her daily adventures with you, as you both call them.'

His chest tightened. 'Then I am finally doing something right. And our time together is healing me too. I have decided I will no longer seek vengeance against Audric. I have decided he will have his due, in his own time, but it does not have to be by my hands. I will not ruin us or our clan's future by taking measures to do so myself. It is not worth it.'

'I thought as much,' she said quietly.

'How did you know?' he asked, studying her.

'It was the brooch on her grave. When I saw it there, it stole my breath.' Trice pressed a hand to her chest. 'I had hoped you had finally let it go, but now I know I was right. I am happy for you. You have a life and future waiting for you to claim.'

'Aye,' he said. 'You are right. I do. Now, if only I knew how to do such. I fear I have allowed my desire for revenge to ruin some of those chances.'

'What do you mean?'

He stared into her searching eyes, so similar to his own. Should he tell her all he had been up to? Did he dare? He sucked in a breath and charged ahead, leaving nothing hidden between them.

'You may have noticed my distractions over the last two months,' said Rowan.

'Aye, Trice replied. 'You have been a bit secretive, and all this business with the Camerons, especially Susanna, had the villagers talking and me wondering.'

'Well, that was a ruse, or at least, it started out that way.'

'A ruse? I do not follow,' she replied, shaking her head.

'I was pretending to be her betrothed in exchange for her help in killing Audric.'

'Rowan!' Trice chided him.

'I know,' Rowan replied. 'It was ridiculous—and you need not worry, the intrigue is over. But along the way, I thought what used to be between Susanna and I long ago was rekindled. I thought maybe we had been given a second chance, that we could have even had a future together.'

'What changed?' she asked.

'She chose her family over me. I was angry that she went back on her promise to help me kill Audric so she could protect them.'

'Was it for a good reason?' said Trice.

'Aye, even though I do not wish to admit it,' Rowan answered.

'And now?'

'What do you mean?'

'If you no longer feel this desire for revenge, then why not take a chance and see if any of it was real?' Trice asked. 'Approach her again without this scheme between you. Offer her the you of now and an opportunity for a future. Leave the past behind and see what happens.'

'I am not so certain,' he replied, watching Rosa.

'What *is* certain? Nothing. And I have always thought you two were a match. A volatile match, to be sure, but a match just the same.'

Rowan laughed. 'I suppose we always were a bit intense, but perhaps now that we are older, we could learn to temper those emotions.'

'You will never know if you don't try, brother. Go to her. Offer her the man you are now. She would be a fool to refuse you, and while Susanna Cameron is many things, she is no fool.' Trice set the grass flower Rowan had made behind her ear.

''Tis no longer so simple,' he replied. 'Her brothers have promised her to Devlin in some misguided belief that it will provide them protection and security in their relations with Audric, which I know is a farce. The old man and his clan are not to be trusted. Despite how much I have come to respect Devlin after all he has done for Fiona, Brandon, and wee William, the very idea of her marrying him makes my stomach turn.'

'Then do something. I've never known you to accept any outcome you have not liked. Why start now?' she said with a smirk.

Rowan nodded. 'You make a fine point. Perhaps I will send word to her this eve when we return.'

'You can be quite persuasive when you set your charm to it. So be charming, brother.'

'I will try, but my charm is a bit rusty from lack of use,' Rowan quipped.

'Until then, you best get busy with that new creation of yours,' Trice added, hugging him before rising to leave. 'As of now, it looks—like a twig.'

'I have only just started, sister. It will be something beautiful. It just takes time and patience.'

'All beautiful things do, my brother.' She winked and left him to his work.

Chapter Twenty-Six

'Enjoy your nap, little one,' Susanna cooed, running her fingers gently over the kitten's smooth belly, which was now swollen with milk. The sweet girl yawned and purred before her eyes drifted closed.

'How is Little Midnight?' Iona asked as she entered the barn.

'I have decided to shorten her name to Dorcha, which means *dark*. I think it suits her. Little Midnight was far too long a name for the wee girl. And to answer your question, she is well and off to sleep after her morning feeding.'

'I see you are quite taken with her. Each day you are up earlier and earlier to see her.' Iona beamed as she began her check upon the animals and gathered their food and hay.

Susanna rolled her eyes but did not refute her sister-in-law. 'I adore her. I only hope I will be able to bring her with me.'

Iona scoffed, pausing her movements. 'You mean you plan to go through with this sham of a marriage to Devlin?'

Susanna shrugged. 'What choice do I have? I cannot refuse and put Catriona or the clan in such danger.'

'And what if it doesn't even work? Audric plays by his own rules from what I know of him. How will you feel about sacrificing your happiness if it served no purpose?'

'And how will I live with myself if something happens to Catriona or the clan?' She stared upon the steady rise and fall of Dorcha's belly. A tiny snore escaped the kitten.

Such contentment Susanna envied.

Iona shook her head. 'You are doing it again.'

'Doing what?'

'Trying to control the uncontrollable and trying to create ultimate safety and security when no one can be guaranteed such. Did nothing we spoke of before set in?'

Susanna frowned. 'I know what you said, but I cannot just let things happen.'

Iona chuckled. 'Nay, you *could* do that.'

'I cannot be so reckless.'

'Could you be in the middle?' Iona asked. 'Could you care for yourself and live the life *you* want while still caring for your family?'

'Maybe,' Susanna answered.

'Maybe?' Iona asked, crossing her arms across her chest.

'Aye.'

'Then do that,' Iona replied. 'That is what I mean. Not all is so black and white.'

'And if I want what I cannot have?' she asked, pressing a kiss to Dorcha's head.

Iona's face softened. 'Then at least you will know that you tried.'

'I hate it when you are right,' Susanna muttered.

Iona laughed and began cleaning out the next pen. 'So does Royce.'

'My lady,' Lunn called as he came in the barn. 'A messenger just delivered this for you. Asked me to pass this along to you with haste.'

Iona and Susanna stilled, bracing for bad news.

'Who was the messenger?' Susanna asked.

'No one known to me, although he wore a Campbell plaid.' Lunn approached Susanna and held out the sealed letter for her. At the sight of the maroon seal and the Campbell crest pressed into it, Susanna's pulse increased. She and Rowan had not had any communication since the afternoon in the parlour where she told him she would no longer honour their original arrangement to have his revenge upon Audric.

When Susanna didn't take the letter, Iona stepped up. 'Thank you, Lunn. I will see she reads it.'

'Thank you, my lady,' he said and left as quickly as he arrived.

'Susanna?' Iona asked.

'I cannot read it,' Susanna stammered. 'We have not spoken since our last disagreement, and I do not wish to know if he hates me.'

'But not reading it will not change the contents of the letter,' Iona stated. 'Wouldn't you rather know where you two stand with one another?'

'Not if it is bad,' Susanna replied, setting Dorcha back into her small pen, tucking her deeper into the folds of the old plaid she wrapped her in.

Iona gifted her a knowing look.

'Fine,' Susanna said, taking the letter from her. She broke the seal and held her breath as she read.

Suze,
If it is not too late, I must speak with you. I have been a fool.
Meet me in the rowan grove tomorrow morn.
Hoping not all is lost,
Ro

In the bottom fold of the letter was a pressed and dried bluebell. Where he had found one to send to her, she didn't know. They bloomed in the spring, not the autumn. But they were her favourite. The fact that he still remembered made her heart swell with hope.

'I must see Royce,' Susanna said. 'Where is he?'

'His study, I think. What did the letter say?' Iona asked.

'That there is still hope. I can still choose my future, so I must go.' She rushed to Iona, hugged her tightly, and then ran from the barn, across the meadow, and into the entrance of Loch's End. She had to speak with Royce before her engagement was sealed by ink and deed. She slid across the stone floor and into his study. He looked up from his ledger with wide eyes.

'Sister?'

'I do not wish to marry Devlin. I want to marry Rowan. I love him, and I believe he loves me. And for the first time since I lost Jeremiah, I want to follow my heart rather than my fear.' Her words were rushed and scrambled, and her breaths afterwards were ragged and uneven. She stared, waiting for his answer.

To her horror, he said nothing at first. Finally he said, 'Sit.'

'I cannot sit. I am not waiting for your approval or your answer, brother. I just wanted to tell you before I went to him.'

He leaned back in his chair and studied her. Then, surprisingly, he did the unthinkable. He smiled.

'Then go to him, sister,' he said softly. 'I will not stand in your way.'

Her eyes welled. 'I do not understand. I thought you

would be angry or forbid me to go. Why are you agreeing? Me not marrying Devlin may lead to a horrible outcome.'

'And so might marrying him. Even if you do, Audric may attack us for another reason altogether.'

'Then why did you go along with the plan for me to do so?' she asked.

'Because you agreed to it so readily, I thought you did not care, Susanna. When I spoke to Iona, she told me otherwise. Seems we still have work to do on not keeping secrets from one another despite the promise I made you months ago.'

'I only agreed to please you and because I hoped it might keep Catriona and our family safe,' she added, feeling weak in her knees.

'Nothing can guarantee that,' he replied.

'I know. I am just figuring that part out,' she said. 'And realising that I can dare hope for happiness again.'

'Go to him,' he commanded. 'You will only have regrets otherwise.'

'Aye, brother.' She rushed to him and hugged him. 'I will. At once.'

He hugged her back. 'And I will see to undoing this engagement of yours.'

Susanna pulled back and met Royce's gaze. 'Thank you,' she whispered.

'You can thank me by being happy, sister,' he replied. 'That is all any of us want and require of you.'

'I will. But now I must go.'

She fled the castle with haste and headed to the stables to have Midnight saddled.

Lunn stood outside the barn with Midnight, waiting for her. She slowed and stood before him. 'Are you ready, my lady?' he asked.

'I am. But how did you know I would need Midnight?' she asked.

'The messenger who brought the note told me. And Cynric and I have seen the way you look at Laird Campbell, my lady. We know how lonely you have been without Jeremiah.' He cleared his throat. 'We want you to be happy. So would he.'

'You two have been the best of friends and champions to me. I—I—' she stammered, unable to finish.

'I know, my lady,' he said, pressing the reins into her hands. 'And it is okay to move on. To be happy.'

She nodded and accepted his help as she mounted, settling into Midnight's familiar saddle.

'Cynric will ride with you, my lady,' Lunn said with a smile. 'He is just beyond the bend.'

'Thank you,' she said and started a fierce gallop. If she hurried, she could make it by nightfall, and she knew exactly where she could find Rowan, the man she loved. She just hoped it wasn't too late.

Chapter Twenty-Seven

Rowan studied his newest creation with wonder. His thumb caressed the smooth metal and its fine chiselled carvings as they reflected in the flickering torches in his makeshift forge. Had his hands finally made something of such beauty? The brooch was perfect and had come out even better than he believed possible. Susanna would love it.

If she comes tomorrow.

He set the small oval brooch in the square of plaid, wrapped it carefully, and tucked it in the leather satchel on his waist belt.

She will come.

Knowing Susanna as he did, he assumed her curiosity would bring her to the grove in the morn to hear him out, if nothing else. Whether she would agree to give him a chance—*them* a chance—he didn't know. She might very well be engaged to Devlin or on her way to marry him already. He cast the worry aside. No good would come from such thoughts.

The barn door opened and slid closed behind him.

'I am finishing up, Hugh. There is no need for you to chase me out,' Rowan said with good humour.

'I could not wait until the morn.'

Rowan froze.

Susanna.

'Oh, no?' he replied, still facing away, so he could gain his bearings. 'Why not?'

'The bluebell. I didn't know you remembered.'

'There are many things I cannot forget about you, Susanna, despite how much time has passed.' He exhaled and faced her. The sight of her almost brought him to his knees. Colour was high in her cheeks, and her eyes were the brightest of blues, catching the light in the forge. She wore her signature dark cloak, and it was pulled high over her hair.

He came to her, his heart pounding in his chest. 'Cool night for a ride,' he said, stopping just shy of too close. He reached out his hand, and it trembled along her own. 'I hope you didn't catch a chill.'

'Nay,' she replied, stepping closer to him and twining her fingers around his. 'We travelled quickly. I was eager to hear what you had to say.'

He met her gaze and faltered briefly before he began in earnest. 'I have been a fool. I was so caught up in the past and in my need for vengeance that I couldn't see you in the future that was right before my eyes.' He paused and continued. 'I couldn't see anyone, not even my daughter. And you were right. I needed to grieve for my son. I needed to say his name aloud, speak of him, and celebrate him, but I couldn't do that until I let him go. And I couldn't do that until I released my vengeance and my anger and my grief.'

Susanna took his hands in hers and held them. Her eyes beckoned him to continue.

'His name was Keir. We named him that because his features were so dark. He had black hair, wavy like his mother's, and dark brown eyes like the bark of a tree. He had a glorious smile and the mightiest laugh. He could make everyone laugh with his antics. I could not bear to remember all of those things about him, so I clung to my vengeance and my hatred. It was so much easier than remembering him and all I lost that day.'

Tears streamed down Susanna's cheeks, and Rowan wiped them away.

'Thank you for demanding I remember him, because it's what he deserved and what Anna deserved,' he said with a sniff. 'And you helped me realise I had to move on. So did Trice. I know that when I thought of moving on, I saw you alongside me. I was a fool to let you go and to let you push me away. I want you in my life if you will have me.'

For long seconds, Susanna stood and stared at him as if he were a strange creature she had never seen before, and perhaps he was. He was standing here, heart in hand, pledging his affection for her and begging her to spend her life with him and to choose him over her family.

Her answer was a crushing kiss to his lips, and he responded in kind with equal parts affection and gratitude. She slid her arms around his neck as he pulled her closer and wrapped his arms around her waist.

'So, is that a yes?' He asked after their kiss ended.

'It is a yes a thousand times over, my laird.'

'You are not pledged to Devlin? And your brother will not punish you for your decision?'

'Nay,' she answered with a coy smile on her lips. 'He was the one who told me to come.'

'You Camerons are always up to something,' he replied. 'But for once, I find I like your surprises. Which reminds me, I have a surprise for you.' Rowan opened the satchel on his waist belt and pulled out the small tartan cloth holding the brooch he had just made. 'While it is no fancy ring or gem to show you my affection, I crafted it with my own hands for you. To show you my pledge and promise for the future and to us.'

Susanna gently accepted the plaid and opened it slowly. A smile bloomed on her lips. 'You have made this? For me?'

He nodded. 'It is a rowan tree. To symbolise where our relationship began and where it was renewed. I find there is always hope and promise in the rowan grove, don't you?'

'Aye. I do. Just as I find hope and promise in you.'

Epilogue

'**W**ho would have imagined this a year ago?' Susanna asked, her head resting in Rowan's lap as she stared up at the cold winter afternoon sky.

Rowan leaned over, blocking her view of the clear blue sky above, but the sight of him made her heart flutter. He skimmed a finger along her hairline. 'Who would have imagined this two months ago?' he teased. 'But I am pleased by such a surprise.'

'As am I,' she murmured, reaching up and running her hand through his lush dark hair before cupping his cheek. Rosa played at the base of the meadow below them with Poppy and a very daring Dorcha. The young girl's laughter coiled into the air, making Susanna smile. Rowan's daughter had carved her way into Susanna's heart since their engagement. She could hardly wait to care for her and try to be the kind of mother the wee girl deserved.

Susanna's siblings were excited for her match and her newfound release from their expectations. Rolf seemed the most pleased by her choice and more determined than ever to resolve the situation with Catriona on his own, despite Royce's objections. Susanna could not fault her younger brother's dogged determination. She secretly hoped he would find the key to unlocking the mystery of Catriona's conception and bring all the messy intrigue to an end so everything could go back to normal. Even Devlin had sided with the decision to end their engagement, pleased with the idea of halting such a match to thwart his father's plans.

'In a few days, we will be wed,' Rowan said, staring off into the distance, his fingers flitting along her scalp. The light skimming touch sent her senses reeling, and her mind drifted to memories of a far different kind. 'Are you ready to be Lady Campbell?' he asked, lifting his brow.

'More than ready,' she replied. 'Although—' she paused and frowned, toying with the edge of his plaid '—I do think the Cameron plaid suits my colouring better.'

He rested his warm hands along her waist and leaned closer, his voice husky and full of promises she could not wait for him to keep. 'Do you need convincing otherwise, my lady?'

'Aye,' she replied, her body humming as his hands slid down her torso.

His lips hovered over her own until she ached for them. He kissed her and lingered before pulling away slowly, his eyes hooded with desire. 'I look forward to the challenge.'

'As do I, my laird.'

* * * * *

If you enjoyed this story,
make sure you're caught up on the first
installment in Jeanine Englert's
Secrets of Clan Cameron miniseries,

A Laird without a Past

And while you're waiting for the next book,
be sure to check out her
Falling for a Stewart miniseries

Eloping with the Laird
The Lost Laird from Her Past
Conveniently Wed to the Laird